Forsaken Soul

Books by Priscilla Royal

Wine of Violence
Tyrant of the Mind
Sorrow Without End
Justice for the Damned
Forsaken Soul

Forsaken Soul

Priscilla Royal

Poisoned Pen Press

Poisoned
Pen
Press

Poisoned Pen Press
6962 E. First Ave., Ste. 103
Scottsdale, AZ 85251
www.poisonedpenpress.com
info@poisonedpenpress.com

Printed in the United States of America

My God, my God, why hast thou forsaken me? Why art thou
so far from helping me, and from the words of my roaring?
Our fathers trusted in thee; they trusted, and thou didst
deliver them.
But I am a worm, and no man; a reproach of men,
and despised of the people.
All they that see me laugh me to scorn...
—Psalm 22: 1, 4, 6-7 (King James Bible)

To Barbara Peters whose talents are the stuff
from which legends are made.

Acknowledgments

Thanks to: Peter Goodhugh, Ed Kaufman of M is for Mystery Bookstore (San Mateo CA), Henie Lentz, Dianne Levy, Sharon Kay Penman, Barbara Peters of Poisoned Pen Bookstore (Scottsdale AZ), Robert Rosenwald and all the staff of Poisoned Pen Press, Marianne and Sharon Silva, Lyn and Michael Speakman.

Chapter One

"I do not wish to cast aspersions on Sister Juliana's virtue, my lady."

A hope you most ardently pray I shall reject, Prioress Eleanor concluded, noting that Sister Ruth's complexion had deepened from its usual ruddy hue into that nobler color oft favored by God's anointed rulers. She willed herself to maintain an expression devoid of all but civil concern.

"Yet I am sure you agree that those virtuous people of the village, who have expressed apprehension in this matter, may not be ignored."

The effort to retain a suitably grave bearing grew more difficult. The youthful leader of Tyndal, a Fontevraudine priory on the East Anglian coast, nodded with visible impatience.

Sister Ruth stiffened her back. "Without question, an anchoress may accept visitors at her window and dispense humble advice. To do so only at night, when Satan lewdly disports himself with his imps, is distressing. Many say that advice given at such unholy hours must be hissed in Sister Juliana's ears by the Prince of Darkness, not by God." Sister Ruth tucked in her chin, hoping to emphasize her stern demeanor, but her effort managed only to double her jowls.

"You were correct to bring this problem to my attention," Eleanor conceded.

"Nor is that all!"

I feared not, thought the prioress.

"None of the worthy women I have found to serve her can bear to do so."

"What complaint could these women possibly have?" Eleanor snapped. "A bishop carefully questioned Sister Juliana, when she requested this entombment, and found her calling to be a true one." She instantly regretted that tone of voice. It suggested she had lost command over this exchange.

The middle-aged nun smiled at her younger leader with naked disdain. "Were our anchoress to levitate in prayer, these women would stand in awe. Had her eyes grown raw with unrelenting tears over mortal sins, they would sing her praises. When she howls at them like a wild beast and screams abuse, they see the handmaid of Satan."

"Perhaps there is a reason…"

"These good women agree that laments are most suitable for any wicked daughter of Eve and rejoice when the anchoress moans and cries out in prayer. Nevertheless, like any person of reason, they grow frightened when she beats her head against the stones until she bleeds or writhes on the floor like one possessed."

Eleanor's eyes widened.

The sub-prioress bent forward as if conveying a confidence. "One woman was certain she glimpsed a dark shadow lurking in a corner of the anchorage. It laughed most wickedly, she said." Sister Ruth resumed her erect posture. "She is but one witness who fears our anchoress is possessed."

Eleanor nodded, but her frown suggested that any perceived concurrence was both hesitant and skeptical.

A loud creak broke the palpable tension in the room.

Sister Ruth spun around, her face a chalky white.

The chamber door was opening very slowly. No hand was visible.

Sister Ruth crossed herself with trembling fingers against the onslaught of Evil.

A large, red tabby slid through the small opening and into the room. When he saw the square-bodied sub-prioress, he sneezed, and then shook himself with vigor.

Sister Ruth drew back her robes.

"We should be grateful Arthur did not honor us with a rat from the kitchens," Eleanor said, smiling down with fondness at the creature now circling her feet.

"Which is where the beast should stay," Sister Ruth muttered as a most brilliant pink colored her neck and cheeks.

"What other witnesses have complaint against our new anchoress?" Eleanor continued, ignoring the remark. Even though Sister Ruth routinely saw the darkest sin in anything of which she personally disapproved, much to the prioress' annoyance, the woman's ideas found company enough in others of like mind. Although Eleanor believed that fear or ignorance were often the basis for such opinions, she also knew how much Satan delighted in the mischief they caused. For that reason, she never ignored what was said, but, in this instance, she found herself troubled as well by the accusations against Sister Juliana.

"What more need you hear? Surely the report that righteous souls fear the anchoress consorts with the Devil and may be possessed is sufficient to take action."

"Allegations are worthy of consideration, but truth demands details and evidence. As Our Lord has taught us, Sister, what lies inside any vessel may be disguised by its exterior."

Sister Ruth blinked.

"Be assured that I will investigate these concerns."

The nun stepped back at the prioress' implied rebuke, then realized she had just been dismissed. With ill grace and only token respect, Sister Ruth bent her head and turned to leave.

All dignity in retreat was thwarted when she ran straight into the sub-infirmarian standing outside the chamber door.

Sister Anne stepped aside to let her superior pass.

Eleanor wondered if her dear friend had barely stifled an outburst of laughter. As she watched the middle-aged sub-prioress march away, arms and legs pumping with purposeful effort, she herself was reminded of a hungry ox, loosed at last from the plow and aware that the evening feed was but a short distance away. She glanced toward the window. The sun's position might indicate that the mid-day meal was nigh.

"Your visit was well-timed!" Eleanor gestured for the tall nun to enter.

Anne put a woven basket down on the table. The delicate scent of cut herbs drifted through the room in the soft summer air. "Then the tale I bear has twice-good purpose."

"What news?"

"According to Brother Beorn, our crowner has returned from court."

Eleanor's eyes glowed with undisguised pleasure. "After the crusader was murdered and Ralf left to stay with his brother, the sheriff, I feared our friend would not return. Has he come back to us for good? His sergeant might be as honest as our crowner but never as clever."

"I believe he has, but I bear sad news as well."

The prioress' hand flew to her heart.

"Ralf is well enough," Anne added quickly, "but the woman he took to wife during that absence died giving birth. Now he is both a widower and a father to a baby girl."

Eleanor closed her eyes, sending a quick prayer heavenward that God might grant comfort to a good man. "Is the child strong?"

"Brother Beorn confirmed that the child resembled her father in health, although I confess his description was not quite complimentary." Anne smiled, but a mist of sadness drifted across her face.

Although they rarely spoke of the death of Anne's own child, Eleanor squeezed her friend's hand with silent understanding. "Those two men have been like oil and water since boyhood," she said to distract the sub-infirmarian. "Might I be right in concluding that our lay brother made some reference to oxen?"

The tall nun laughed as she bent to stroke the cat stretching up against her leg and purring for attention.

"What name did Ralf bestow on this wee babe of his?"

"Brother Beorn did not say."

"We shall learn it." Eleanor began to pace, her mind racing to consider what this tiny new arrival might need. "I am delighted with this news! Ralf must have brought a wet-nurse back with him, but surely she would not wish to stay so far from the comforts and worldly advantages of the king's court. The little one will need a nurse from the village as well as a good woman to care for her after weaning." She gestured at the sub-infirmarian. "If Ralf resumes his work of ferreting out the lawless, he will have little time to seek such a woman, let alone watch over a motherless child. We must find someone reliable to replace the woman he brought."

"Perhaps Gytha knows a suitable person?"

Eleanor nodded. Her maid, now a full-grown woman of seventeen summers, knew everyone in Tyndal village. "And the priory must also show our pleasure at his return. Prior Andrew will invite him to share a humble meal with us."

"Sister Matilda's meals may be simple but never humble," Anne replied.

Nodding with amused agreement, Eleanor peered into the herb basket lying on the table. "What have you harvested?"

The sub-infirmarian picked up a handful of fleshy green leaves with sharp maroon tips. "Houseleek will serve to ease any insect bites our monks and nuns have suffered with the coming of the warm weather, I think." Replacing that, she fingered some white flowers. A strong fragrance filled the room. "An ointment from this Madonna lily may ease Sister's Ruth's corns." A glee untinged by suitably pious benevolence teased at the corners of her mouth.

Eleanor turned to stare out the window as if something unusual had just caught her attention. "How fares Brother Thomas?" she asked, her tongue stumbling on the monk's name.

"I want to try an infusion of chamomile flowers for easier sleep and a mix of crushed, sweetened rosemary to chase his melancholia away."

"He has grown so thin and pale since our return from Amesbury. I would believe he was a ghost if I did not know otherwise."

"Sleep, even when it comes, rarely refreshes him."

"Brother John has found no solution? Can he offer no comfort?"

Anne hesitated as she considered how to phrase her response. Eleanor might know that the sub-infirmarian still spoke with the man she would always call *husband*, but the nun wished to protect the prioress from the details of how often they did meet or the particulars of these otherwise chaste encounters. "So far he has failed, much to his sorrow."

"I thought the festering wound was caused by his father's death, but surely there must be something else troubling Brother Thomas."

"Brother John fears that Satan has infected our brother's soul with some foul pestilence. If prayer, fasting, and self-mortification fail to cure him, he believes we must take more severe measures and use exorcism to cauterize the decay brought by the Evil One."

The prioress shuddered. "May God be merciful and chase the imp away! Yet I hear a note of disagreement in your words. Does exorcism not find favor with you?"

The nun shook her head. "Brother Thomas continues to give most godly comfort to the sick and dying in our hospital. How can such a man be owned by the Devil?"

"Still, the Evil One is a clever creature," Eleanor replied, "and Brother John does not often suggest such a remedy. For those reasons, I am disposed to take his recommendation; although it is drastic I would agree."

"I beg you to let me try other methods first! I did persuade Brother John to wait before he came to you for permission to perform exorcism."

"You are very much the child of your physician father."

"I do not deny the strength of evil or of God's grace, but I have also learned that skullcap is often useful in these matters and vervain may chase malevolent spirits away should rosemary and chamomile fail."

"God shows grace in many ways. For this reason, I have never denied the power of the healing arts when used with His direction." Eleanor hesitated. "I agree that a man, who continues to offer a gentle touch to the dying and spends his days in kind acts, is not likely to have given his soul into the Devil's hand. Yet, if he has not, what could be the cause of our brother's torment?"

Anne shook her head with frustration. "I wish I knew. When I begged him to confide his grief, he said only that his dreams were indescribable and the source inexplicable."

"Has there been any improvement after he began this latest task?"

"I believe so. He told me that carrying medicines at night to the sick and aged in Tyndal village has brightened his spirit. If sleep fails him, he would rather help those who cannot come to our hospital, yet need the ease our herbs can offer. Bringing mercy is far better, he said, than pacing the monks' cloister garth, which does little to chase away his own suffering."

Eleanor did not reply, nor did her expression betray her thoughts.

"Before an exorcism is done, I would try other remedies that wise men say will chase feverish dreams away while our brother continues his nightly mercies. These methods will take time to brighten the dark shade of his humors, but they are far kinder than exorcism."

"Your advice is always worthy. Of course, you have my permission, and I pray daily that our brother's melancholia will be cured. Along with your herbs, his extra acts of kindness may be enough to strike Satan's hot hand from his heart."

"God has smiled on us for many months now. May He do so in this matter as well."

"Aye, except for Brother Thomas' suffering, we have been blessed with peace. I must believe that God saw how greatly we have suffered from worldly violence and mercifully blessed us with a long reprieve from so many mortal woes."

"With one exception, I fear." Anne grinned as she gestured toward the now firmly shut door.

"Sister Ruth may think murderous thoughts on occasion," the prioress laughed, "but our sub-prioress loves God too much to ever act upon them."

Chapter Two

The summer night air had never felt so thick, Brother Thomas thought as he trudged along the path to Tyndal village. Each muscle in his body ached with the effort. Had he ever loved the summer season? Perhaps in the years before he became a monk. As a boy?

How long ago that seemed. He struggled to recall something of the time but could only see a fleeting image, albeit one of flashing color. Indeed he no longer expended much effort to recapture such memories. What sickening man wants to remember pleasures he had in life?

"Sinful musing," he muttered to himself. Brother John had told him to concentrate on the joys awaiting him in Heaven when earthly troubles bore down with crushing weight. Were he a true monk, Thomas thought, such thoughts should make his heart rejoice. Instead, they only ground a sharper edge on his anguish.

Thomas cursed the humid thickness of the still night air. His burning eyes longed for the soothing cool of autumn weather. Surely he would suffer less if he got more sleep. How many nights had it been since he had slept longer than an hour or two?

With so little rest, he had begun to see and hear strange things: naked, rampant imps dancing in the cloister garth; disembodied voices calling his name with such sweetness that he wept with longing; faces of people, some long dead, whom he had once loved.

If he did not believe that his soul would tumble into Hell, he would welcome death. But the Devil would rejoice if he committed self-murder, and Thomas was in no mood to give the fiend any more satisfaction than the creature already enjoyed with him.

At least he now had these nightly distractions. When Sister Anne suggested a new task to fill his sleepless hours, he accepted with eager gratitude. By providing aid to those who suffered far more than he, the monk found some relief. He might be the most wicked of men, but at least he could ease pain, bring comfort, and hold the hands of the dying. In addition, the walks into the village fatigued him enough to blunt the sharpness of tortured dreams when he did sleep.

Thomas exhaled a deep sigh. Poor Brother John was grieving over his failure to cure the melancholia. His confessor was a man of compassion and faith, but nothing John had suggested eased the feverish dreams, the taunting visions, or the coal-dark burden in his heart.

John himself believed in self-flagellation, but Thomas had stopped the practice when he found it gave him a troubling pleasure, a feeling he distrusted and disliked. On occasion, he found some spiritual ease when he lay face down on the stone floor of the chapel, but the moment he began repeating prayers, his soul filled with noise and peace took flight. God must flee the chapel at the very sight of me, Thomas had decided.

Nay, Brother John was innocent of failure. He could not staunch a hidden bleeding when Thomas was incapable of pointing out the lesion from which it flowed. Lust, especially for another man, was sinful. That simple thing he might have confessed, as he had done once. What he could not explain was the sweet tenderness woven into his physical longing for both Giles and the man at Amesbury. Wise men knew that God drew battered souls with tender gentleness while Satan lured a man's soul with glittering lust. For this reason, the combination of purity and transgression in his heart confused him.

His shoulders fell with despair's cruel weight. Maybe his confessor was right about the cauterizing effect of exorcism.

As matters stood now, Thomas' soul was dying of putrefying wounds.

As he approached the edge of the village, he stopped and rubbed his eyes. These questions inevitably circled back on themselves while God refused to give him answers. Perhaps he should be grateful for small mercies. Lust had ceased to bother him, except in dreams, and his current disinclination to sleep limited those occasions. While he was awake, he was blessed, as it were, with impotence.

"Very well," Thomas laughed. "Hasn't God graced me with some benevolence then? It seems I must be content enough with that."

He continued on to the village.

The path from the priory into the village of Tyndal now merged with the more traveled road from the west, one that was uneven and deeply rutted by the wheels of lumbering wagons. Thomas focused on keeping a steady pace without stumbling and dropping the vials he carried.

For the most part, the village was dark, whether the rude dwellings of the poor or the windowed houses of more prosperous families. No one here wore furred robes, but a few earned more than subsistence required. Whatever the nature of their daily labor, most were weary enough to sleep when the moon gained supremacy. Candles rarely flickered long after the sun had set.

The only brightness came from the inn at the fork in the road, one of the branches leading to Norwich with its great cathedral, relics, and abundant herring for those partial to the fish. Travelers from the west, on pilgrimage to Norwich's shrine of Saint William, brought profit to the inn, but the most business nowadays came from visitors to the priory's hospital. That was due to Prioress Eleanor. The inn had been a paltry thing until she arrived and lent her support to the healing skills of Sister Anne.

Before that time, East Anglian fishermen, and those that farmed the damp land in this remote area, rarely had the coin for decent ale, and never wine. The hospital had brought demand for finer craft and more trade. As a consequence, Tyndal village had grown richer, hosting a regular market day as well as attracting merchants who catered to those who sought cures for gout, bad digestion, and other ills of leisure. Sister Anne had many remedies for the afflictions that plagued courtiers, and they were willing to pay for them, afterward finding solace in the pleasures offered by a well-appointed inn.

Thomas' destination was just beyond it. Although it was not his nature to be sanctimonious, he lowered his eyes to avoid seeing the lewd glow. Inns held too many memories he wished to forget, and he increased his pace to pass quickly by. Joyous shouts and loud singing assaulted his ears. Shuddering despite the muggy heat, he muttered a plea for protection against the lure of worldly delights he had enjoyed in the past.

Briefly, he hesitated. Did he not hear that Crowner Ralf had recently returned and might his friend be at the inn? Thomas turned to look back. He had grown fond of that rude but honest man. The former soldier and the unwilling monk had become friends before the crowner had deserted the village for the court. Thomas had missed him. Should he not seek him out, share some ale, and welcome him home?

Nay, I shall not, he said to himself. I would not be cause for any wicked rumor to reach Prioress Eleanor. I am no minor clerk, rather a monk, and have no cause to be drinking ale at any inn. Firmly bowing his head, he gripped the sleeping draught he had brought for old Tibia and hastened away.

The woman's hut was but a few yards further on. The dwelling looked quite dark as the monk approached. No window fronted it, but there were spaces enough in the walls to show any light if a candle had been lit. Was Tibia fast asleep without this potion? Or was she gravely ill and in need of aid? Fearing the latter, his heart began to pound.

He tried the door. Although the alignment was askew and the door caught in the hard earth, it finally opened to a firm pressure from his hand.

"Mistress?" he said, his voice rising above the noise from the inn. "Are you ill?"

Nothing.

He began to ease himself inside.

"Careful, Brother. Wait for me. I don't want you to trip over some pot." It was a woman's voice, roughened by age, the tone flattened with an effort to disguise pain.

Thomas leapt back and turned.

"You're wondering that I am not in my bed?"

The woman limped closer, a dark shadow outlined against the light from the inn. Pulling herself forward with a thick bough, her progress was slow. Her back was bent so cruelly that Thomas was doubtful she could see much beyond the earth under her feet.

"You think I should lie still on my straw, waiting for my fate because I must die soon?" She hissed these words as she stopped in front of him and then laughed. The sound was sharp like the snapping of twigs.

Thomas drew away from the over-sweet foulness of her breath. "Nay," he said, "yet I wonder that you can do otherwise." Not a kind statement, he realized and chastised himself for his thoughtlessness.

She waved impatiently at him. "For God's sake, Brother, step aside. I can no longer stand."

He moved away from the open door.

"Nay, not inside." She pointed with one trembling, gnarled finger. "Help me to sit. That stool. There."

As he eased her down, he marveled at the lightness of her body.

"Ah, he is so youthful," she sighed.

Thomas quickly understood that she was not speaking to him. Had her wits wandered? Did she imagine some long dead companion sat beside her, or a sister, maybe a husband?

"The young see in themselves only the beauty they'll lose." Tibia chuckled as if sharing a joke with her invisible friend. "And us? We're just crones to them, as if we've never been else. But we know better." She began to rhythmically tap her hand against her knee. "When we see these wrinkled faces in rain puddles, we can still see the shadows of proud breasts and straight limbs in all our drooping flesh. Isn't that so? And white teeth, too, in these empty mouths."

Thomas shivered. "May I bring you something to eat or drink?" he asked, eager to recall her wits if nothing else.

Turning her head, Tibia looked up at the monk. Her narrow-set eyes blinked nervously as she struggled to remember who he was.

To ease any fear she had, he grinned like the foolish youth she had just described.

"Signy fed me bits of softened meat at the inn," she replied, the unseen companion now forgotten, or else dismissed back to the spirit world. "A good woman. Some claim she holds her head too high for a tavern wench. I wouldn't. She comforts me. Why not find kindness when she lays a gentle hand on my arm? It's a rare enough thing," she cackled, pointing her twisted finger at him. "Old women know how cruel men can be."

Was this woman a witch or simply mad? What should he make of her words? Thomas grew more uneasy and bent forward to look at her sharp-featured face, hoping to learn something from the look in her eyes. The angle of her head made it impossible. All he could see was white hair that provided but scant covering to the top of her head.

"Aren't you the silent one, Brother! Am I so disgusting? Or do you think me sinful for feeding this..." She brushed one hand lightly over her breasts. "...decaying flesh? Should I have prayed instead?"

"You may be old but are not yet dying," Thomas replied. His words might have been innocuous, but his tone was sharp with irritation. She was no witch, he thought, just a troublesome hag. He bit his lip in repentance, cursing the weariness that made him impatient and harsh to a querulous old woman in pain. "As for the innkeeper's niece, I do not listen to mean-spirited gossip," he added quickly.

"Ah, charity! That's always the greatest virtue, isn't it? Never hope. Why's that? I've always wondered." Tibia laughed but there was no joy in it. "Ah, Brother, forgive me. You came here with warm compassion, and I burn your ears with blasphemy. I confess it. I have sinned. Will you forgive me in God's name?"

"God forgives everything." Thomas extended his hand. "Would you not go inside and seek your bed? Sister Anne has sent a sleeping draught."

Briefly, Tibia struggled to stand, then gave up with a loud gasp. "Lift me, if you're willing. Take me to my straw pile," she whimpered. "Were my son alive, he'd have made me a softer place to lie in and stayed while I fell asleep…"

Thomas felt a twinge of guilt. "Then after you drink this, let me wait in his stead until you sleep," he said, bending to pick her up.

She uttered a sharp cry as he set her on her feet, and then pushed weakly at him when he took one arm to steady her. "You're most kind, Brother," she hissed in pain. "Please sit at my side. As you offered. Tell me of God's grace. That would bring comfort. I must think on dying."

With that, she slipped through the small opening to her dwelling.

Thomas followed her into the darkness.

Chapter Three

Signy reached out, desperately grasping for the wall to steady herself.

Her head spun. A cold sweat rolled down her temples and cheeks. Then her fingers did find the wall and she leaned against it, pressing her face against the rough surface as if greeting a dear friend. Slowly the nausea eased, but the sweat did not dry in the oppressive air of the upper rooms.

It is over, she thought. It is done with. Yet she trembled with the weakness of a newborn babe. The innkeeper's niece squeezed her eyes shut to keep from weeping.

Below her, the patrons of her uncle's inn shouted. A few sang bawdy songs, and their raucous joy rose with the stench of their hot bodies.

Signy took a deep breath, taking in the familiar smell to reassure herself that the world was no different than it had been but a few minutes ago. Turning around, she leaned her back against the wall. A sharp twig protruding from the hard clay wall scratched her arm. From the thatch above her, she heard a familiar rustling. Rat or mouse most likely, creatures she hated, but tonight their stubborn presence was a source of comfort.

"I loathe Martin," she muttered and felt better for having said it. Why should she feel otherwise? He was a man who took whatever he wanted, discarded it at will, but always left evidence of his possession like gangrene in a poisoned wound.

"And I hate his foul jests," she said.

Bringing Ivetta here on a regular basis, as if the inn were a brothel, was just one example. Why not swyve the town whore midst the wood splinters on the floor of his cooper's shop, when he wanted a woman, or rent out his stinking bed when he had a paying customer for her?

"Because he wished to mock me," she answered herself.

Signy pushed herself upright, walked slowly to the top of the stairs, and looked down at the milling crowd below. The inn was a profitable enough business, so why did her uncle permit this blatant whoring? Surely it did not bring him that much extra coin.

"I like the king's face on silver as much as my kinsman," Signy whispered, "but I would have spat in Martin's face, not grasped his hand in agreement, when he suggested this arrangement."

Of course she had particular grounds to hate such a proposition, the cause of which her uncle was quite ignorant. But Martin knew her reasons well and found especial pleasure in the distress this whoring brought her. "I may not be chaste," she said, as if arguing with some critic in the shadows, "but I have never given myself for gain."

Not that many of the men below had not hoped otherwise when she first came to serve at the inn, but her uncle soon knocked several heads together. The word quickly spread that the innkeeper's niece might be a buxom lass, but her body was not for hire. Now she might still suffer ribald jests but only the occasional, rude touch. The former she answered with light and practiced retorts. The latter she greeted with the prick of a pin she kept secreted in her sleeve.

Signy looked behind her at the closed door. The nausea returned, and she quickly shifted her gaze around to the room below. Straightening her back, she started down the narrow stairs. "Business is good," she said aloud. That would please her uncle as much as it did her.

Halfway down, she stopped and bent to look toward the inn door. Old Tibia must have left, she thought. Her heart ached for the poor soul, alone in the world and growing aged without kin to take her in. Although she and her uncle might disagree about allowing Ivetta, the harlot, to ply her trade in the room above, they did not argue about giving the old woman a meal and a cup of weak ale.

In the past, the woman had often sat at that bench near the door and earned enough crumbs by selling remedies to ease mortal ills to keep herself alive. She enjoyed an especially brisk business in herbs that counteracted the effects of too much ale and was known to have tonics that helped men plagued by impotence. Even after the priory hospital became so popular, she kept her following of those who preferred not to share their particular sins with lay brothers, many of whom were reputed to be gossips. In the last few months, however, Tibia had plied her trade less and less.

Signy shook her head. The old woman must be suffering so much pain now from her back and leg that death would be a joy. Youth surely had its curses, but those attendant upon the aged must be harsher to bear. Was there some merit in dying before the hair turned gray?

She glanced back at the now invisible room above, shuddered, and hurried down the remaining stairs.

Easing her way through the crowd of men shouting orders for food and drink, she caught sight of Ralf the crowner, still in his corner and staring at nothing, grim as ever. Through the crush of milling bodies, she watched him for a moment without danger of being seen. He had reason enough these days for that dour look after the death of his wife. A pang of sympathy did prick her heart, and she asked herself if she had finally forgiven him for using her so cruelly that brief time now past.

She rolled the thought around in her mind as if seeking out any hidden bitterness. One part of her argued she should not condemn him. After all, wasn't it simply a man's nature to care little if the soft body he rode so casually offered that sweet ride out of love? Another now roundly cursed that she had been born one of Eve's descendants, creatures with much cause to resent God's decision to make them helpmeets to Adam. "Our Lord should have chosen some other to serve instead—like the perfidious serpent," Signy muttered.

As she watched Ralf pick up his pitch-sealed jack of ale, hesitate, and then drink with eyes shut, she felt a sharp pain in her heart. How many times had she watched this small habit of his and smiled?

She clenched her fist and hurled silent abuse at his head. The very next moment, her heart cooled her fury and she concluded she was being unfair to the man.

He was rude, prickly as a hedgehog, but a good man who had loved another for many years. Of course she had heard the tales before she took him into her bed, but she imagined she could turn his heart away from a woman who was now a nun. Instead, he cried out Sister Anne's name while swyving Signy.

"Had he wanted something more than a mere vessel in which to release his seed," she muttered, "I could have been patient and taught him how kindly I could love. Instead, he ran off to court and married a woman with land. Fa!" She spat. "No better than his greedy boor of a brother, he is."

An arm brushed against her breast.

Signy felt her face turn hot with angry humiliation, and she reached for her pin.

The man looked down at her, blinking with drunken concentration. "I meant nothing. I was pushed," he slurred, nervously casting his glance sideways to measure the distance to the inn door should the innkeeper seek amends.

Signy nodded forgiveness and then pushed a path through the bodies toward the door herself. When she reached cooler air, her thoughts slipped back to the deceitful crowner. At least she had not quickened with child from her brief bedding with Ralf before he deserted her. She shook with a brief chill.

A pregnancy would have caused her much difficulty at the inn. Although some in the village suspected that she had granted her favors to the man, there was no obvious proof that she had shared her bed with Ralf. Rumors were whispered, but they often were even where there was no truth in the tales. Had she provided evidence with a rounded belly, however, many would have called her *whore* as they did Ivetta, and men would have expected similar service.

The moment her courses failed she could have sought out old Tibia. Sin though it was, women in the village often did, willing to do penance rather than chance hunger by failing to help at harvest time or see yet another wee loved one die. But this would have been Ralf's child. Would she have rid herself of a babe she might have loved? With clenched fist against her heart, she thanked God she had not had to make that choice.

"Sweet Signy!" a merry fellow shouted as he exited the inn. "The ale tastes bitter without you to serve it."

"Yet it seems you have drunk enough of it not to know which soft hand passed you that last jug!"

The man belched with good cheer, gave a genial wave, and staggered down the road to his bed.

Watching him, she mused how strange it was that reputation depended on what rumors were about and the credence given them. As long as a woman was not flagrant with her lovers, others could pretend she was virtuous if they had little else to quarrel with her about. That was a fragile state of affairs, but, truth be told, she had taken few enough lovers to keep the rumble of gossip low. Ralf had been the first in a long time, and she had lain with him only once. Since then, she had been chaste enough, although some now claimed she had caught Tostig's eye.

She sighed and walked back into the inn. Would she mind if that were the case? Despite coming to the inn many evenings and speaking at length with both her and her uncle, the tall Saxon had yet to claim any love for her, nor had he even suggested they lie together. Perhaps his only interest at the inn lay in the priory ale he had to sell.

Signy glanced back in the direction of the now-invisible crowner, tossed her head, and picked up a sweating jug. Tostig was a handsome man, she decided. If he begged sweetly, she might consider taking him to bed. That was a thought pleasant enough to soothe her bruised heart.

She smiled and served a table of thirsty men.

As she looked around for others in need of food or drink, she was relieved not to see either Hob or Will. If God were kind, they would have left. Of the two brothers, Hob was usually harmless. Although sullen in nature, he avoided confrontation when by himself. Will, on the other hand, was both choleric and brutal. That noted, the brothers caused trouble when Will had had too much to drink. Although prone to starting fights, he was a coward when attacked. Hob, it was, who had to protect his elder brother with his fists.

Signy slammed the jug down on a table. If she ever did inherit this inn from her childless uncle, as he had promised, she would hire a strong man to throw such fellows out. "Under my ownership," she muttered softly, "this inn will countenance neither harlots nor fights."

"A bowl of your fine stew, served with your pretty hands, would be a pleasure, lass!" shouted a man nearby, his gaze savoring the curves of Signy's heavy breasts.

"Would your wife like to know how our cook prepares it?" the innkeeper's niece replied with forced humor, softening it with a dazzling smile.

Chapter Four

Crowner Ralf wiped his hand across his mouth. "Not drunk enough to feel happy," he muttered, staring into the brown liquid that still half-filled his leather jack as if accusing the ale of some crime. Were he to think more on that, he might have confessed that little had ever brought him profound contentment until recently, but he was rarely in the mood for contemplative debates. Tonight was no exception.

Earlier, he and Tostig had met at the inn to celebrate the crowner's return from court. That they had done with pleasure enough, but his friend from childhood was a prudent man and left, like any responsible merchant, at a sensible hour. Thus Ralf was left alone, accompanied only by all the reasons why he had not been in the village for over a year.

Some time ago, he had glanced up to see Signy climb the stairs to the private rooms above. Resting his bristling chin on his hand, he let himself enjoy the sight of her soft buttocks swaying under the fabric of her robe. A tall and buxom woman, she gave this inn its especial brightness and had once shared his bed with ardent willingness.

He sighed and stroked the tabletop with lingering remorse. Had he not called her by another woman's name when he was riding her, she might have continued to pleasure him, but his mistake had quickly cooled her eagerness. Since Ralf was not a complete boor, he did understand why and had even apologized, but all efforts to make amends were greeted with a broom to his head. He had not approached her since. After that night, she always sent another wench to serve him whenever he visited the inn.

This evening, although she stopped to speak to Tostig, she had turned her back on the crowner, ignoring him as if he did not exist and had not been absent from the area for well over a year. He had been hurt at the snub, and, when she disappeared through the crowd of men, Ralf realized he still regretted what had occurred between them. Although much had happened since he tried to escape his especial grief in mindless service to his unpleasant elder brother, he had retained a fondness for a woman he believed to be kind and sweet-tempered—unless provoked, of course. Now, he suspected she might have transferred her affections to Tostig, a pleasing thought overall.

Or was it? He frowned.

In any event, Tostig had said nothing about any feelings for Signy. He had not even spoken her name after the innkeeper's niece left them. The man instead had amused the crowner pleasantly with village news and asked about Ralf's brief marriage as well as tales from court.

Did that mean Signy had not captured his heart?

Perhaps he should simply overlook Tostig's reticence to talk of any woman. The man had rejected all idea of marriage when his parents died and he chose to raise his younger sister, Gytha. The girl herself was now of marriageable age, but her doting brother had given her more choice about a husband than was considered wise. Since she had yet to settle on anyone, a few eager suitors now urged Tostig to simply decide for her, as was more proper. He ignored them.

"There's a spirited girl," Ralf said with a grin when Tostig told him that she had just rejected a goldsmith of acceptable means. "When she finds a husband she likes, he had better be a worthy fellow or he will have you to deal with." And maybe himself as well, Ralf thought. He had always liked the lass.

Ralf sat back. Out of old habit, he began to scan the crowd. Most of the faces were familiar to him. Some of the tradesmen had grown grayer, stouter, or even frail. Sitting with them now were sons too young to have joined their fathers when Ralf was last here but since grown old enough to take on a man's responsibility as well as vice.

Was Ivetta the whore still stripping these lads of their virginity, he wondered, or was she finally too raddled for that? Tyndal was not big enough to have an excess of young girls, lush and ripe for the swyving by rampant young men. The town prostitute had often provided that service, although it was not uncommon for a daughter to be churched before a father could push her to the church door for a wedding.

A movement at the corner of his eye caught Ralf's attention, and he turned to see Will and Hob coming down the stairs, stumbling like a pair of drunken goats. His mouth filled with a foul taste and he swallowed some ale as antidote.

When they were all younger, the brothers were town bullies, picking on the weaker like the cowards they were while leaving him alone because he always blackened their eyes first. Martin Cooper was part of that gang, he remembered, and had added cruel jests to the brothers' usual ill behavior. Most of the damage left by all three was minor enough in the life of any boy: some broken noses, a few burns, and one lost ear. There were also the inevitable, broken maidenheads, although more than usual were unwillingly burst as he had heard. The girls denied all. Out of fear, he suspected.

Once, however, the boys had gone too far. A lad had died of hanging when the rope caught in the tree. They panicked and ran, leaving him to jerk in the air and then choke to death. The boy's mother had discovered his limp body and raised a hue and cry, but the boys suffered no consequence.

In fact, after the crowner's jury found the death accidental, she was fined for falsely raising the hue and cry. After the decision was announced, Ralf and Tostig had discussed whether the verdict had been decided more on other considerations than the event itself: two of the boys were the blacksmith's sons; the dead lad's mother was believed to be a meddler in magic.

Tonight, the two brothers passed near enough that Ralf could smell their sooty sweat, but the men were too deeply involved in some argument to pay him heed. The crowner was glad enough of that. Just remembering the death of that young boy had made his fist itch to strike. When he had been named crowner, it was the memory of this tale, among other things, that caused him to swear never to choose the easy answer to any crime.

As he watched the two men disappear, he recalled Tostig remarking that the younger brother had become almost respectable over the last several months, although he still bloodied his knuckles in Will's defense when necessary. Had Hob changed that much? Although Ralf had seen the younger blacksmith grow less wild over the years, he believed that few men ever truly repented until they were on their death beds, knowing they must face God's judgment.

The crowner poured himself more ale and raised the jack to drink. "Maybe some do, a bit," he whispered, setting the jack down. After all, he was not drinking himself into oblivion tonight. The reason was his wee babe, a daughter he adored. Why find some empty solace at the inn when he had a child at home who would smile when he picked her up for a hug?

"After all the horrors I saw in my soldiering years and the cruelties I have seen men commit against each other, how can this leathery heart still melt so?" A veritable miracle, he decided, his mouth twisting into an embarrassed grin as he pushed the drink further away.

He never thought fatherhood would affect him so. Perhaps his own father had been right when he called Ralf a disappointment, the contrary one, compared to his elder brothers. A man was supposed to want strong sons, but he had roared with joy when he learned his wife had given birth to a lass. But how could he not love this beautiful little girl? Weren't her cheeks pink like a fine apple and her ten fingers perfection in miniature?

Shifting on the bench, he knew he must find her a new wet-nurse very soon. As he was rocking the baby to sleep in his arms last night, the woman his brother had sent complained bitterly about the rank pig swill and steaming piles of manure all too near the house on the land Ralf had acquired through marriage. He might have been pleased that the manor was situated close to Tyndal village, but few women, used to the comforts of such things as castle latrines, would enjoy what the remote and lonely land of East Anglia had to offer. He had promised the woman he would send her back to Winchester soon enough.

Aye, the land stank of dead things from the sea and hobby-lanterns danced above the fens on misty nights. Yet he loved this place despite all the sad memories it evoked. Perhaps he was happiest back at Tyndal village after all. Old habits must die hard, he decided, and suddenly realized he was hungry.

He waved at a serving wench and asked for stew. When she put the bowl down in front of him, the pungent smell of well-spiced rabbit cooked with onions brushed aside his mild alcoholic haze and led his stomach to rumble with pleasant anticipation.

As he plunged his spoon after a bit of meat and onion, he caught sight of Signy waiting on a group of men nearby. He felt a twinge of lust as he recalled how those rounded thighs had held him fast in the night. Then he shook off the image and filled his mouth with flavorful stew.

Two men beside him roared out an irreverent song, slamming their jacks on the wooden table.

Ralf turned to grin at them.

It was just then that a woman's piercing scream from the upper loft shattered all merriment.

Chapter Five

Thomas heard shouting and grew cold with fear. He quickly took a deep breath but smelled no smoke. That brought him hope, but what besides fire would warrant such an outcry?

He bent to listen to Tibia's strong, steady breathing. It would be a blessing if she could sleep like this until morning, and if there was no purpose in doing so, he would not rouse her.

A fire was the most probable cause for the uproar, a horror that could destroy the village so swiftly, but he still could not smell smoke. Might it have been an attack by lawless men? That was doubtful and had never occurred in his memory. There was no reason to believe it had now. Puzzled, he rose to investigate first before carrying her from her bed.

As he squeezed through that narrow hole that served as entry to her hut, he saw a crowd of villagers milling about just outside the inn. "No flames or smoke at all," he noted with relief, then grew curious. Why did they seem so distraught, yet remain as if awed by something? He pulled the rough door closed and went to discover the reason for the commotion.

"What took place?" he asked, walking up to a broad-shouldered man who stood at the far edge of the crowd.

"The Devil flew into the inn's loft, I heard." Rivulets of moisture twisted through the stubble on the man's face.

"Did you see him?" Thomas asked, noting that the hot summer night was insufficient cause for such rank sweat.

"Nay, but I have more sense than to let Satan come close and grasp my soul with his twisted fingers. Someone in the inn wasn't so clever and now lies there a corpse, or so I was told. That's why I stand here."

The Devil would not be put off by such a short distance, Thomas thought, but decided there was no merit in frightening the man further. If it was Satan, perhaps he could be of service. Sinner he might well be, but he still bore a monk's tonsure. Oddly enough, he found himself eager to confront this tormentor of his and pushed his way through the crowd toward the entrance to the inn.

"Don't go in there!" someone shouted at him.

"It is a monk from the priory. Prioress Eleanor has sent aid!"

"Brother Thomas!" another cried out. "Praise God and the holy priory for sending you to us!"

"May God forgive my sins!" A fat man collapsed to his knees as the monk passed. "Save us from the Evil One, and I will bring the priory an offering at daybreak. I swear it, Brother!"

Thomas hesitated a moment, recognized the man as one more prone to fair sayings than fine acts, and hurried on through the inn door. Shutting it carefully, he pressed his back against it, made the sign of the cross for protection, and looked around for imps or their fiendish prince.

There was nothing. He relaxed. How shabby an empty inn looked, he caught himself noting, and was oddly troubled by the observation.

Near the bottom of the stairs, he saw Signy standing beside her uncle and walked toward them. Their faces were pale; their staring eyes dark with fear.

"What happened?" he asked gently.

Startled, Signy gasped and her hand flew to her heart. "How did word reach the priory so quickly?"

"It has not," Thomas said. "I was sitting with old Tibia after she took a potion sent by Sister Anne. When I heard shouting, I rushed here to find the cause."

The innkeeper grunted. "It's well you did. Our crowner is in the loft alone, except for a corpse and a whore. Some claim Satan is flying about up there with his dark angels. Now that good King Henry is dead, the Prince of Darkness has little reason to show respect for a king's man. What's needed upstairs is a man of God to get rid of any rank spirit and save the crowner!"

"The Devil may be evil but he is not stupid," Thomas replied. "King Edward is coming home from the Holy Land." Looking up the stairs, he could see little and heard only the thud of footsteps mixed with muted speech. If Ralf was confronting Satan, they were both behaving in a most courteous fashion. "Satan knows how much God favors a crusader king and would face our crowner knowing that."

"I am so grateful the herb woman left the inn before this happened!" Signy hugged herself to keep from shaking. "Is she well, Brother? Should I go to her now that you are here?"

"The drink caused her to fall into a deep sleep. Methinks she will be well enough until morning." He turned to the innkeeper. "You said our crowner is in the loft with a corpse and a harlot. Then the Devil came? Or was this in reverse. I do not understand."

The man puffed his florid cheeks out. "My business did not need this. It is hard enough to keep good customers with the common twists and turns of trade, but news of violent death in an inn scares people away faster than rotten meat."

Thomas raised an eyebrow at the reply. If the innkeeper was now worrying more about trade than fork-tailed imps, he was recovering from his fright. Any conclusion that Satan had made a personal appearance here was also growing less likely.

"A man is dead," the man continued. "When the news spread, someone claimed to have seen a black-winged imp with a bloody mouth fly out the door. My customers fled and now rumor is rife that my inn has been taken over by the Prince of Darkness." The innkeeper waved at the crowd outside. "My trade suffers! The ale I bought turns stale, and the stew grows rancid. Those men outside should be drinking and eating in here." He blinked, then began to grin at Thomas with new hope shining in his eyes. "Could you do an exorcism to scare the Fiend away, Brother? Done while the whole village could watch? Doesn't the Devil flee in a great puff of smoke, or something like that, to prove he's left?"

"Uncle, I think we might show some concern for the safety of our crowner—and the whore as well," Signy said through clenched teeth.

The innkeeper's expression did not suggest he was regaining much interest in either.

"Has anyone called for his sergeant?" Thomas asked.

The innkeeper shrugged and looked at his niece.

"Not yet," Signy said. "Ralf ran upstairs as soon as he heard a scream. He has not come down or asked us to do anything yet."

"He must be safe enough," the innkeeper added. "I may have heard some curses but haven't yet smelt burnt flesh."

"Then I shall join him," Thomas said, looking up at the loft.

"Take care, Brother," Signy cried out. "I will send someone for Cuthbert."

"If you get rid of the Devil while you are up there, Brother, spread the tale." The innkeeper winked. "I will double my next gift to the priory hospital."

Thomas nodded and started his climb upward. If the innkeeper even paid his expected tithe to the parish church, he thought, Prioress Eleanor would count it a minor miracle.

◇◇◇

Thomas gagged as the stench from excrement and vomit hit his nose and bore into his stomach.

"Get out of here," Ralf roared at the sound of the monk's retching.

The harlot, Ivetta, cowered naked on a bed in a corner of the room. She held one arm across her breasts and a hand between her thighs. "It's a monk," she squealed.

Ralf turned around, his expression softening with both fondness and amusement. "What brought you here, Brother? Does the Virgin now send your prioress visions or is her new anchoress truly an all-knowing saint?"

Thomas swallowed hard, then coughed. "I was close by, sitting with old Tibia, and heard the shouting. What is going on?"

As the crowner rose from his crouch, he pointed to the corpse. "Martin, formerly a cooper," he said as calmly as if he were making polite introductions.

The dead man lay on the floor, a dull, rough sheet twisted around his naked body. Both were spotted with yellow, brown, and blood-red stains. Considering the pattern of body fluids scattered around the room, the cooper must have violently flung himself about before he died.

"It was the Devil did it," Ivetta whimpered.

"Or else you because he wouldn't pay your fee," Ralf snapped.

Thomas looked about for something to cover the woman, then spied a crumpled gown on the floor nearby and tossed it to her. "Why do you think it was Satan?"

She snatched the thing and fingered the coarse cloth as if finding some comfort there. "You should have seen Martin's eyes. Just before he started to jerk about, they grew so big! They changed color from blue to black. He must have seen the Evil One!"

"If his eyes were big, maybe he did. The sight of you, in any light, would cause a man's parts to shrink." Ralf was back down on his knees.

She spat at him, then pulled the round-necked tunic over her head and let it fall carelessly around her body.

The crowner rolled the corpse over. "What think you, Brother? I smell no fumes from Hell. I'd swear the Devil had less to do with this crime than his handmaid."

"The stench seems mortal enough, but I would not conclude much else from that." Thomas continued to study the pale-faced woman in the corner.

"What handmaid, Crowner?" Ivetta cried, suddenly aware of what Ralf was suggesting.

"Did Martin refuse to pay his entry fee when he found the doorway fouled?"

Ivetta flew at Ralf, her fingers bent like eagle talons.

Thomas grabbed her before she did damage to a king's man. "Be still, woman! You were witness to what happened. We must hear the details from you."

She pushed the monk away, then gestured at the man kneeling on the floor. "Do you think he will listen to a whore, Brother?"

"If you doubt he shall, then believe that I will." Thomas reached out as if offering peace.

"Why are you not terrified of a woman like me?" She stared at him.

"The founder of my Order sought out women in brothels to spread God's truth. In consequence, I fear you not and would hear what you have to say."

"What does that matter if you do?" Ivetta shrugged. "He'll hang me for this in any case."

"Our crowner is a fair man."

"You heard what he just said."

Thomas glanced down at Ralf and wondered himself why this man, who had always shown more love of truth than anything else, had spoken so cruelly to this woman.

"I have naught to say," the woman said. "Why waste the little breath I have left, talking to a man who has already condemned me." Ivetta fell silent. The sulky expression in her eyes did little to mask the pallor of fear on her face.

"Go back to the priory, Brother. This murder has naught to do with you," Ralf said as he rose and wiped his hands on his leather tunic. "It has all the common marks of a man's act, not the Devil's."

"Then may I tell the crowd outside that Satan had no direct hand in this?" Thomas asked. If he could not serve God in this matter, he could at least do something for priory business since it was priory ale that the innkeeper bought.

"Aye, this is solely the king's affair," the crowner said, glaring at the woman in the corner.

Chapter Six

Signy sat down on the bench near the doorway to the cook shack and turned her face away. She was not pleased.

Ralf was scarlet with anger and frustration. "I only ask to learn what happened."

"You have already made up your mind."

"That is what Ivetta claims."

"As you know, Ralf, I am no friend to the harlot, but I might agree with her in this."

"I have not determined guilt!"

Signy looked heavenward as if seeking guidance or, more likely, patience. "Very well, the tale is simple enough: I took food and drink to Ivetta and Martin, both of whom were alive when I left."

Ralf waited for more, then growled, "Did you see anything unusual?"

"*Unusual?*" she mimicked. "Perhaps you imagine that I stayed to watch them couple?" Her face flushed. "Do you think me the kind of woman who spies on such things? Or maybe you believe my uncle sent me as a third to increase their pleasuring?"

"I meant none of that," Ralf roared. "Just answer my question. What did you see when you were in that room?"

"First, I knocked at the door," Signy's pitch dropped with mock gravity. "Martin opened it. I entered, laid the tray on the table, then left. Question Ivetta. She knows more than I could possibly."

"She refuses to talk to me."

"Do you blame her? Even I heard you shout at the woman, and I was below the stairs."

"She was in the room where he died, and I can count the reasons why she might want to kill him." Ralf rubbed his fingers as if feeling good coins.

"You have spent too much time with your brother, Crowner. I see that you will now take the easiest route and choose the simplest answer without further care for justice. Is Ivetta not a whore? Are her shameful ways not reason enough to condemn her for other crimes?"

Ralf slammed his fist against the side of the wall and cursed.

Signy jumped to her feet. "Methinks all women are whores to you. You certainly treated me like one. Why should I answer you either? I have no reason to suppose you would believe me any more than you do Ivetta."

"You are no harlot! I wronged you. I confessed it then. I repeat it now. Is that not enough?"

Signy's eyes flashed with anger.

"But you have recovered well enough if the tales I hear are true."

"And what lies do you choose to believe?"

"That Tostig would marry you."

"Have you heard this from him or, for that matter, from me?"

"What need have I of that, when all others speak of it?" he shouted.

Signy's blue eyes began to glow like sapphires in the hot sun. "Indeed you have just proven that you are no different from either of your brothers. Rumor becomes truth if it suits you. Otherwise, you might have asked yourself whether Tostig would even consider marriage to a woman like me." Disloyal tears began to flow down her cheeks. "After all, is he not your friend? As such, he knows you bedded me, and, like all men, he wants his woman unbreached until he comes with his own lance raised."

"I said nothing…"

"And the moment after a woman does open her gate to the brave knight, he calls her *whore* and mocks…" She turned away and, with one swipe of her hand, destroyed the tears that had cruelly exposed her vulnerability.

Ralf groaned. "This is getting nowhere. If you hate me still, I cannot blame you, but I must hear from you all you know of what happened tonight."

Signy folded her arms. "I took food and drink up to the room for Ivetta and her customer, as I said. I shut the door and returned to serve those downstairs. We all heard Ivetta scream. You were there yourself as witness after that." She turned around and glared at him. "Do you accuse me of murdering the cooper?"

"Did you?" he barked. Immediately both repentant and exasperated, he covered his eyes with his hand.

"I must have, hadn't I? No one else poured the wine or took it up to the room."

"This is murder, Signy. Do not mock or I must ask if that is a confession."

"*Mock?*"

Ralf waited. A muscle twitched nervously in his cheek. "Why do you say it was the wine that killed him? I did not mention anything."

"It matters not what I do or do not say, Crowner. Arrest me if you want. Chain Ivetta and me together and take us both off to dance in the air if that suits you best. You'll hang whomever you wish on this no matter what the truth."

Ralf pressed his fingers into the corners of his eyes as if to numb a very sharp pain.

Chapter Seven

A pottery jug shattered against the wall. Ale splattered across the stone floor, altar, and the prie-dieu. The orange cat flew from his nest on the narrow bed and raced toward the safety of the public rooms.

Prioress Eleanor was suffering from a most uncharacteristic rage.

"I hate him! God curse him!" Her hand shook, but she gripped her aunt's letter from Amesbury with the force of one who would take it to the grave with her.

Gytha peeked through the entrance at her mistress, then very quietly slipped back from the prioress' private quarters, and left the chambers.

"May his soul crackle and burst in the bubbling pitch of Hell!" With her free hand, she raised a pewter tray as if to send it after the broken jug, then dropped it, and collapsed to her knees.

Clutching the letter to her heart, the leader of Tyndal began to weep with a rare anguish. "Nay, I did not mean any of that. May God forgive me," she sobbed. "I do not want him cursed!"

The prioress crawled to her prie-dieu. She laid the letter out as if to read it again and ran her hand over it most gently. Then she slammed her fist down and shoved the offending thing onto the floor. "How dare he do this to me?"

She pressed her forehead against the prie-dieu until the carving bit into her flesh. "My heart broke vows for him. My body suffered lust for him. At night, when Satan sent his imp dressed in the body of that cruel monk, I coupled with the incubus and took joy in it! Now I learn he is a spy, a viper at my breast!" With each phrase, she beat a fist against her heart.

With a cry of almost animal pain, Eleanor flung herself on the floor in front of her altar, covered her face, and howled for mercy and solace.

Comfort was slow in coming, but at last her sobbing did quiet, and reason tentatively slipped back from its brief and unexpected exile.

The prioress of Tyndal raised herself to her knees and sat back. "Should I not be grateful?" she sighed. "I might have learned this secret in any number of other ways." Someone besides her aunt, some enemy who did not have Eleanor's best interests in mind, might have used the knowledge against her. Sister Beatrice, however, not only understood the pain and anger her letter would cause but would also keep the revelation close to her heart.

As she knelt, her emotions teetering on the brink of another burst of despair, a soft body bumped against her and rubbed against her hands. Looking down, she did smile and picked up the large orange cat, holding him close to her heart. "Ah, sweet Arthur," she sighed as he began to purr, "men may be cruel and faithless, but you remain my only perfect knight." Rising to her feet, the prioress of Tyndal rubbed her cheek against the soft bundle of fur.

After a few moments, convinced that he had done what was required, the great tabby squirmed out of her arms, leapt to the floor, and returned to the aforementioned bed where his recent nap had been so abruptly interrupted.

Eleanor picked up her aunt's letter, and then held the item at arm's length. "He is still a traitor," she said to the missive, her voice brittle with scorn. "I am a weak woman, Eve's child, created as an afterthought from a mortal man's rib. Brother Thomas, on the other hand, is Adam's descendant, the creature He made first as His more perfect reflection. As the superior being, blessed with logic and reason denied women, shouldn't Brother Thomas have understood that he could not serve two masters? Did he not understand when he came to Tyndal that he owed me protection and obedience just as the beloved disciple was commanded to do for Our Lord's mother? He should have known better than to commit such a heinous transgression! How dare he be so deceitful?"

Or was he? And, if he was, should she assume that he was truly disloyal to her?

Eleanor carefully reread her aunt's letter. Sister Beatrice had not, in fact, condemned the monk for duplicity. While praising him for his dedication to God's work in ferreting out those who plotted against Church power, she had also carefully emphasized his loyal service to Eleanor and her family at Wynethorpe Castle and more recently in Amesbury Priory.

The prioress walked over to her window and stared out at her priory lands. Was her aunt suggesting that his fealty to any spymaster might be weaker than the oath he swore to her as the leader of this priory? To say so directly would be dangerous, lest the letter fall into the wrong hands. In fact, as she went over the phrasing again, she smiled. If a certain man of significant religious rank read this missive, he might have been quite amused by the naiveté of one woman finding joy in the discovery that her niece's monk had such a high-ranking patron.

Eleanor chuckled with almost wicked delight. The man was a fool if he thought her aunt was no wiser than some wide-eyed child. But aunt and niece knew well enough how to read the other's meaning in cautious phrasing. Surely Sister Beatrice had meant to give her practical solace to ease the news of Thomas' deception.

"He has shown unquestionable loyalty," Eleanor conceded, "especially at my father's castle when he had no real cause to do so. If I handle this matter with wisdom, I may yet bind him more firmly to me. Although I'd be foolish to assume he would serve my interests first, should his spymaster's demands conflict with mine, I have been forewarned in time to prepare for that trial of wills."

Then she gazed down at the shards from the broken jug and sighed. "Meanwhile, I have sinned by letting the Devil infuse me with the flames of wrath, thereby melting all logic with searing rage. Of course I must choose carefully when it is best to fight and secure my right to his loyalty. There are times I shall concede defeat, but my brother Hugh used to say that any successful warrior will retreat if that means winning the ultimate victory."

She cleaned up what pieces of the shattered pottery she could find and laid them on the table next to the reprieved platter. Gytha should not have to pick up what she had so wickedly destroyed, the prioress decided, and swore to do penance for this act.

Then Eleanor sat at the edge of her bed and rested her hand on the sleeping cat. "Nor should I let my ungodly lust for the man give the Fiend cause to prance about. My aunt's advice last year at Amesbury should be burned into my soul. 'Love and its chaste expressions are not the sins. Vice comes from the selfish greed of mortal flesh when a man and woman couple'," she repeated. "Since then, when lust burns through me like hot metal, I have found some cooling comfort in her words—and in her assertion that Brother Thomas would ever be my liegeman."

"My liegeman?" The pain from those words pricked tears in her eyes again, and she swallowed them as anger returned. "That he shall be, for cert! I may never bed him or bear his child, but I have the right to demand a far higher devotion from him than that of *husband*. He is *my monk*!"

"My lady?"

Startled, Eleanor spun around.

A pale-faced Gytha stood in the doorway. "Are you well?"

"Aye, well enough." Eleanor said, raising her chin with recovering dignity. After all, no matter what happened with Brother Thomas, she did still have a priory to run.

"Crowner Ralf begs an audience, my lady, but I will send him off if you…"

"Nay, bid him enter. I would never turn our friend away." She glanced through her window at the position of the sun.

"And bring something to hush his stomach for I do recall that its roaring often mutes any message he brings!"

◇◇◇

When Gytha opened the door and gestured for Ralf to enter the public chambers, the prioress nodded for her to stay. The maid placed food and drink on the table and retreated to a distance sufficient to allow conversation but still provide proper attendance.

"I am grateful you would see me, my lady."

"You are always welcome at Tyndal Priory and have been much missed." The prioress' eyes grew sad. "When we got word that you had buried a wife, we longed to offer consolation. I have prayed for her soul and that your heart may heal in good time."

Ralf's brow furrowed.

It was an expression Eleanor knew well. "I would love to see your daughter," she said, quickly changing to a happier topic. "How is she?"

A grin broke across his face. "Fat, pink, and beautiful, my lady!"

"Then she is nothing like her father," Gytha interjected, then flushed with embarrassment at her impertinence.

Ralf stiffened for an instant, and then turned to Eleanor's maid with a softened look. "She has my lungs if not my face. In this way, my paternity has cursed her young life, but on balance she has found a most adoring father in me."

"Then she has exposed the soft heart you have taken much care to hide," Gytha replied, an impish glow in her eyes.

Ralf grinned like a boy.

"What do you call her?" Eleanor asked.

"*Sibely.* It was her mother's name. I wished to honor my wife for bringing me such a joy at the sacrifice of her own life."

As if remembering a task, Gytha jumped up and disappeared into the prioress' private chambers but not before Eleanor noted moisture on her cheeks.

"I know you came to us for some reason, Crowner," she said. "How may we help?"

"I have a corpse…"

Eleanor threw open her arms. "And when do you not? Ah, Ralf, I jest, but forgive this frail woman and give me your news."

"A poisoning, methinks, a deed I need confirmed…"

"…by our sub-infirmarian who was once an apothecary." Ralf nodded.

"Should I know the dead one's name? Perhaps there are kin in need of comfort."

"Martin, the cooper, my lady."

Eleanor frowned. "Without doubt, he was not a godly man, but neither did he have wife or children, or at least none that he would claim. Would you prefer to send the body with Cuthbert? I can report back to you on what Sister Anne observed."

"Nay, I must hear what she says and ask what I need to know." Ralf lowered his eyes. "My absence from this coast has been long, my lady. Much has changed."

Eleanor considered his words for a moment, then nodded. "Very well, I shall let our sister know that you will be bringing her a body for examination."

"I fear that the favor I beg is greater still."

The prioress gestured for him to continue.

"As a former soldier, I know violent death well, but I have little understanding of poisonings, a form of murder more common amongst those of higher rank methinks."

Eleanor struggled to contain her amusement. Crowner Ralf might be a man of rude manners, but his birth was not as low as he would prefer to suggest.

"I beg permission for Sister Anne to come to the inn and see the corpse where it lies. I have oft found that a knowledgeable eye recognizes important details in such situations. If we move the body, I fear we might destroy valuable clues."

"Perhaps it would be best to send…" she hesitated, "…Brother Beorn?"

The crowner coughed, perhaps to keep himself from speaking his true mind about the lay brother. "As much as I respect his skills, they are not as fine as...I do not want anything missed out of ignorance."

"Then I will ask Sister Anne if she is willing to venture forth. If she is, I will arrange for proper escort."

"I am most grateful, my lady."

"Something else is worrying you, Crowner." Despite the warmth of the East Anglian summer day, the prioress hid her hands in the sleeves of her habit. "I pray that this priory is not involved this time."

"Nay, my lady. It is not." Ralf shifted uncomfortably. "Yet, as always, you see into my soul most clearly."

"You are a friend, Ralf. What else troubles you?" Had this something to do with his baby? Eleanor wondered.

The crowner's wind-burned face flushed an unnatural red. "My lady, I have a problem that requires delicate handling."

"Speak freely."

"I need help with a woman..."

Had it not been for the bleak expression on his face, Eleanor might have laughed, for when did her dear friend not have trouble with the gentler sex?

Chapter Eight

Thomas twitched. His eyes opened wide. Had he fallen asleep?

His arms were stretched out in the shape of a cross; his feet were folded on top of each other, all in imitation of the crucified Jesus hanging upon the cross on the altar in front of him.

None of this brought the comfort he longed for, or even the condemnation he expected. All he felt were the sharp edges of the rough, uneven stone floor pressing into his body.

He rose awkwardly and carefully stretched the stiffness from his legs. His arms tingled as they recovered from their numbness. "Might I do better if I went back to the hospital and served the sick?" he asked the twisted figure above him.

After waiting for some response, he shook his head at his obviously vain hope and left the chapel.

Had he truly slept? He asked the question again as he shut the door to the church behind him. If so, the sleep was not restful, images from the inn last night flashing in his mind like a hobby-lantern in the fens. Each time he had breathed deeply, the dead man's stench assaulted his nostrils, and the figure of trembling Ivetta filled his heart with a troubling, albeit vague, apprehension.

Now that he was awake, however, what bothered him most was a change he had seen in Ralf. Although the pair had worked together in the past, and even called each other *friend*, this was the first time Thomas had noted deliberate callousness in the man. The crowner was harsh with scoundrels, and his rough ways had often caused unintended offense or hurt feelings, but the monk had never seen him act with cruelty to an obviously frightened witness.

The cooper's death quite literally reeked of murder. Why, then, would Ralf dismiss a good witness like Ivetta with such mockery when he had always sought as much information as he could obtain? Surely he knew that scorn would only silence her? Ivetta might be a prostitute, but the crowner had never cared much about such things, especially when he was in full cry after the truth of a crime. Yet last night he had acted no differently than his brothers might have done, either sheriff or the churchman.

As for Ivetta, she had good reason to assume that any representative of the king's justice would treat with little kindness those who plied her trade. Her expectation that a crowner would simply cart her off to some dank place, where she might rot of the damp long before she ever came to trial, was not unreasonable. Thomas had expected Ralf to calm her fears, at least long enough to get her tale, even if he suspected her of murder. Instead, he had rained abuse down on her head, effectively stopping any attempt at defense she might make or willingness to give information pointing to a killer.

On the other hand, Ivetta and Ralf had surely known each other from childhood. Thomas had come but recently to Tyndal. Perhaps the crowner had reason to assume her guilt—and maybe she had cause to mistrust him. Whatever the truth, Ralf had been gentler to the innkeeper.

Since the monk had stayed last night to assure the crowd outside the inn that the Devil had been permanently routed back to his home in Hell, Thomas heard the outraged roar from the merchant when he was told that the room upstairs must remain untouched, corpse included, until further notice.

"Do you have any idea how this will affect my purse?" the innkeeper shouted.

In the past, Ralf would have had little patience with anyone who worried more about coin than solving a murder—and taken less care to hide his contempt. Instead, the formerly gruff crowner eased the man into agreement with smooth grace.

Had his friend chosen to learn the delicate skills of diplomacy during his time at court? Or had his nature changed? Was there a side to the man that Thomas had never seen, one that others, who had grown up with him, knew well?

If the crowner did have a part touched by the Devil, why had Tostig remained his devoted friend—or Sister Anne for that matter? The brewer of ale might be called a good man, but the monk believed the sub-infirmarian to be most saintly.

Thomas frowned in perplexed thought as he trudged along the path to the hospital. "None of this is my worry," he concluded at last. The murder may have sent a spirit to God's judgement uncleansed, and he might even pray for the cooper's soul, but the crime itself was a matter for secular justice.

"Nonetheless, I am uneasy," he whispered, "although I do not understand why."

Thomas turned and gazed back at the dark-stoned church he had just left. Although the shimmering white sun had not yet reached its zenith, the air was growing thick with damp heat. The black curtain in Sister Juliana's anchorage window barely moved with the weak sea breeze, and the white cross emblazoned on it almost sparkled in the sunlight.

What was she doing? he wondered, distracting himself from his troubling thoughts. Was she in prayer, or had she sought rest on her stone bed after her night vigil?

Ever since he had met the woman at Wynethorpe Castle, he had felt both attraction and revulsion whenever he was in her presence. These warring emotions were complicated by his inability to decide whether she was simply mad or truly touched by God. Even his astute prioress might have no answer to this debate either, or so he suspected. She and Juliana may have been girlhood friends, but Thomas guessed much had changed between them in the intervening years.

Whatever his opinion of her, Sister Juliana had arrived here in the spring and was permanently entombed as an anchoress.

Soon after the last rites were performed to symbolize her death to the world, and the door to her small cell slammed shut, the distressed from the village began arriving at her window.

This was not unusual. Anchoresses often received those tormented by their sins, but they did so primarily during the daylight hours. This anchoress received only at night.

He had learned of this quite early on. When he had grown weary of his nocturnal pacing around the silent walkways of the monks' cloister garth, Thomas went to the church to beg for comfort. Her anchorage was near the path he took, and he grew much amazed at how many others were rendered sleepless by their sorrows. There was always some shadow pressed against the wall, whispering at the curtain. Once he caught himself concluding with some irreverence that the Church might soon proclaim her the patron saint of the sleepless.

Yet, for all his discomfort with her, he had been tempted to kneel at the window himself and seek what she might advise. Then a dark shape would approach, and he had scurried off to the gloomy chapel. At Wynethorpe, he feared she had glimpsed his soul in all its pitiful nakedness. If that were the case, he wondered what her response would be if he came to that small and curtained opening. Would she offer gentle comfort or call for God's flaming wraith to scorch his soul? He shook these musings aside with a shiver and turned his thoughts to those who had visited her.

Sister Juliana did not seem to mind if someone came more than once. Thomas had seen the baker's wife every night for awhile, although not of late. Hadn't Signy approached her for some reason, and maybe old Tibia as well? And now that he thought more on it, he wondered if he had seen Ivetta at the window too. Tostig had sought her advice, although fewer men than women came to the anchoress' window.

Why did women seem to come more often than men? Was the cause to be found in their greater mortal frailty? Nay, as he thought more on it, he realized that men were more likely to seek wisdom from pious hermits while women sought out the anchoress' window. God must not care who gave moral direction as long as souls were saved.

But what could an innkeeper's niece and a village whore have sought from an anchoress? Ivetta had continued her trade. Her soul was as fouled by lust as it had ever been, so the road to chastity had not been her concern. And what had troubled the innkeeper's niece? Signy seemed no more sinful than any other woman in the village. On the other hand, the baker's wife had certainly found some answer because her husband's bread began to rise again shortly after her visits to Sister Juliana—or so the story went. Perhaps Signy's woes had more in common with those of the baker's wife, something to do with stews and ale.

"Ah, well," Thomas said, entering the hospital courtyard. "I have sins enough of my own with which to struggle. Whatever problems bring Ivetta and Signy to see the anchoress are not mine to solve. It is time I got back to His service."

But the monk, like any other man, was still nibbled by curiosity. As he started down the rows of straw beds, filled with bodies whimpering in pain and terror, he caught himself asking again why Sister Juliana sat by her curtain only after the sun set. Unlike most mortals, she must be very bold to defy the Prince of Darkness, when he tortured man's spirit the most, and offer refuge to quivering souls during such bleak hours.

As he recalled his meeting with her, in the swirling snow on the walls of Wynethorpe Castle, he decided Sister Juliana most certainly did have that courage.

Chapter Nine

Sister Anne agreed to visit the inn.

Eleanor chose to accompany her.

When the prioress heard the growing rumor that many had seen Satan swooping about the inn when the cooper was murdered, she decided that an immediate monastic presence was required to calm village fears. Of course, this vigorous foray against the Fiend would not only drive panic away, but it might also free the villagers from thoughts about malign imps and thus send them back to memories or observations that should help find mortal killers.

As a result, when the religious contingent from Tyndal Priory walked to the inn, Sister Anne may have borne her worldly knowledge of herbs and potions, but Prior Andrew carried a large cross.

Eleanor left the good prior downstairs to speak with the fearful and curious while she and her attendants accompanied the sub-infirmarian upstairs with the innkeeper and Ralf. With one hand on the door, she suddenly realized what might be seen in the room behind it and shuddered. Death might mean that a soul had taken flight from earthly ills, but slaughter never brought any spirit delicate wings.

"Stay back by the stairs," she commanded the two beardless novices beside her.

Except for those cursed with sensitive noses, few noticed the common odors of everyday life, but murder exuded a fetid stench. Even Sister Anne, used to the overly sweet stink of mortal decay, hesitated at the door to the room where Martin's body lay rotting in the heat.

Both Eleanor and Anne covered mouth and nose with their sleeves before stepping into the room. The innkeeper was willing enough to stay without. Once Ralf had joined them, Eleanor shut the door, deciding that she and Anne were sufficient attendance on the other. "No one else need suffer this," she said.

Anne stepped over dried excrement and around stains where urine had darkly colored the wooden floor. When she reached Martin's corpse, her expression grew thoughtful, then sad. She knelt by the body and began her examination, raising the eyelids, opening the mouth, peering in, sniffing, testing limbs for rigidity, and feeling flesh for marks or other signs.

At last she rose, looked about, and walked around the room. After examining excrement and vomit, she went to the table where a jug lay on its side next to an upside-down pottery cup. She bent and looked into the jug but quickly saw it was empty. She sniffed at it, then finally studied the stains left by what had been spilled. Anne frowned and ran her fingers over the dark marks.

"This was most certainly not a natural death, Ralf, a finding you did not need me to make. Clearly Martin suffered convulsions before he died. His pupils are dilated, and his mouth is blue." She pointed to vomit, smears of excrement, and the table. "You were right to leave everything in place and let me see all this. One thing by itself might mean many things. It is the entirety that points most accurately to a conclusion."

"A poison?" Ralf asked.

"So I would say."

"Which one?"

"I suspect yew, but I would like to ask for more detail from any witnesses before I settle on that one in particular. Precision in this could speed discovery of the killer."

"The only witness was Ivetta, a woman…"

"…who practices a most sinful trade," Anne finished.

"If you will tell me your questions, I will ask her myself."

"Surely you questioned her last night," Anne said. "What did she tell you?"

The crowner's face turned scarlet.

The prioress raised an eyebrow but said nothing.

"She refused to talk to me, Annie."

"That has never stopped you before, Ralf." Anne bent to closely study a rough spot on the table.

"Your offer to protect our virtue is both admirable and kind," Eleanor said.

Realizing that she was letting him save face, the crowner nodded with a sheepish look.

"As you have said yourself, justice must be served with efficiency," the prioress continued. "I believe it would be best if Sister Anne asked her the questions directly. If Ivetta's testimony raises other questions, then our sub-infirmarian can resolve discrepancies immediately. Otherwise, there might be much going back and forth which consumes valuable time."

"Could you bear to do this?" Ralf asked, looking over at Anne who had returned to communing only with the dead man.

Anne smiled at his question, then nodded at the corpse. "Methinks you should know my answer."

"Remember that the sainted Magdalene is one of our especial protectors," Eleanor said. "I am sure she would be pleased if we exposed this poor sinner to the joys of a more prayerful life. I will ask Brother Beorn to accompany Ivetta to the priory. Sister Anne can question her in my presence."

"I will await your news, my lady," Ralf said.

"Then let us leave and give back this room to the innkeeper. If the corpse has surrendered all the secrets he ever shall, methinks it is time enough to send the cooper to his grave."

"I will not argue that!" the crowner said, then swung open the door and immediately took in a deep breath of fresh air.

Chapter Ten

Had she been unwise to volunteer help in this matter of murder, Eleanor asked herself as she hurried along the path to Sister Juliana's anchorage. Did she not have problems enough of her own, especially with Sister Ruth's ongoing complaints about the anchoress? As for the revelations about Brother Thomas, she was still unable to force her mind firmly to the dilemma with full reason intact.

She quickly exiled that second thought before tears as traitorous as her monk once again breached the weakened walls of her resolve. The cooper's murder was easier to contemplate.

Most would argue that this crime was no concern of those enclosed behind monastic walls. They might well be right, but if honest men saw Satan strutting amongst them because of this misdeed, then surely the religious of Tyndal were duty bound to help send him back to Hell.

Besides, Ralf had asked for her aid. Not only was he crowner but he was also her friend, a king's man who always honored her authority at the priory and had helped her two years ago when she had needed a favor, one that might have caused the crowner much grief had his brother, the sheriff, ever learned of it. She owed him something in return. The least she could do was interview two women.

"A simple enough thing to accomplish compared to what I must do now," the prioress sighed as she approached the anchorage door. There were times she wished she had never agreed to the admission of Sister Juliana as anchoress at Tyndal. Today was one of them.

The lay sister who had most recently, and even more reluctantly, agreed to serve Tyndal's recluse stood next to the anchorage entrance. The firmly bolted door was very thick, a precaution suggested by the bishop who had performed the entombing ceremony. Some women had chipped their way out, he said, when this austere life had begun to drive them mad.

Eleanor nodded to the lay sister.

"She often barricades this from the inside, my lady," the woman said, unbolting the door.

"I sent word that I wished to speak with her."

The lay sister knocked.

The great door squeaked open.

With head bowed, the woman inside fell to her knees, her hands steepled in an attitude of submissive prayer.

How gaunt Juliana has become since her arrival at Tyndal Priory, Eleanor thought as she stepped into the tiny room. On those occasions, when she had brought Brother John for spiritual advice and discussion, she had asked if anything was needed. The only thing the anchoress ever requested was time for confession.

Although Eleanor knew that any mortal, who vowed to resist all evil, was tormented by Satan with exceptional vigor and vivid temptations, she found herself asking how many lusty imps the Devil could possibly send to a room barely large enough for an altar and small bed.

"You have rejected yet another servant," the prioress said. "May I know why?" Space for an even smaller servant's room had been included when the anchorage had been built, but Juliana had refused any resident attendant. Instead she was using the space to dig her future grave in the floor with her bare hands.

"I am sure Sister Ruth has given reasons, my lady."

"I would hear the cause from you."

Juliana's lips twitched into a humorless smile. "I do not wish anyone to attend me."

"You have no choice in this. Your duty is to pray, seek God's wisdom, and comfort those who are compelled to seek your advice. Another must cook, clean, and care for you should you fall ill."

"When I begged an anchorage, I asked to be granted a forest hut where I could tend to my own needs. There, apart from all other mortals, I would have had the silence to hear God's voice even while I tended to those few vegetables needed for my daily meal."

"That was rightly denied by the bishop. No woman may be granted a hermitage."

"Then permit my only other request."

Eleanor threw up her hands in frustration. "As you should know well, I shall not assign a monk or lay brother to care for you!"

"I cannot pray with women in my room."

"You could not pray if a man was left alone with you! How dare you even ask that I permit such a thing?"

"What if I told you that God demanded it?"

"You cannot, for He would not."

"As Brother John told me, Robert of Arbrissel went to brothels. When he emerged, he did so cloaked in greater virtue than when he entered. I do not ask that a manservant enter my room, only that he serve my needs through that tiny space." She pointed to a small opening in the wall that provided a view of the church itself.

The prioress went to the curtained window in the other wall and glanced outside. No one was there to hear what she had to say. "As you should understand, your demand is outrageous. Why not permit a sober, modest, and elderly woman to perform the same service?" She gestured at the empty servant's room. "You have always refused to allow anyone to stay there. What quarrel do you have with someone who lives without?"

"As I told you long ago, apart from your own, I cannot abide the sound of a woman's voice. I would not speak to those who come to my window if God did not command it as atonement for my sins."

"Not even the voice of Sister Anne who has had to come often enough to treat your wounds when you beat your head against the wall?"

The anchoress bowed her concession in silence.

"Juliana, you are taking advantage of our friendship in the world by continuing to insist on such a shameful thing. No prioress, or prior in any other double house, would listen more than once to such a proposition. If they were merciful, they would set you a severe penance. Most would conclude you were possessed by Satan. I would prefer to do neither. If I continue to hear complaints, however, I may have little choice except to take harsh measures to end them."

"I have never wished to couple with any man. As you know, I did not have to take a nun's vows to become an anchoress. I chose to do so, and my vow to remain chaste is a true one."

Eleanor spun around. "I may believe that, although many would not. Even if your chastity remained inviolate, you must understand that such an arrangement would be a cruel test of any man's vows?"

"There are those who would either welcome it as a test of their virtue or else not find it troubling at all." Juliana flattened herself on the floor. "My lady," she whispered, "you know me well. Believe me when I swear my plea has no taint of wickedness."

"I might indeed," the prioress sighed as she took her childhood friend by the arms and raised her. "That said, there is another reason to deny your plea. The sons of Adam rarely allow the daughters of Eve authority, for it was our ancient mother who took the apple from the serpent, offered it to Adam, and gave God cause to slam shut the gates of Eden. Men need little to remind them that tragedy results when women are not closely ruled; therefore, the virtue of our Order, where Eve has power over Adam, must remain undoubted. Even if I wished to do so, I could never grant your request."

The anchoress' eyes turned dark.

"I promise that I shall persist in searching for a woman who will serve you with the silence you require and who will not otherwise trouble you. In the meantime, the current lay sister will continue attending to your needs twice a day, and I command you to cease barring your door to her."

Juliana covered her eyes and groaned.

"As you said, you willingly took a nun's vows. Need I remind you that one of those was obedience? Do not attempt to take any further advantage of our old friendship. Not only do I command you to stop begging me to grant this wicked plea, but I order you to treat all women who serve you with the sweet kindness Our Lord embodied."

The anchoress bowed her head but remained silent.

"On the other hand, I must ask if any of these women has done you harm? If so, tell me for I shall not tolerate that."

"Their only vice lies in their sex, my lady."

"Then you owe them the compassion God grants all women, for you share their frailty."

"I shall obey, my lady," Juliana whispered.

"There is one other matter."

"I beg that you teach me all my sins."

"The visitors to your window. They are mostly women and come only at night, when they should be safe in their beds. It is the hour the Devil loves most…"

"No one at my window has been attacked by imps, my lady. If God had not taken away what desire I might have for sleep, these mortals would have no one to bring His balm to their battered souls. Show me the possessed, if I speak with the Fiend's tongue. That is how I answer those critics who wish to cover innocence with the stench of their own filth."

For a long time, Eleanor studied the bent figure of her old friend, then blessed the woman and left without speaking further.

The door slammed shut. The bolt was drawn.

Sister Juliana remained on her knees, staring in silence at that heavy wooden door which had failed to protect her from the world she hated.

Chapter Eleven

Ivetta grumbled as she focused on the callused heels of the lay brother leading the way. Walking through the nuns' cloister made her nervous, and she was not at all pleased about coming to the priory. There was something unnatural about all this hush, she concluded, but then she was happiest surrounded by the deep voices of men and the soaring laughter of women.

Her bad-temper had begun even before Brother Beorn arrived at her hovel. Ivetta had just awakened, a time of day not reckoned her most cheerful, and then vomited. She felt as sour as her mouth tasted when the lay brother informed her that Prioress Eleanor had some questions about the cooper's death. Would she come with him to the priress' chambers?

As if she had had any choice!

Out of the corner of her eye, she watched two nuns pass her in the walkway. The elder was short and square. The younger still possessed a soft, youthful roundness. "And that blank stare of holiness," Ivetta muttered, not quite under her breath.

The older nun glared, twitching her nose as if she had smelled the smoke of Hell emanating from the whore's robe.

Brother Beorn turned around. "Did you ask a question?"

Ivetta shook her head, and the unlikely pair continued on. At least the dark frown with which he had graced her was no different from the glare he gave everyone else. In all the time she had known him, Brother Beorn had never suffered from hypocrisy. Other than children, to whom he showed a saintly patience, he disliked all mortals equally.

When they reached the stairs that led to the prioress' chambers, Ivetta grimaced. The very thought of climbing them exhausted her. Nor did she want to talk about Martin Cooper's death. Who would, under the circumstances? Just as he had gotten into bed with her, he had begun his death throes. Ivetta dry-retched as the memory returned. Sweat began to drip down her cheeks.

These holy virgins would never understand what she had suffered that night. What did they care about a woman's passions? Martin had been different from her other men. When he took her in that open field the summer she turned thirteen, she forgot the weeds that scratched her back and remembered only the sweet scent of flowers. Since that day, she did whatever he wished, opening her legs for a price and giving him the coin. None of that mattered. Other men might ride her, but they all remained faceless and transitory. Martin had possessed her.

Brother Beorn cleared his throat.

Ivetta began to climb the stairs.

◇◇◇

"Thank you for coming here, Mistress," the Prioress of Tyndal said.

Mistress, was it? Ivetta spat out the bitten-off nail she had been worrying about with her tongue.

With a courteous manner but inscrutable tone, the prioress began to introduce her companions.

Gytha smiled, a look completely lacking in condescension.

Tostig's sister and a decent enough sort, Ivetta had always heard. The brother had never sought her services, and he was polite enough when he passed her on the road.

"Sister Anne, our sub-infirmarian."

So this was the famous healer? Ivetta had never met her. The only time she had ever needed potions and herbs was when she missed her courses. In her profession, that meant one thing, and she knew well enough how to handle the problem. A priory hospital would not serve her there.

"I am called Eleanor, Prioress of Tyndal."

A woman reputed to see any evil that skulked behind men's eyes. Ivetta quickly lowered hers and bobbed an awkward obeisance. But surely this prioress was too far removed from earthly concerns to recognize all the imps that squirmed in her soul? Most of her sins were common enough and well-known anyway. As for the uncommon ones, what did she have to fear from a woman who had rejected the world?

Ivetta's brief impudence withered the moment she looked up. She most certainly had much to fear, and those grey eyes now studying her did hold a scorching heat. Unless some priest came fast enough to forgive her on her deathbed, she knew she would instantly fall into the deepest regions of Hell. But she had little choice, did she? She could not afford to repent just yet.

"You have nothing to be frightened of here," the prioress said. "Our only purpose is to hear details of Martin's death."

Ivetta realized how tense her muscles had been. She shrugged her shoulders to ease the tightness.

"The crowner can be harsh…"

"He wants to hang me."

"He is a fair man. You grew up in this village so must know him well…"

"With respect, my lady, you were not there last night. He wants to hang me because I am a harlot."

"As was the sainted Magdalene. Our Lord did not turn his back on her, nor do we. Will you have some refreshment?"

The Prioress of Tyndal rose, carried a mazer of wine to Ivetta, and offered both bread and cheese.

The woman snatched the wine and gulped it down.

The prioress carefully refilled her cup, then placed the platter near enough for Ivetta to reach. "Should you be hungry," Eleanor said with a nod as she settled herself back into her chair.

Ivetta stuffed some cheese into her mouth. Hungry or not, she could no longer afford to turn down any offer of food.

"Please answer honestly. We are not here to condemn, indeed we wish you no harm. Anything you remember of the cooper's murder might be helpful in finding the one who killed him."

"I know nothing of murder, my lady."

"But Sister Anne does. You may mention something, no matter how small, that would help her piece together what killed the man. I do not expect you to know how it happened, only to relate the events of that night. Will you answer the questions I must ask?"

Ivetta nodded, snagged another hunk of cheese and reached back to tear off a large piece of bread. Taking a bite, she discovered that the heavy loaf was no lordly one. Instead it was rough with bits of broken grain. She looked at the prioress holding a similar dark-colored bit in her hand. Contrary to tales she had heard from some of the men she served, these religious were neither fat nor arrogant. Not only had this prioress personally served her, but the monks and nuns of Tyndal must eat no better than villeins.

"Do not fear plain speech," the prioress said. "As for your trade, who amongst us is not a sinner?"

Her smile is not the haughty look with which one of her station might greet one of mine, Ivetta noted.

"Nothing you say will cause offense. Our desire may be for the chaste and sequestered life, but that does not mean we are less mortal than you or do not suffer from human error. The world is no stranger to us and even less to Sister Anne who was an apothecary with her husband before she joined the Order."

Ivetta tossed her head in the maid's direction.

Eleanor nodded. "You may go, Gytha. Should we need anything more, I will send for you."

When the young woman had closed the door, Ivetta drained her cup again. "Martin said he had a night's work for me, my lady. This was always done in the same room at the inn. When I arrived, he was already there."

"Did you contract with the innkeeper for the room or did Martin?" The prioress sipped her wine.

"Martin did."

"Were you to serve him or others that night?"

"I never knew. He always collected the price first so I was not surprised to see him."

"Was there anything different about the arrangements last night?"

"Not that I knew."

"Had the food and wine been brought up before you arrived?" Anne asked.

"No." Ivetta turned away. "If a man wanted refreshment, he was told to sup with the others downstairs after my allotted time was done."

"Yet there was food and drink that night…"

"When Martin wanted me for himself, or with special friends, he always ate before we bedded. There was a game we often played when we were alone, you see. I pretended to be a beggar woman…do you want those details?"

"Perhaps you need only say if you shared either food or drink after it had arrived that night," Anne replied with a hint of amusement in her eyes.

"I did not have the chance. I never ate until I had sated his other needs and he had fallen asleep. That was part of our game."

"And in this way your life may have been saved," Eleanor said, her expression growing solemn. "So you came up to the room. Martin was waiting for you, but the food and wine had not been served. He was by himself…"

"He was not alone, my lady."

"If refreshment was ordered, then they were friends rather than strangers staying at the inn?"

"Friends. Hob and Will, the blacksmith brothers. Many times in the past he has shared me with the elder if there were no others in need of my service."

"Was that the arrangement for the night?" Anne asked, glancing at Eleanor. No mention had been made of the blacksmith and his brother.

"I assumed as much when I first arrived, but the three were arguing."

"What was the dispute?"

"Martin was ridiculing Will's manhood."

"And Hob's as well?"

"Nay, only Will's. His sex had become a cowardly thing on the tilting grounds, as I have oft discovered." Ivetta snorted. "As for Hob, he has spurned my talents for a long time. For all I know, the heat of the smithy did melt his rod as well."

Eleanor coughed to hide her mirth.

"You say the *three* were arguing?" Anne asked.

"When I walked into the room, I heard Martin tell Will that he should dress in women's attire because his sex was no bigger than…" Ivetta shrugged. "Will's face was scarlet and he tried to strike out but tripped. Methinks he had drunk too much ale already. Then Hob swung at Martin. I did not want to get hurt so I backed out of the room."

"Did Martin often insult Will in this manner?" Eleanor asked.

"Often enough."

"Did you shut the door when you left?" Anne continued.

"I might have done, but the tavern wench arrived just then with a jug and plate. I stood aside to let her enter, and she shut the door behind her."

"Which woman served?"

"Signy," Ivetta replied, then spat.

Anne raised an eyebrow at the prioress.

"Did Hob and Will stay in the room with her?" Eleanor continued.

"For a short time. When she shut the door, the men stopped yelling." Ivetta hesitated. "One must have felt her up because I heard her screeching. Then Hob threw open the door and dragged his brother out by the collar. They went down the stairs, shouting at each other. I paid no further heed to what they said or did since they were well on their way."

"You went in then?" Eleanor asked.

"Signy slammed the door in my face."

"You waited outside?"

"For a few minutes. They must have had some heated words because I could hear their voices above the din, but not what they said. When the wench left, I went in to Martin and then shut the door behind me."

"Did Signy say anything to you?"

"We are not friends. She may be the innkeeper's niece, but she is still a tavern wench and can handle her own problems with the men."

Anne nodded. "What do you remember next?"

"When I came in, Martin was sitting on the bed, drinking wine."

"Was he distraught?" Eleanor asked.

"He was smiling, my lady, as if quite pleased. Had I not seen the fight amongst the men, I would never have imagined it had occurred."

"Did he both eat and drink, or only drink?" Anne asked.

"I do not know what he did before I came back into the room, Sister. I only saw him drink."

"Please go on."

"We did not play beggar girl and knight as we often did. He began to strip me and fumbled at it. He was trembling so, I assumed he was especially impatient to mount me. Then his eyes grew dark, almost black. I recall that because they were always the most beautiful blue..." Ivetta began to chew on a finger. "His trembling changed to fits..." She could not go on.

"Do you remember the color of his skin, lips?" Anne asked.

Ivetta squeezed her eyes shut. "Only his eyes."

The sub-infirmarian shot a glance at her prioress.

"I know these details are horrible to bring back to mind, but we must hear the whole tale." Eleanor's voice was as gentle as a soft touch.

"He began to scream and jerk about. I knew something was horribly wrong." Ivetta rubbed her hand under her eyes to dry the wetness there. "I screamed for help. He got twisted in the sheet, vomiting and...it seemed forever before the innkeeper came. By then, Martin had stopped breathing… Don't ask me more, please!"

"I have no wish to be cruel, but God's justice requires your strength in telling all you can recall." Eleanor reached out with commiseration to the woman.

"The next thing I remember was the crowner taunting me!" Ivetta shouted, and then began to sob without attempting to hide it. "He was a beast to say what he did, accusing me of murder. Martin was not… Oh, my lady, I may be the vilest of God's creation, but even soulless creatures know tenderness. I loved him! And I am bearing his child!"

Chapter Twelve

"Devoted lover?" Ralf snorted. "Martin? He may have liked to swyve Ivetta from time to time, but he never would have let her keep the babe had she told him of it."

The prioress remained silent, her gray eyes darkening.

"Surely you do not mean…" Anne pressed her hand against her waist.

"He hired her out. She let the cooper take whatever she earned, and he paid as little as possible for her keep in return. A pregnant whore brings little trade, Annie. He would never have tolerated the loss of income. Is this sweet love?"

"Perhaps he had gained affection for her after all this time," Anne interjected.

"A bull would sooner grow wings. By all reports, Ivetta is skilled at her craft. That may satisfy a man's hungry yard, leaving behind some short-lived taste for the food, but it rarely fills his heart with tenderness."

"What of Hob and Will, the two men who were alone with Martin that night? They argued with the cooper. How quickly the number of your suspects has increased from one to three," the sub-infirmarian concluded.

"A number enlarged by the very woman who may have poisoned him and wishes to point us in some other direction."

"There is also the innkeeper's niece," Eleanor said. "She, too, was alone with him."

Ralf shook his head. "Signy is innocent," he mumbled.

"We cannot ignore her. After all, she delivered the food and drink and apparently had heated words with the cooper. At some point, Signy, Hob, and Will were all alone with Martin for a while. After that, when Ivetta entered the room the second time, Martin was drinking the wine. Any one could have poisoned the drink before she arrived."

"So claims the harlot," he replied. "Shall I mention that the goblet was empty, as was the jug that contained it, by the time I got up the stairs?" Who might have done that and for what purpose?"

"Who was in the room when you arrived?" Eleanor asked the crowner.

"The innkeeper and Signy were just in front of me as I climbed the stairs. They could not have destroyed evidence without my seeing the act. Only Ivetta was alone with the corpse and the method of killing him. For all her cleverly professed affection for Martin, she had the best opportunity to do the deed, then destroy the poisoned wine."

"For just a moment, let us assume that one of the others killed him. What reason might either Hob or Will, perhaps both, have for doing such a thing?" Eleanor continued.

Ralf shrugged. "They have long been friends with the cooper and used to his ways. The brothers drank, and when they did, they got into fights—with Martin as well as others. The difference is that all was forgotten by the three men before the aching heads were healed. That has long been their pattern."

"Ivetta said that Martin was mocking Will's impotence. Was that a longtime jest?" Anne asked.

The crowner frowned. "That I had not heard. If true, would it be cause for murder? I wonder."

"Would it be if he had said the same about you?" Anne snapped.

Ralf's face turned scarlet.

"I have made my argument," the sub-infirmarian replied.

"And Hob?" Eleanor added.

"As a boy, Hob always followed his elder brother in wickedness. Then he changed his ways but still works at the smithy with Will, and thus is not removed from that influence. Tostig claims Hob has grown more independent in the last several months, however. Of the two, the younger has long been the more restrained, but he is fiercely loyal to his brother. Of all their family, only they remain on this earth. So I could believe Hob might have struck out to protect his brother, but I doubt he is a murderer. Nay, I still think the whore had more reason to kill than either man."

"Because she was with child?" Anne asked.

"Surely it is not the first time! Maybe she thought this quickening would change a bawd into a husband. Her value as a common woman is diminishing, and even she must have realized that Martin would have been contemplating the acquisition of a younger harlot. Perhaps she thought he owed her the security of marriage, and, when he laughed at the prospect, she killed him."

"Slipping ground yew seeds into a man's wine suggests some planning, Ralf."

"Are you certain that was the case, Annie?"

"Before I heard what Ivetta had to say, I suspected yew or nightshade. Now I am fairly sure it was the seeds from a yew tree. There were tiny bits left where the wine had spilled. The symptoms described and what I noted about the corpse were consistent with that kind of poisoning."

"Something easily slipped into a drink?" Eleanor asked.

"The taste of wine, especially a flavored one, hides many things. The poison can work quickly, and we do not know exactly when the cooper might have started to drink it. Of course, it could have been put into the stew, both food and drink were brought together, but little of the stew had been eaten. A potion slipped into wine is more likely to achieve the murderous effect than something scattered over food. Some men reach for the cup before the spoon." Anne hesitated. "I fear that yew has also been used to abort unborn babes, usually with cruel consequences to mother and child."

"Of course a prostitute would be familiar with it." Ralf paused to let the comment sink in.

"Or an apothecary and many more women than we might commonly assume. Dangerous though it is, the method is well known, Ralf."

"Which reminds me that we have yet to consider any motive Signy might have," Eleanor said.

"None!" Ralf struck a fist into his other hand.

"Why are you so convinced?" Anne asked.

He threw up his hands. "Ivetta has committed sins that would make the Devil blush. Signy is a decent woman."

"Very well, Ralf, but we will question her shortly." Eleanor's stern expression was enough to quell any potential argument.

"I am grateful." Ralf lowered his eyes.

The sub-infirmarian tilted her head and studied the crowner in silence.

"She refuses to speak with me," the crowner sputtered in response to Anne's unspoken query.

"Why am I not surprised?"

Ralf threw up his hands. "Very well, I will not arrest Ivetta yet, but she is still my strongest suspect. Signy is innocent, but you may well learn something valuable from her. The innkeeper and other possible witnesses, I will question myself, including Will and Hob."

"I praise the wisdom of your direction, Ralf," Anne said wryly.

Eleanor laughed to lighten the mood. "Our priory is attracting the most interesting visitors these days. A prostitute and a serving wench? The Kingdom of Heaven must be nigh when such come to a priory and give up the secrets of their souls."

Anne nodded. "Ivetta was quite blunt in telling her tales. I wonder what the innkeeper's niece might have to say..." She hesitated, then gave the crowner a mischievous look. "...about many little things."

Although Ralf's muttered response was not completely clear, the two nuns later agreed that he had first complained about being a much maligned man with nothing small about him, and then had uttered a most impressive oath before stomping out the door.

Chapter Thirteen

"You're a godly monk, Brother." Old Tibia's voice began to slur as the sleep-inducing draught took effect.

Godly was not a word he would have used to describe himself, Thomas thought, but opted not to contradict her gentle words.

"And have a consoling angel's smile."

"You are most kind, but I am a sinful man like any other. I will convey your gratitude to those who make this potion. I am but the courier who delivers restful sleep from the priory."

Tibia laid a light hand on Thomas' arm and watched him as she did. "You don't draw back at the touch of this crone?"

"Why should I?"

"Most bearing the tonsure do. How can a feeble old woman like me corrupt chastity? I've oft asked that." Her expression suggested some distant memory had drifted like a cloud's shadow across her face. "If the sex that bore them troubles monks so, how could they have been good sons? But you, you're like a proper son, Brother. Touching you with a mother's hand comforts me and makes the absence of my own boy more bearable."

"We should praise the God who sent me to you."

She turned her sharp-featured face from him.

Remembering his earlier, less compassionate thoughts about her, shame filled his heart. Why was it that we sing paeans to lush but wicked youth, he asked himself, and mock the hooked noses and hollow cheeks of those whose souls were soon to see God?

Should we not pray instead for these scars left by grueling life and condemn the plump callousness of youth? At the moment, age's pale warmth seemed preferable to Thomas than the heat of youth. What joy had the latter ever brought him?

"Is your mother dead?" Tibia's voice was just a whisper.

"Aye, as are the women who took me in as a babe and young boy."

"Your father?"

"He also."

"More recently? There's fresh sadness in your voice."

"The brothers and sisters at the priory are my kin," he replied, realizing that there was much truth in what he said, more than he had intended.

"A kind family," Tibia murmured. "Your holy prioress brought good with her when she came to Tyndal Priory. The Evil One stays where he should in his stinking pit longer than he did in the past."

"Like the beloved disciple, who took care of Our Lord's mother after the crucifixion, I gain honor by serving Prioress Eleanor," Thomas said. The words might have been spoken out of common courtesy, but his heart meant them.

The old woman suddenly gazed up at him, all sleep fled and her eyes shining with wide-eyed zeal. "And now the priory has a new anchoress. A holy woman, for cert!"

"You think her blessed by God?"

"Her advice brings hope to us in the village. And I've heard it true that pilgrims, even from London, delay their journey on the way to the shrine of Saint William to crouch by her window."

Although he had seen some whom he had not recognized at Sister Juliana's window, he had no idea that her reputation as a woman touched by God had spread quite so far abroad. "Have you spoken with the anchoress yourself?"

"What woman hasn't?" Tibia sighed. "A friar traveling through the village preached that women are the most sinful creatures. We destroy any hope men might have to return to Eden." She closed her eyes as if wearied by the effort to talk. "That's hard to bear. Since I've committed much wickedness, I know I must take my share of blame. But those words must weigh heavy on a virtuous woman. If the Anchoress Juliana can spread balm on my evil heart, she'll do more for the innocent."

"Nevertheless, she cannot give you God's forgiveness."

The silence grew long, except for the sound of the old woman's steady breathing. Had Tibia finally fallen asleep? He bent over to listen and decided that the potion had finally worked.

That was just as well, he decided. His curiosity about Sister Juliana and her advice was sparked, but he should not question this poor soul about her experience with the anchoress. As a priest, he might be able to hear any willing confession. As a mere man, he had no right to pry into what had transpired between the old woman and the young anchoress.

As Thomas rose to leave, he heard old Tibia mutter something. Was she just talking in her sleep or had she spoken to him? He leaned over and brought his ear closer to her mouth.

"A priest may bring a father's forgiveness," the woman said clearly enough, "but we all long for a mother's embrace. A holy woman brings that from God, Brother."

Startled by her meaning, he drew back.

Tibia now slipped into a sleep so deep it foretold the peace of death.

Chapter Fourteen

Aided by the full moon's ashen light, Thomas hurried along the path to the priory. His mood was darker than the Devil's heart.

After leaving Tibia, he had taken one more potion to a man who suffered a deep and oozing sore in his throat. As the monk helped him drink a measure of poppy juice, the man screamed, his eyes wide like a wounded animal, terrified by the unimaginable pain before the numbing drug took affect. Glancing up at the wet cheeks of the man's wife, Thomas knew that both of them would call God merciful if He took the man's soul quickly, even though that aged widow would be left to the care of their son's spouse, a woman of few mercies and even less charity.

"Is there any earthly happiness for mortals?" Thomas growled as he entered the priory grounds near the mill. His eyes were gritty with fatigue—or was it bitterness?

He rubbed angrily at them.

The light might be bright enough to see along the path, but the shadows cast in front of him were sinister, twitching like tortured souls in Hell. Although daylight might reveal the cause to be as harmless as wind-stunted brush moving in a sea breeze, Thomas found night to be an ominous time. When God's sunshine deserted the earth, Satan most certainly rejoiced, ruled his kingdom with bleak terror, and filled the hours with hideous deeds.

The monk shuddered. Madness lay in these thoughts. Surely, if he were able to sleep, he would awaken to a more joyous view of God's creation and cast his foe, the Prince of Darkness, out of his heart. Thomas quickened his pace as he passed the creaking mill wheel.

Of course there were men who experienced an honest pleasure in life: those with loving wives and children; some who found salvation in killing infidels and gaining prestige with a well-honed sword; or men filled with such rapturous faith that they longed only for God's company, either in a hermitage or the cloister.

Thomas did not regret the lack of a wife, although he was sometimes sorry he had never fathered a son. Nor did he wish for the military life. Despite his bastardy, he might have gotten horse and armor from his father had he shown talent in warrior sports, but the monk had always preferred jousts with sharp wit to those with lances. The Church was the only logical place for a clever by-blow with reasoning skills, high enough birth, and a pleasing manner but no lands to tempt noble fathers demanding more than a handsome face for their daughters.

As for faith, he had always assumed the truth of what the Church taught but rarely thought much beyond that, unless struck by terror that his sins were so horrible that his soul must plunge directly into Hell. In short, his piety was of the common sort and made him unsuited to the monastic life. Might he have felt differently if he had not been forced to take the tonsure? He doubted it. As a clerk in minor orders, he had prayed respectfully but mostly out of habit and duty. Of course he wished to serve his Lord, as all Christian men did in this land, but he had never, until now, hungered for God's voice.

Even before his imprisonment, he had never found tranquility on his knees before the altar. Now that he sought it after the events at Amesbury, God seemed to be taking a most cruel pleasure in mocking his pathetic attempts to pray. The only time he found peace was in the comforting of the sick at the hospital or helping his prioress bring justice to the aggrieved.

At this moment, the monk almost wished his spymaster had an assignment for him. Perhaps that would distract him from these gangrenous musings?

Thomas rubbed his eyes again with the heel of his hands and cursed. All these thoughts were wicked self-indulgences. Had he been in his narrow bed dreaming of heaven, or on his knees praying to God, Satan would not have found such joy in pricking his soul like this. No matter what his doubts, was he not still a priest sworn to serve God? His duty was to fight the evils that tortured him, not give in to mortal weakness.

Despite his clenched fist, Thomas knew that such fine thoughts were as hollow as his heart. His dreams were never of heaven, and the only thing Thomas ever heard, when he lay on the rough-cut stones of the chapel, was the chatter of rats and his own babble of repeated prayers. Death might well be kinder, he often thought. Even the certainly of Hell seemed preferable than the spiritual torment he now suffered.

Thomas stopped and shook his head as if that would scatter his brooding thoughts. His hard bed in the monks' dorter would give him no relief tonight. The looming, dark outline of the priory church was just in front of him. He might as well try prayer again. At least God must surely understand that he wanted to be a true liegeman, even if he did fail in practice.

As he neared the church door, he glanced at the anchorage. For once, there was no one at Sister Juliana's window. Dare he kneel there at last and seek whatever curse or blessing she might have for him?

He stumbled toward it, weary with fear and sleeplessness. Had some unseen force taken him by the arm and pushed him there? Whatever the cause, he did not even try to resist. At the curtained window he dropped to his knees and started to weep, his cheeks stinging as if the tears were made of vinegar.

"What brings you here, Brother Thomas?"

How did she know it was him?

"I remember that sigh from the time we met in the snow at Wynethorpe Castle."

"You recall that, Sister?" Thomas' voice rose with terror. If she could not see him, how could she distinguish one stranger's moan from another?

"Memory's vivid colors dance in my heart. In this way I am reminded of the reasons I left the world."

"Then I should not remind you of such troubling times," Thomas replied, struggling to rise without success.

"Stay, Brother. I hear your heart's dreadful groaning. God must hear it as well."

"If so, He brings no comfort." Thomas blinked, hearing the anger in his voice. "Forgive me. Those were the Devil's words."

"Nay, they were a man's cry for help. Are you afraid because you curse God? You are not the only one to do so. Priests may teach us to emulate Job and praise God even when He torments the just, but I say that others have cursed Him and gained His sympathy. Remember Jesus when he cried out from the cross: 'My God, my God, why hast thou forsaken me?' If the perfect son speaks so to the perfect father, may you not do the same?"

"None of us is the Son. Surely the wise men are right when they say we must follow Job's path and his strong faith."

"Will you listen to men or to God? Those who boast they know God best often fail to understand the sweet humanity of His son."

Silence fell between them, and a light breeze dried the tears on Thomas' cheeks to salt. The hot summer air, that had weighed him down earlier, now rested with a light touch on his body, but he had lost all desire to stand. He sank back on his heels.

"Even if God were to forgive a man for railing against Him, there must be sins that He will not forgive," he whispered.

"And that man sees the sin he committed and begs for mercy with an honest heart? Do you not believe in perfect grace? If you have no faith in flawless mercy, you deny God's perfection. In this way, you allow that He is capable of sin. Such is blasphemy."

"Then why will He not bring me solace and the understanding I long for?"

As Thomas waited for her answer, an owl hooted in the distance as if mocking his impatience.

"Surely you have asked this question of your confessor?" Juliana asked. "Tell me what he said."

"That I have not prayed loudly or long enough. I am too wicked a man…"

"Hush! Perhaps your confessor fails to understand that God cares less about the loud gnashing of teeth than whether the heart is ready to hear Him."

"My confessor is a priest, through whom God grants wisdom and guidance. If we listen to our own hearts, we may confuse the Devil's voice with that of God."

"You are a priest."

"Aye."

"Then are you not allowed to know God's will?"

"I am not worthy."

"No mortal is, Brother, but understanding how unworthy you are is the first step to cleansing yourself of worldly error."

"I am frightened."

"As you should be. Truth's light shines in men's eyes with such painful intensity that most turn away from it. It is far easier to look upon the cancerous rot of their willful and arrogant ignorance which Satan has glazed with the sheen of righteousness. Yet are we not commanded to obey the holy spirit of the law, not the imperfect letter, to reject a fine appearance for the plainness of truth? Those who repeat the well-worn phrases of prayer may still be good men, but they will never match the blessedness of those who follow the example of God's only son."

"What am I to do?"

"Be silent in God's presence, and He will send you guidance."

Surely it was blasphemy to deny the power of spoken prayer? Thomas began to sweat, his head light with dizziness. "Your phrases are sweet in the ear, Sister, but I must listen to you with caution. Do you not recall how Saint Paul said, in a letter to Timothy, that women must be silent and not teach for they are the daughters of that great transgressor, Eve?"

"I would not dare to speak with my own mouth, Brother. Without question, I am a frail woman, a creature of no consequence. Nevertheless, as you know well, I am not the first woman through whom God has chosen to speak."

Was he wrong or had the tenor of her voice deepened? Women, who swore themselves to God's service, often acquired a sacred masculinity through their vows and faith. He himself had witnessed this transformation after entering the Order of Fontevraud where women ruled men. If God had chosen this anchoress to convey His wisdom, Thomas should listen and not argue. If not...

"How can I know whether or not you speak with God's voice?" he whispered.

"Alas, I am unable to prove this to you. When morning comes, my throat is raw from speaking words I cannot even remember. My heart fills with anguish, and I beg God to choose someone else as His voice. No one knows better than I what a foul creature I am, so I spend my days punishing myself for my unworthiness and longing for forgiveness. Give me your blessing, Brother, for I most certainly need it!"

Although his voice shook, Thomas did as she asked, then rose and walked to the chapel. Was this strange woman, who counseled weary souls in dark hours, God's true instrument? Or was she the handmaid of that most clever Prince of Darkness?

While his manly reason reserved judgement on this, his heart recalled what old Tibia had said earlier that evening, words that now filled him with a rare calm.

Chapter Fifteen

The sound of feminine laughter shattered the concentration of the prioress at prayer. Unlike some of her vocation, Eleanor believed laughter to be one of God's most gracious gifts to his mortal creatures. Instead of being offended at the interruption, she rose from her prie-dieu and thanked Him for His charity.

When she entered the public chambers, she saw Gytha and Signy standing near the window, their backs turned to the prioress.

How lovely the innkeeper's niece is, Eleanor thought, as she watched the light dance in Signy's hair, brightening the red-gold strands scattered amongst the blond. This was a woman who could easily ensnare a man's heart.

Not long ago, Gytha had confided her suspicions that Tostig might have fallen under the woman's spell, a development the loving sister found pleasing. Although Ralf had said nothing about it to her, Eleanor knew from other sources that the crowner had also been shown much favor by Signy in the days before he left to join his elder brother. Even now he seemed fiercely protective of her in the matter of the cooper's death. Did an easy capturing of a man's affection have any significance in this particular murder?

The women turned.

Signy knelt and asked for a blessing.

"Thank you for coming here," Eleanor said. "The day is fair, and I regret darkening it with grim questions about a slaying. Nonetheless, justice demands it."

"As does our crowner," Signy replied, her voice betraying a hint of discontent.

"A man with many flaws." Eleanor nodded in acknowledgement of the woman's displeasure. "In that I would agree, but one of them is not an unwillingness to seek the truth."

"My lady, I know I am here because I would not answer his questions the night Martin was killed. Despite my anger with the crowner, I most certainly have no quarrel with you. I will cooperate in any way so that justice may be rendered."

At the prioress' nod, Gytha slipped out of the room, leaving the two women to talk in private.

Eleanor poured dark golden ale from a sweating jug and passed the cool mazer to the innkeeper's niece. "We all hold secrets in our hearts," she said, "and I shall not stand in judgement on anything you might tell me. If it has no relevance to the death of the cooper, I will promptly forget it. Is that fair?"

Signy nodded.

"Then I may conclude that neither of us wants a killer to escape because some detail, no matter how inconsequential or even humiliating, was ignored or kept hidden out of shame or pride?"

Signy lifted the cup to her lips but failed to hide a rising color in her cheeks.

"God knows everything about us. Only His judgement matters, not the flawed opinions of mortals, including prioresses."

"Ask what you will. I shall be honest in my answers."

"Please tell me what you remember about the night Martin died."

Despite the prioress' encouragement, Signy had very little to tell. Ivetta had given more detail.

"Where did you get the food and drink? Did you deliver them directly to Martin's room?" Eleanor asked at the end of the brief tale.

"The food was from the common pot, my lady. A stew of meat with wine, ginger, and onions. I poured the ale myself. Both I took directly up the..." Signy stopped, her lips now moving silently as if they insisted on finishing the sentence. "Nay, I did not do so!" she continued. "I stopped to speak with my uncle for a moment and put the platter and jug down on a nearby table."

"Do you remember if anyone was sitting there?"

"Three men had just left." She thought for a moment. "The table was empty. Had it been occupied, I might not have taken my eyes off such tempting fare, lest a man take a spoonful of something he had not paid for."

"Who was nearby?"

"I do not recall, but anyone leaving or coming into the inn would have passed by. I was standing near the door…"

"Would your uncle remember?"

"I confess the subject of our conversation was a heated one, and he might not have noticed anything. I faced the door, not he, yet surely I would have become aware if some suspicious person had approached the platter. As for my uncle, I cannot truly speak for him."

"Perhaps Crowner Ralf can ask him."

"He must, I am sure."

Eleanor deliberately took her time to sip some ale, waiting to see if Signy would continue. "What was the quarrel you had with your uncle?" she asked.

"Did I say *quarrel*, my lady?"

The prioress simply raised her eyebrows, sufficient reminder of the promise to speak with honesty.

Albeit with evident reluctance, the innkeeper's niece nodded her concession. "It was about his willingness to rent a room to men who want a woman for the night. I did not like the practice."

"I commend you in that."

"My lady, forgive my sin in this matter, but I claim no virtue in my objection. Were I a man, I might permit the custom as well, for the little whoring does bring some extra coin. However, my uncle has no living kin and has promised the inn to me when he dies. No woman may allow whoring in her business if she does not wish to be called *bawd* herself."

"Thank you for your honesty," Eleanor said. "I can also understand how this dispute might have kept you both from seeing much that went on nearby, but I beg of you to please think back and try to recall any faces, or voices, of those who might have been close to hand. Did you see someone who hesitated, even for a brief moment, by the food and drink? An odd gesture perhaps? One caught out of the corner of your eye but quickly forgotten because of the nature of your discussion?"

Signy frowned. "There were many villagers there that night with much coming and going. The way to the inn door sometimes filled with customers, and a few may have bent close to the food and drink in an effort to squeeze by others. That said, I still do not recall anything unusual." Her lips curled into a thin smile. "Our crowner was there himself and might have seen something of note, should he bother remembering."

Eleanor nodded with encouraging sympathy.

"In the past, I might have suggested you ask old Tibia. She always saw things others did not, and she was at the inn for a bit of stew and ale that night." She shrugged. "But I doubt she cares any longer about what goes on around her. With all the pain she now suffers, those sharp eyes have surely dulled. It is a blessing that she still eats. Even the king's man might notice more than she."

The bitter tone whenever Signy mentioned Ralf was not lost on Eleanor. "After you parted from your uncle, you said you delivered the food and drink to the room but did not say if anyone was with Martin."

"Hob and Will were there. The three were arguing. When I entered, Will made lewd remarks about me, which caused much merriment for the cooper. I immediately set the tray and jug down on the table. Normally I would stay to make sure all was satisfactory and as requested, but I was both angry and fearful. I wanted to leave."

"Was Ivetta there?"

"She was." Signy squeezed her eyes shut. "She was there when I brought in the tray."

The prioress reached out and took the woman's hand. "I beg forgiveness for the pain my next question must cause, but I would not ask for such details if I did not think they might help the cause of justice."

Signy nodded but kept her eyes shut.

"Did any of them rudely handle you?"

Tears edged Signy's eyes. "Martin grabbed me and told Will to…"

Eleanor forced herself to remain silent.

"Hob pulled Will away before he could do more, and the two brothers left the room. Martin and Ivetta were laughing with such foul delight, I was able to escape."

"Were you ever alone with any of the three men?"

"Ivetta was there the entire time, my lady. She had arrived before I did and was alone with Martin after I left. While Martin held me, she was the one to lift my gown so Will could put his hand between my legs…" She burst into tears.

Eleanor pulled the innkeeper's niece into her arms and comforted her. Perhaps that would be all she could learn, she thought, but as Signy wept, the prioress' thoughts shifted from anger to puzzlement. Was there significance in the difference between the tale told by Ivetta and the one she had just heard from Signy?

Chapter Sixteen

"If you want information, Crowner, talk to Will or Hob." The innkeeper scowled as he recounted the dead rabbits lying on the table in front of him. "Ask the whore too. I'm a busy man."

Ralf shoved the carcasses to one side and leaned toward the man. "The night of Martin's death. I want details from you."

Clearly annoyed at the interruption to his concentration, the man separated the rabbits once more, pointed a pudgy finger at the first one, and started yet another count.

"Answer my question. I'm not here to watch you pretend King Edward is stopping for his first good English meal since leaving on crusade."

The innkeeper's resigned sigh was as huge as he was. "Martin made the same arrangements he always did when he had Ivetta to himself for the night. He paid for the upstairs room and a proper meal to go with it. Something to break his fast the next morning as well, although he never got to that this time, did he? Now there's a difference for you!" The innkeeper moved the carcasses to one side and dumped a basket of fish in their place. "Twelve rabbits," he shouted to somebody. "Skinny. Tell Hanry to bring me fatter ones, or I'll buy elsewhere."

Ralf was sure the conies were poached but had usually ignored this one practice on the assumption that most lords were in little danger of running short of rabbits to feed upon. "Did the harlot come with him or later?"

"Later."

"You got your share first?"

"I own the room, not the whore. He paid me what I asked when he made his arrangements. Ask her when he gave her whatever he thought she was due—or what, if that means anything to you."

The crowner glanced at the fresh, glistening trout. The innkeeper had never cheated on the quality of what he served at the inn, giving fair value for anything sold. He might bluster and rant about prices and business above all else, but he was an honest enough man. Ralf decided he would probably tell him the truth despite his obvious reluctance.

"So Martin went up to the room alone?"

"Aye. He paid and climbed the stairs."

"The harlot came next? No one else?"

"You think I have the time to spy like a woman on her neighbors? I've a business to run, something you seem to have forgotten."

"You keep your eyes honed well enough for anyone who might cheat you of a tiny silver farthing or cause trouble."

The innkeeper solemnly considered that for a moment, then his features relaxed as if he had concluded the observation was a compliment. "Hob and Will arrived, then the whore. The brothers often joined Martin upstairs for ale." He snorted. "And more if the cooper was feeling generous."

"Who served the food and drink?"

"My niece. Perhaps you might find some answers there, if you sing sweetly enough."

Ralf's face grew hot. "I am investigating a murder, not playing minstrel."

Glaring at the king's man, the innkeeper growled like an apprehensive dog. "She has yet to kill a man, Crowner, although she might have had cause—one time or another."

Ralf swallowed a retort.

The man swept the fish back into the basket. "On her way to deliver the fare, she stopped to talk with me. She did not like that I rented the room upstairs to men who pay to swyve Ivetta."

Shrugging, he continued, "Not that I fault her, but the coin was reliable and Ivetta is clean. No one has claimed to have caught any sickness from her. Had anyone complained that they had done so, I would have banned her."

The crowner nodded.

"While we talked, she put the tray down. Perhaps someone dropped the poison in the food then?"

"Did your niece always serve them?"

"Aye. She knows our inn depends on its reputation for good service given in exchange for good coin. She might not like doing it, but she understands business."

"Did she say anything later about what she saw that night?"

"I didn't ask her. Look, my niece has never been happy about this agreement. I do not want to start a quarrel so I never bring it up. See no point in inviting her woman's squall. Now that Martin's died, the whoring upstairs is done. It's one thing to rent a room for a purpose I can turn my back to, but I don't want the reputation of running a brothel. Ivetta can whore from now on in her own hut, if she can find the custom without her bawd."

"Whatever you may have wished, your niece chose to confront you about the arrangement anyway. Was that a common practice of hers or had something different happened to cause it that night?"

"Nothing odd. That's just a woman for you, continuing to argue about settled matters." Shaking his head, the innkeeper lugged the fish basket over to the door. "These are ready to gut," he shouted.

A man as tiny as the innkeeper was huge rounded the corner. With ease, he hoisted the basket onto his shoulder and disappeared in the direction of the inn's cookhouse.

The fish had looked good, Ralf thought, his stomach issuing an appreciative rumble. Maybe he'd return for the evening meal. "Where did your niece put her tray down?" he continued.

"At the table near the door." The innkeeper waved for the crowner to follow him into the public room, then pointed out the specific place.

"And who passed by while you talked?"

"My back was to it. Ask Signy if you want details."

"No one was sitting there? On such a busy night?"

"You were near. Why don't you ask yourself if you remember anyone?"

Ralf walked over to the innkeeper and jabbed a finger into the man's chest. "Mock and you may find your inn is filled with my men often enough to frighten away anyone with the slightest fear of the king's justice."

The man stepped back. "No need, Crowner, no need! I have told the truth. I saw nothing, remember nothing, and am too busy to care what anyone is doing. Were I to notice such things, I might be crowner instead of you." He yelped as Ralf shoved him. "A jest! 'Twas a jest!"

Ralf did not step away. His teeth were so close to the innkeeper's nose he could have bitten it off.

The man bent back as if he feared that was exactly what the crowner had in mind. "For God's sake, I know nothing more about what happened that night. The harlot screamed. I ran to see what had happened. My niece has told me nothing. Ivetta has lost her bawd and has not returned here. Martin is dead. Business has suffered. What more do you think I can tell you?"

"Hob and Will? Did they quarrel with Martin and did they do so often?"

The innkeeper blinked. "Quarrel? You know the three well enough to answer that yourself. You are all of an age."

"I have not been here for many months. Things change. Answer me."

"They haven't. They fight when they are drunk, and then buy each other ale the next night. Sometimes Will stayed to share Ivetta. That angered Signy more than when Martin had the whore by himself because it meant she must serve refreshments more than once."

"Were they sharing the whore that night?"

"Martin slipped me extra and ordered more food and wine when they did. I never knew until then. Don't think it was always planned. That night I knew only that he was with Ivetta, and he died before he could pay me the additional. And he was good about that. He was an honest man about it."

"How about Ivetta? Did she have any quarrel with the cooper?"

The man laughed. "He never beat her. She ate well enough and drank more. Her clothes were no worse than any harlot might expect. Many wives would be happy with a man like Martin, let alone a woman of her trade. And, unlike a spouse, Ivetta didn't have to make his clothes or cook his meals. Why would she want to kill him?"

"I'll be back," Ralf said. He shook his head in frustration as he walked away.

The innkeeper shouted after him: "When you do, bring some of the king's coin. Leaving that corpse upstairs cost me two day's business!"

Chapter Seventeen

Ralf did not get far from the inn. As he stepped out the door, he saw Thomas walking away from him. "Have you visited Hell of late, monk? You look like it," he shouted at the monk's back.

Thomas spun around. "I must therefore be grateful that all vanity was forbidden me when I took the tonsure, Crowner." He cocked his head to one side and studied his friend with much care. "But I fear you have much the same appearance," he said at last, breaking into a grin. "However, now that I look more closely, I see no difference in your face from the last time we met."

"It is dusk, monk. When did you begin leaping priory walls at night for bright village joys?"

"I am bringing a sleeping potion to old Tibia and have just delivered dill water to a young mother." He pointed behind him. "The babe is colicky. Neither she nor her husband sleeps much at night."

"Are these evening visits Prioress Eleanor's idea?"

"Sister Anne's but our prioress saw the charity in it."

"You say you are visiting old Tibia?"

Thomas nodded.

"Then I will walk with you. I am on my way to see Will the blacksmith."

"How goes the murder investigation?"

"Slowly enough."

Thomas nodded in sympathy at the angry edge in the crowner's voice. "Too many suspects or not enough?"

"In this village, there were few who did not dislike Martin, including me. If someone had taken a cudgel to him at long last, I would not be surprised. What troubles me is the use of poison. Have you heard about that?"

Thomas nodded. "Sister Anne told me. You'd find that a more common method in places other than this fish-reeking coast."

Ralf chuckled. "Still longing for the stench of London streets, monk? You may have the king's court, if you want it though. I would not even give a clipped coin for that."

Thomas shrugged. "All my thoughts of London have faded like a lady's fine silks in the sun." That was true enough, but the memory of his rank prison cell had not.

"An interesting image, monk! Many streets are indeed colorful with the effluence of both man and beast, but the sun does not fade the odor." The crowner slapped Thomas on the shoulder.

"As for the court, I have no experience of it, being a simple monk. We rarely come so close to God's anointed." Folding his hands into his sleeves, Thomas looked at the man with affection. "It pleases me to see you laugh."

They stood together in companionable silence, watching several gray and white mews fly overhead, engaged in raucous avian conversation.

"Back to murder," Ralf said as they walked away from the inn. "Poison is the weapon of someone who cannot or will not face his enemy, man on man. That is my opinion. In court, there are enough cokenays dressed in multi-colored robes that would use it, but I know none such here. A woman might though. Have you heard any rumors?"

"None involving mortals. You accused Ivetta. Why?"

"I think she did it. She was alone with Martin the longest." Ralf gestured back at the inn. "Just talked with our fine inn-keeper who said his niece usually took up the meal but that night had a quarrel with him and set the tray down on a table while they argued. Thus the drink and food remained unattended. According to him, someone might have slipped poison into it on the way out of the inn." He snorted. "That seems unlikely. Too much luck involved."

"Unless someone did not care when he killed Martin and had the poison ready for just the right moment?"

"The king might have his food tasted for such a reason, but we deal more directly with disagreements on this seaweed covered coast you love so well. That idea would have merit someplace other than Tyndal village."

Thomas laughed. The ongoing joke between them had become a comfortable thing.

"Martin has been a bully since boyhood," Ralf continued in a more serious tone. "If he angered someone, he would have been stabbed or beaten bloody coming home drunk from the inn not long after any offense. Who in this village would lie in wait with a vial of poison? Perhaps tied up in the sleeve? I can name no such man."

"A woman then, as you suggested."

"Ivetta."

"You haven't arrested her."

Ralf scowled. "I may think her most likely, but I cannot come up with a reason why she would have murdered him. That's the trouble. She's followed the man like a bitch in heat ever since he broke her maidenhead years ago in the field over there. If she never cared that he turned her into the village whore afterward instead of marrying her, why would she want to kill him so many years later? She may have had cause, but I have yet to discover a recent one."

The two men stopped as they came to Tibia's hut.

"You have not yet talked to Ivetta?" In the growing dark, Thomas could not see the crowner's face, but the man's long silence answered eloquently enough.

"Your prioress agreed it was best if she talked to her," Ralf admitted at last. "Knowing how persuasive Prioress Eleanor can be, I might even hope that she could get the harlot to confess to murder. Or, if not that, persuade her to repent her sinful trade, although I cannot imagine Ivetta in a nun's habit myself. Your prioress will also speak with the innkeeper's niece to ask what she might have noticed." The last was quickly mumbled as if in afterthought.

"As we both have learned, the leader of Tyndal can pry secrets from most men, let alone any woman. Your request for her help was a wise one."

The crowner flushed. "It was her suggestion, monk. I am grateful."

Thomas nodded. Having witnessed the harshness with which Ralf had treated Ivetta, he knew his prioress must have greater success gaining the prostitute's confidence. Why would anyone, especially a frightened woman, confide in a man who gave every sign of wanting to hang someone, anyone, as soon as possible? As for Signy, he had heard rumors enough that the rough-mannered Ralf had offended her deeply not long ago.

Suddenly Ralf's expression brightened. "As for help, Brother, why don't you ask old Tibia if she noticed anything that night? I saw her in the inn sucking at a bowl of stew."

"She suffers great pain, Crowner. I fear the only thing she can see is her path to heaven."

"I had an aged aunt with eyesight better than any hawk. On her deathbed, she told her son, in front of his wife, to give up the mistress he thought he had well-hidden. Don't let an old woman fool you into thinking she has one foot in God's hand."

"If she is alert enough to remember anything, I shall ask her," Thomas agreed.

Still grinning at the memory of his cousin's discomfort, Ralf set off in the direction of the smithy.

◇◇◇

Thomas peered through the thick darkness of old Tibia's hut. His heart beat several times before he finally saw her in a corner, sitting on a stool. "It is Brother Thomas," he said in a soft voice.

"My son!" Tibia's voice was flat with pain. Her hand reached out toward him, fingers clawing as her breath came in gasps.

"I have the potion," he replied, quickly pulling the stopper from the neck of the jar.

She grasped the small container and gulped the liquid like a starving babe at its mother's breast.

When she was done, he helped her ease off the stool and lie on her matted straw.

"I remind God daily to take note of your kindness to this crone," she whispered.

"God knows everything," he replied. From the sweetish stench of old urine and the musty smell of decay, Thomas suspected the straw had not been changed for a very long time. Tomorrow he would come earlier and bring fresh straw for a clean bed.

"He needs reminding, Brother! I'd not have Him forget you." Tibia's laugh was sharp.

"Have you no family at all?" Thomas asked, looking with pity at the cruel poverty of the small space.

"Hell's full of my kin."

"None of your husband's family…"

"Husband?" She snorted. "My son could've been the spawn of many, Brother. When my father and mother died, I lived by whoring. Young flesh draws a high price." Her voice grew muffled as the mixture began to dull her senses and ease her pain.

Perhaps God did need reminding if a young girl was allowed to suffer the loss of her parents and then all virtue in order to survive, Thomas thought. A chill sadness took hold of him.

"Shocked, holy man? Or disgusted by my sins?"

"Only grieved that you should have so much sorrow."

"Don't be, Brother. It doesn't matter that no one's alive to call me kin, or would if I had any, but I've known some joy. When I quickened with my son, I stopped whoring." Her eyes glittered in the small light. "Nay, I didn't find virtue. I fell in love with the babe too quickly to rid myself of him, as I knew well enough how to do."

Thomas smiled at the softness in her voice, then caught himself wondering if his own mother, a woman he never knew, had felt the same about him. He looked down at Tibia, but she had turned her face from him and did not see his especial sympathy.

"I sold herbs and potions to feed us both. Some say charms as well, but many point out the Devil in others so no one will see the Fiend in themselves." She turned back with a toothless grin. "Look at me, Brother! Why would I dance naked for the imps at midnight? Satan himself would not couple with this body even if I offered my soul."

The monk sat back in shock. Surely there were no limits on what the Evil One might do to gain a soul for Hell? "I have seen you consulting with Sister Anne about cures," he said, quickly changing the subject.

"She is a good woman. Taught me much while I could still walk upright and visit the priory hospital."

"Did your son not have a wife?"

There was no answer.

Thomas fell silent and listened to Tibia's breathing deepen into sleep.

His heart now overflowed with compassion for this woman. On impulse he bent to kiss her rough cheek. No matter what his particular distress, he was surrounded by many who would care for him if he suffered the physical pain this woman did, and do so with tenderness. Her lifelong suffering and loneliness was greater than anything he could even imagine, and he quietly berated himself for his own selfish moaning.

As he slipped out the door and walked back to the priory, he remembered that he had not asked old Tibia about what she might have witnessed at the inn. He shrugged. Why trouble the poor woman right now when she endured so much agony. The questioning could surely wait.

Chapter Eighteen

"You're standing in my light." Will lowered his hammer as sweat made pale and twisted paths through the black ash on his face, arms, and chest. The air stank of hot metal and unwashed flesh.

Ralf did not move. "I offer you a bargain then. I will give you light if you will enlighten me."

"Not changed at all, have you? Landless Norman spawn with naught to do but torment honest tradesmen. You always were a troublous cur. Only Tostig could stand you, but I've oft thought him a cokenay, since he doesn't keep a woman and hasn't shown much longing for the cloister." The smith smirked and rubbed his hand under his nose. "Which of you holds the lance, I wonder?"

Ralf grasped his sword.

Will reached over for his tongs and picked up a white-hot coal.

"Drop it, Will!" a voice shouted. "'S Blood! The man will skewer you before you ever decided what to do with that." Hob emerged from a hut near the smithy, wiping his hands on a ragged piece of cloth. A muscular beige dog, with blotches of pink scarring along one side, followed him but carefully kept his distance from the elder blacksmith.

Sparks scattered as Will tossed the coal back into the fire.

The dog yelped and ran back to the dark interior of the hut.

"Lout! Are you trying to burn the village down?" Hob grabbed a bucket and dashed water on some ominously glowing embers. When rising steam confirmed all danger of fire was over, he turned to Ralf. "Why bother us, Crowner? You have Martin's murder to solve. Or is the killer too clever for your frail wits and your pride demands you punish someone to prove your manhood? There's no other reason for you to be here."

"You and Will were the last to see Martin the night of his death. Witnesses heard you quarrelling with him." Ralf had eased his weapon back but kept his hand on the hilt. "I think you killed your boyhood friend."

"Talk to the whore, Crowner. We left. She was alone with him." Will snorted, his eyes still dancing with eagerness for a fight.

"Use what little wit you own," Hob warned his brother. "He has no reason to accuse us. If you lose your temper, you'll only give him cause to arrest you for that alone. Let me speak for both of us."

"Maybe Ivetta tells a different tale." Ralf addressed Hob but kept an eye on the brother.

"Tell me why we'd have wanted to kill him. Will and I often fought with Martin, as you would remember if you have even half a wit. It meant nothing. Ivetta had reason enough to hate him though."

"Why would a harlot suddenly want to kill her longtime bawd?"

Will shrugged. "She was too well-used for Martin. He liked a tighter hole."

Hob put a cautioning hand on his brother's arm. "It wasn't only that," he said. "She boasted to us that he'd promised to marry her at last."

Ralf frowned. "Another one of Martin's jokes?"

Will spat just in front of the crowner's feet. "She should've known that no man will buy where he can get it free. But Ivetta always was a bit slow. Much like you."

"That night, he was going to tell her that he had no intention of taking her to any church door. Not only that, he'd no longer be her bawd," Hob said, glaring at his brother. "He had hopes of a younger woman."

"So he'd leave her to spread her legs in whatever dry ditch she could find," Will added, licking his lips suggestively.

Hob threw his hands up in exasperation. "Don't listen to him, Crowner. None of us would have left her to starve or beg on the king's highway."

"Would you have married her instead?" his brother asked.

Hob shook his head. "Martin mightn't have married her either, but he never would've shoved her aside without…"

Will roared with laughter. "That's not what he told me! He jested that she'd soon find only lepers and friars to pay her with whatever they could beg from honest folks."

"You said she had reason to hate him, enough to kill." Ralf directed this to the younger brother.

"I didn't say she killed him, only that she had reason to hate him. We didn't have cause, and she was with him last…"

"She only had grounds if he told her what you say he was planning. Did he tell her or did he not?" Ralf shouted.

"Why should I know?" Hob yelled back. "I wasn't there." He tossed his head at his brother. "And neither was he."

"Martin was cruel in his jesting," Ralf said, turning to Will. "You knew that best of all and often came to blows…"

Will's face flushed with blood lust, and he clenched his fists.

Hob stepped in front of him. "Stand back or I'll let him run you through, Will."

With but a brief hesitation, his brother did.

Ralf also retreated a step. "Do you believe he meant to toss Ivetta aside or was that just another of his callous jokes? After all, she was bearing his child."

Hob's mouth dropped open. "May God have mercy on her, Crowner! We did not know…"

"Did Martin?"

"It wouldn't have mattered what she claimed," Will growled. "Enough men had mingled their seed in her. What reason had he to believe he was the father any more than…" He grinned. "Me, for instance, or one of the priory monks?"

"Was there another woman or was that false, said only to wound her more deeply?"

Will began to shift from foot to foot like some eager boy. "You'll like this one, Crowner."

"Shut up, Will!" Hob snapped.

Ralf looked from one to the other. "What do you mean?"

"He had another, for cert!" Will leered at the crowner. "Signy, the innkeeper's niece."

Ralf swallowed hard, his face turning pale.

Will the blacksmith bent over, holding his sides as he roared with laughter. "Can't you share the jest, Crowner? Or does it trouble you that she found Martin more pleasing in bed than she did you!"

The crowner lunged.

Hob leapt between the two men and shoved his brother backward through the door of the hut. "Leave us in peace," he shouted from inside, over the barks of the unseen dog. "My brother may be rude, but neither of us had aught to do with murder."

Feeling his face seared by humiliation, Ralf shut his eyes.

Suddenly, he heard a hiss behind him.

Drawing his sword, he spun around.

A very pregnant cat sat nearby and glared. Her eyes glowed red in the light of the dying fire in the forge.

"Devil, thy true name is *Woman*," the crowner grumbled, replaced his weapon, and strode out of the smithy.

Chapter Nineteen

Ivetta leaned back against the lime-washed, straw and clay daub of the stable wall and absently ran a hand around her quickening belly. Had the babe grown? She smiled.

But the memory of Martin's death quickly shattered that brief happiness, and she began to whimper like a hurt child. "He was jesting. It was what he always did. He never meant what he said!"

That horrible night, she had thought his trembling hands spoke of his especial eagerness to mount her. He must be excited about becoming a father at last, she remembered thinking, and his cruel words about the babe had meant nothing, nothing at all.

When he then began to jerk and twist so oddly, she imagined he had found some new way to pleasure himself, but she grew perplexed when he did not enter her and had twisted around to look at what he was doing. The memory was as vivid as if she were seeing it all again, every hideous detail of it.

Martin had fallen to the floor, twitching and clawing at himself. His lips were painted white with foam, his bowels had loosened, and his eyes were wide with unholy terror.

Was it then she had screamed?

She opened her eyes and looked around wildly as if she had just awakened from a nightmare. Staring at the familiar shape of the inn brought her comfort, and the image of his twisted features began to fade. Surely this must all be just a bad dream, she thought.

"Martin will be waiting in that upstairs room. He'll laugh when I walk in, slap me on the tout, and tell me he never meant a word he said."

Won't he?

She had not told the prioress what Martin had said when she revealed she was with child. There was no reason to mention any of that, was there? It had nothing to do with his murder, and God's holy virgin could not possibly understand what often passed between a woman and her man. How could she explain to such a woman that he had often said one thing while thinking another? Despite what others might conclude from his words, she always understood what Martin truly meant.

She had heard many call him cruel and selfish but she knew better. Hadn't his smile betrayed his joy when she gave him her news? Surely he had only meant to be considerate when he said she could birth or bury the child for all he cared. Foolish man! Of course she was happy but he had only wanted to make sure she was.

She shut her eyes again and tried to remember his exact expression. Wasn't that a delighted smile he gave her? His lips were twisted as they always were when he spoke mean words, but didn't that sparkling in his eyes shout a most paternal happiness? An uneasy doubt pricked at her heart, but she quickly disregarded it.

And then there was that business about Signy. At first, she had grown angry when he said he would soon replace her in his bed with the innkeeper's niece, but her temper had cooled when he began to fondle her as he always did. No matter that she did not like the idea of another in Martin's arms, but a man must have a woman lest his seed grow weak and die. Accordingly, she had decided he could swyve the tavern wench for relief if he wanted, while she herself was big with child, but it would be a temporary thing as it had always been.

Yet he had been cruel to tease her and bring up things she'd rather never remember like the other women he'd bedded. Of all times, why did he also have to do it that night when she was so happy about their first son and the coming marriage he had once promised her?

And why did he have to die? Who would have been so pitiless as to kill him, especially before he could marry her? As his wife under law, she would have gained possession of all he owned, a portion for herself and the rest for their child. Now she had nothing and might starve before the babe was even born. She began to shake with icy terror and pulled herself closer to the stable wall for support.

When she felt some ease, she loosened her grip on the rough surface and looked with longing toward the inn where her beloved had died. A figure coming along the path from the priory caught her eye.

Ivetta tensed. Anger rose with the heat of Hell's fire from her belly, and an idea burned itself into her mind. Why had she not thought of this before? Now she knew what had happened that night. Like a wild woman, she flung herself away from the stable.

"You killed him!" she screamed and ran toward the innkeeper's niece.

Startled by the screeching woman racing toward her, Signy stopped so quickly that she stumbled, lost her balance in the rutted ground, and fell to her knees.

In an instant, Ivetta was on top of her, pummeling Signy with both fists. "You murdered him because he loved me! You knew you could never have him to yourself!"

The innkeeper's niece twisted first to one side and then the next, shouting for help and trying to protect her eyes and face. Being far taller and heavier-boned than Ivetta, she finally dislodged her attacker and jumped to her feet. "You're mad!" she shouted.

Ivetta struggled to her feet. "Lecherous woman! Martin only bedded you out of pity. When he came back to me, he mimicked how you had howled with longing, and then writhed with lust under him."

"How dare you call me wanton!"

A crowd was now gathering outside the inn.

Ivetta noted the growing audience and gleefully threw her arms out to them. "May not an honest whore expose a dishonest one? Of course, I can. Shall I be more specific to prove the truth of what I say?"

A few voices urged her to continue.

"Do you deny that you have a red mark on your left breast, just above the tit? Was that where the Devil bit you when even he failed to sate your lusts?" Ivetta shouted.

Signy froze.

"And the mole on your pryvete?"

"Liar!" The innkeeper's niece screamed, covering her ears.

Ivetta threw her head back and laughed.

Signy began to weep.

A heavy-set man suddenly appeared at the doorway of the inn, then pushed his way through the crowd toward the women.

Seeing the innkeeper amongst them, a few men left, assuming the entertainment was over. Others stayed to watch what would happen next.

"Go back inside," he ordered. "This is but a spat between women, of no greater import than the sparring of two cats over a vole. Tonight we have a band of jugglers passing through, far better amusement than this silliness."

In good humor after such merry sport and needing ale to wet their throats on a summer eve, the crowd dispersed, most returning to the inn.

The innkeeper took the trembling Signy by the arm. "Come, niece," he said gently. "Dry your tears. The cook needs help with the fish."

By then, Ivetta had disappeared into the shadows of the slowly fading light.

Chapter Twenty

Eleanor's eyes widened. "I never would have thought such a thing."

Ralf stared at the rushes on the floor. Although no one could read his expression, his shoulders were rounded as if heavy melancholy had weighed them down.

"Nor do I now," Sister Anne replied. "Signy may have faults like the rest of us, but I cannot imagine why she would bed a man like Martin. I had never heard that she was fond of the rougher sort."

Ralf glanced up and blinked as if waging war against enemy tears.

"Perhaps I misspoke," Anne said, her tone softened by compassion. "When a man chooses to ignore sweet courtesies and fine fashion, he may still own a gentle heart. Martin was a cruel man. I meant the latter when I spoke of roughness."

"The innkeeper's niece is a woman beyond reproach," the crowner replied, his words barely audible. "Were she otherwise, Tostig would not…" He coughed uncomfortably.

"Of course, Ralf." Anne nodded.

"None of us gives credence to this comment by the smithy." Eleanor's dismissive gesture gave emphasis to her words. "Nonetheless, it provides me with cause to call Signy back. I wanted to clarify some details of her story. And," she continued, "I have more questions for Ivetta as well, although the latter may find a second visit to the priory more unwelcome than the first. I fear the contemplative nature of our life failed to attract her."

Anne raised a hopeful eyebrow. "Our Order has welcomed women of her trade who repent. Not all religious houses do. Her exposure was surely all too brief. Perhaps another walk through our cloister would open her heart to the murmured wisdom of Saint Mary Magdalene."

"That is a miracle for which we might well pray." The prioress smiled before turning her attention back to the crowner. "Meanwhile, I shall see what more I can learn that relates to murder."

"My lady, you are most kind to take on this task," he said, this time meeting her gaze. "The cooper's death does not affect Tyndal Priory, and I shall never forget your generous help when I could not get answers."

"God requires it. First, our priory does serve both the spiritual and many temporal needs of this village. Second, when any mortal falls victim to violence, even one as sinful as Martin, all men are blighted. Whether they follow a secular or religious life matters not. Because you are striving to emulate God's most perfect justice, Crowner, we have good reason to assist you in that pursuit." Her smile was warm with affection.

Ralf flushed unhappily. "I could never achieve perfection, my lady. My soul is so fat with its many transgressions that even the Devil must doubt he can find room for my spirit in Hell."

"All I said was *strive*, Ralf," she replied, her tone turning curiously chill. "With God's help, we imperfect mortals may even succeed on rare occasion. As for the number of our sins, we all suffer from mortal flaws, whether sworn to enforce an earthly king's law or that of God."

Not long after, the crowner left—as did Sister Anne. When the Prioress of Tyndal's eyes darkened to that color of storm clouds scudding above the North Sea, even friends felt safer elsewhere.

◇◇◇

Eleanor marched into her private chambers.

From his nest in a worn piece of wool, the cat raised his head and scrutinized his mistress as she stood over him. His yellow-green eyes were round with grave concern.

"What a hypocrite I am!"

She picked the cat up and carried him in the crook of her arm to the nearby chair. "My perfect knight, I need your soothing company for I am most distraught. Did you overhear my words? Did I not speak convincingly of our duty to strive toward perfection in justice?"

As soon as she sat, the cat circled into a comfortable position on her lap.

"I am wallowing in self-pity. My heart rots with foul anger. The putrefying stench of my sins overcomes me, and my prayers bring neither answer nor comfort."

Arthur, it seems, was less troubled and quickly fell asleep.

"Why should Signy not hide secrets from me that might bring disgrace, perhaps even connect her to murder? My own soul thrashes in a reeking slough. Would I readily speak of my shame, except to a confessor or my aunt?" She threw her head back against the chair.

Startled by the abrupt gesture, Arthur leapt to the floor but remained at her feet.

"And Ivetta? She is an honest whore while I most truly resemble a whited sepulcher, filled with dead bones and uncleanness." She bent over to stroke the wary cat and sighed. "*Strive*, was the word I used," she whispered. "*Strive.* That is all God asks, and I must never say He fails to answer my prayers. My greatest fault lies in not listening for His consolation."

Muffled voices from below her window caught her attention. She stiffened. Were visitors arriving to disrupt this time she needed for musing, she wondered. With relief, Eleanor recognized the familiar laughter of lay sisters passing by, and she slipped back into her troubled thoughts.

"This matter of Brother Thomas has cast my wits into a dungeon and chained them with rough iron to the stone wall," she continued. "There Lust, Jealousy, and Anger are let loose

like mad dogs by Satan to torment my frail reason. I should
have asked our abbess in Anjou to send the monk elsewhere
many months ago!"

She sighed. "But cooler logic showed me the selfishness of
doing so, and I did not. Now that I know his traitorous secret,
do I truly have any better cause than my lust to cast him forth?
Even if I did, my request might be refused. Perhaps I would be
wiser to keep my knowledge hidden. The Abbess herself might
have been involved in making the decision to send him here."

Eleanor patted her lap and the cat jumped back causing the
prioress to smile in spite of herself. "Besides, you and my aunt
seem to find him pleasing, snake in the garden though he might
be," she said to Arthur. "Dare I ignore your greater wisdom and
my aunt's pointed remark that he has proven his keenness for
justice and the willingness to serve me? Surely I am out-argued
by you both and must concede the debate."

Arthur started to scrub her hand with studied care.

She laughed. "That rough tongue of yours is far more effective than any hair shirt, good sir!"

A fly buzzed by, slow and lazy with the summer warmth. The
cat tensed, eyed the threat, then jumped down to the floor and
began stalking it with due diligence.

"Perhaps a hair shirt would scour away this feminine imperfection of rampant lust and recloak my soul with a cooler,
manlier reason? While I sit immobilized by my weaknesses, a
soul draped in evil, one that has broken God's commandment
against murder, walks free in Tyndal village. My sins will mul-
tiply even more if I allow myself to be blinded by my frailty
over Brother Thomas and not help bring that viler creature to
earthly justice."

Eleanor fell into a meditative silence.

The cat, meanwhile, twisted and jumped at the diverting
insect.

"As my aunt told me, lusting after my monk gives Satan joy,
but there is no sin in finding pleasure in the company of the man
if that leads us both to better serve Our Lord. God gave Eve to

Adam for companionship. Surely she found a like contentment with him before their fall from grace. That proves there is no wickedness in chaste affection."

She rose and walked over to the window. The sun was favoring the land outside with benevolent warmth. "Nonetheless, no man may have two masters."

The fly disappeared out the same window, leaving the cat baffled.

The prioress clenched her fists. "And I shall claim first loyalty! Brother Thomas is my liegeman. I do not know the reason he became a spy, nor do I understand why he was sent specifically to Tyndal Priory." Her lips curled with grim humor. "Perhaps the assumption was that I, a simple woman with few years on earth, would be easily deceived and manipulated. Until now, that was certainly true; but anyone who underestimates the niece of Sister Beatrice is the greater fool."

The breeze shifted and brought the smell of the eastern sea into her room. Eleanor breathed deeply, finding calming pleasure in it.

"And now that I have been alerted to my monk's other duties, this unnamed but arrogant churchman who claims his obedience would be well-advised to reconsider his methods." Folding her arms, she looked back at her cat. "Of course, I shall let Brother Thomas leave Tyndal on missions to serve God, as he has been wont to do already, but henceforth he shall do so only by my grace! Perhaps I may even enjoy my next encounter with the priest, who comes with overt lies to purloin my monk, and shall consider how to make it quite clear that I am willing to let my monk serve God's justice elsewhere, but only when it suits me."

She looked heavenward, her eyes narrowing with ardent determination. "As prioress of Tyndal, I may rightfully lay claim to the obedience of my flock. Brother Thomas is mine and shall be only mine until God takes either of our souls to judgement!"

With that the prioress bent to pick up the disgruntled insect hunter and carried him out of her private chambers. Whatever grief Brother Thomas might bring her heart, Eleanor still had properties to manage and a murder to solve, whereas Arthur must clear the kitchen of thieving rodents.

When they departed, a small mouse, that had been lying very still in a far corner, quickly disappeared through a crack in the wall some feet away. Were it able to thank God for the life-saving distractions of a languid fly and a woman's angst, this one tiny creature most certainly would have done so.

Chapter Twenty-One

Hob slammed his hand on the table. "Martin told my brother that he had bedded Signy and would have her again! Will spoke the truth. As you should know, he's not clever enough to tilt with words. His knuckles may be sharp but not his wit. In that he hasn't changed since we were all lads. If you think otherwise, Crowner, you're deaf and blind, or else a fool."

"Sharp knuckles and dull wit, eh? Then I conclude he may kill me like he did Martin." Ralf gestured for more ale.

Hob tensed, then shook his thoughts away and accepted the proffered drink. "My brother's always had a hot temper, but he would no more kill a friend than I would." He took a long swallow of the ale. "Martin, I mean, not you."

"Nevertheless, I must arrest him for menacing me. I may care little myself for his foolish words, but I am the king's man and must demand reparations when my lord's honor is insulted." The crowner spat before drinking. "I wonder what your brother might say about the cooper's death if he knows he will never again see daylight if he does not deal honestly with me?"

"Why arrest a man you know to be no wiser than a child? You've spent too long with your elder brothers if you want to condemn a simple man just for behaving with no more sense than a king's fool." He watched Ralf, waiting for a reaction. When the crowner shrugged, he continued, "Will means what he says in heat but forgets it all the morning after, especially with Martin. The cooper was as close to us as if he, too, had been born of our mother."

"I will think about that. As for what I have remembered from my youth here, I know that Martin always did own a cruel tongue." Ralf leaned closer. "What did he say that made you and your brother quarrel after you left him? And do not deny that you did. You were seen. I suspect the cooper said something that finally gave one of you reason to seek revenge."

"May not brothers disagree? Must that be cause for suspicion of murder?"

"Abel and Cain bickered as well. Their example gives me good cause to wonder."

Hob rose from his seat, his face reddening. "Are you suggesting I plan to kill my own brother?"

A tentative growl was heard from under the table.

"Sit down and quiet that cur of yours. Will safely walks this earth with you as far as I know," the crowner snorted. "I'm only interested in Martin's death. It may well be true that the three of you have been like brothers since youth, but something happened that night—or perhaps before and the flame only burst out then. Knowing his unkind ways, I think Martin struck flint to rock and brought forth a hot spark from someone. If so, either you or your brother might have killed the cooper, perhaps with good reason. I would be willing to consider that in exchange for a confession."

"Will is right. You have always believed you were cleverer than the rest of us. As a boy you may have tried to cover yourself with village mud to look like us, but your Norman nose betrayed you. It still points up at heaven."

Ralf barked a laugh. "I do not mistake you for Will. Do not confuse me with my church-bound brother who exhales corruption with every prayer. I always thought you a better man than…"

"You did not say that when we were boys and the witch's son died. Then you blamed us in equal measure."

"And would do so again. But no one listened to my unbroken voice, and you were all held blameless." The crowner reached toward the other man with a conciliatory gesture. "That day, I think you took on a man's gravity, Hob, and changed for the better."

Hob drained his cup.

Ralf poured more for them both.

"What do you expect me to say, Crowner? I'll not speak ill of my elder brother. I owe him fealty as my kin. To you, I owe nothing."

"You may owe me your life if you act wisely. Speak the truth."

"My brother is innocent of murdering Martin. On my faith in God's mercy, I swear it."

"Then what was the quarrel?"

"A private matter."

Ralf cupped his hands around the mazer and took his time glancing at the crowd. This gesture may have been intended to give Hob time to conclude there was prudence in providing more detail, but he found himself troubled. Wasn't someone missing from the inn this night?

He closed his eyes. It was Signy he didn't see, he realized. She was not serving. A sharp pain stabbed at his heart. Quickly shaking the thought off, he went back to studying the men around him while he waited.

Hob bit his thumb.

The crowner was losing patience. He turned to face the younger blacksmith, his expression as chilling as winter ice.

"A matter between men," Hob offered, a slight tremor in his voice.

Ralf nodded but his manner suggested no compassion.

"He would beat me if he heard I spoke of it."

"You may cast dispersions on my Norman nose, but you cannot claim I have ever failed to honor my word. If the cause does not bear on murder, your words die in my ears."

Hob fell silent and scowled.

"In a brawl, I'd say you might be a match for your brother but the hangman always wins. Think on that."

"Enough talk of hanging, Crowner. Martin mocked Will for impotence. I told my brother to forget it, but he wanted to fight the man. *Fight*, I said, not murder."

"Give me more detail."

"When Martin offered to share his whore the last few times, my brother was too drunk. His manhood lay limp in spite of Ivetta's talents. The other night, Martin ridiculed him for that. Will hit him, but I dragged him away before he could do more, telling him he would catch Martin soon enough with his own pole down. Then he could scoff at him in return. There was little to fight about and more downstairs to drink."

"But not before you tried to rape the innkeeper's niece."

Hob paled at the anger in Ralf's words. "Not I, Crowner. Martin and Ivetta were both jeering at Will when Signy walked into the room. Martin wagered Will could not swyve her. The cooper and the harlot held the wench, and, like a fool, my brother fondled her. I yelled at him and pulled my brother from the room. For that, we quarreled."

"Did you leave the inn with him?"

"You claim to have witnesses. Ask them. I've nothing to fear."

"I want your version."

Hob frowned at his mazer, as if blaming it for being empty, then poured more ale and continued. "We came to blows outside the inn. I don't recall who might have seen us except old Tibia. That I remember because she hurled insults at us, as she is wont to do, and passed on by. Ask her, if you don't believe me. She might talk to you, if her humors are balanced."

"What happened next?"

"Will's temper cooled. We went home."

"He could have returned to the inn."

"He didn't. When we got back, my brother grew quiet and sat out in the smithy for a long time before going to bed. In the past, when we had argued, he'd find his pallet and pass out, yelling and muttering at me until he did. My brother has never been inclined to musing so his odd behavior troubled me. I watched until he finally sought rest. He couldn't have gone back to murder Martin."

"He might have slipped out later."

"I heard the commotion from the inn not long after. Unless my brother's been granted invisible wings to fly him there, he did not do the deed."

Ralf fell silent. Perhaps this tale did prove Will was guiltless. Or not. Hob might have made it up to protect his brother. Or he might have told it to place himself innocently at home at well.

The crowner gazed at the groups of men nearby. Although he had never liked either brother when they were all boys, he had grown to tolerate Hob and even find some decency in him. Were he forced to swear an oath, Ralf knew he would have to say that Hob's tale rang true enough.

Rubbing his hand against the stubble on his cheeks, Ralf groaned silently. If neither Will nor Hob was the killer, then suspicion fell back on Ivetta or else, to his greater unease, Signy.

Chapter Twenty-Two

Thomas stopped a few yards past the inn.

Outside her hut, old Tibia and a man were in close conversation. Not wanting to interrupt, the monk decided to wait until they were done before he delivered the sleeping potion. As he walked slowly back along the path he had just traveled, he began to ask himself what business this Will Blacksmith could possibly have with the herb woman.

The man is not known for his charity to any soul less fortunate than he, Thomas thought, so I rather doubt the visit has aught to do with alms or the offer of kind companionship.

Curious and a bit troubled, he looked back at the pair.

Tibia was sitting on a high, three-legged stool, her eyes wide and unblinking like a painted figure in a manuscript. The staff she used to help her walk lay across her knees.

The blacksmith squatted on his haunches close beside her, his mouth next to her ear as if imparting some secret.

She shook her head and turned away from him.

Will reached for her arm and roughly pulled her back.

"Monk I might be," Thomas muttered, "but I will not tolerate any harm done to an old woman." He hurried toward to the hut.

Tibia's eyes brightened as she saw the monk approach. "My son!" she cried out.

Will dropped her arm and gaped at the monk as if he had just seen a ghost.

"How cruel is your pain tonight?" Thomas stopped and glared at the blacksmith.

Will jumped to his feet and gestured for the monk to leave. "Wait your turn! I have business with the herb woman."

"Indeed?" Thomas stepped closer.

"He did," Tibia said, then turned to look at the blacksmith, her eyes blinking in the reflected light from the inn. "But he's done."

"For the sake of charity, old woman, give me what I need!" Although Will addressed the old woman, he glanced back at the monk. His expression was both confused and wary, his tone pleading.

"I don't have it. I can't forage for such things anymore. Ask someone else."

"Tell me what's needed and where to find it. I'll get it for you. You're the only one..."

"Go away." She waved at him. "I'm tired. Don't want to talk to you. Come tomorrow. I'll think about it." Her staff started to roll off her knees, and she made a feeble attempt to catch it.

Thomas picked it up. "I think your departure would be a wise act," he said to the blacksmith, holding the sturdy branch in a position to strike if need be.

Will's face darkened with anger and he raised one clenched fist.

"God'll curse you if you hit a monk," Tibia said. "And if He does, there's nothing I can do to help you."

"Tomorrow, then." With a curse, the blacksmith spun on his heel and strode away.

"Did he harm you?" Thomas asked, kneeling beside her.

"Nay," Tibia sighed, her look growing distant. "You're a good lad to me." She reached out and patted his hand. "When I birthed a kind son, God did bless me."

Thomas opened his mouth to protest but quickly thought the better of that. What reason was there to waken her from all too brief but sweet imaginings? "Are you in pain?" he whispered instead.

She looked down at him, her eyes refocusing as her mind returned to the present. "It's now when I recall what it was like to be a younger woman, Brother, and in full possession of my powers." Her chuckle was like a rasp on iron. "For just a few moments, I do forget suffering."

"Then you do not need this potion?"

She reached out for the flask.

Noticing how two of her fingers were bent backward from the joint disease, he realized that she was probably in constant pain. Any relief was but the difference between the bearable and the intolerable. He gave her the sleep-inducing drug.

"I may yet awaken in the night. My pain overcomes me of a sudden." She smiled, her mouth innocent of all but two yellow fangs and a few other teeth that had turned black. "Is it safe to take all this at once? I don't want to send my sinful soul to God by chance, without a priest to hear my last confession."

"Sister Anne is careful about such matters. You may take this one draught with confidence but not more."

"Stay, if you will. For a few moments? Unless another sufferer waits for the mercy you bring." She eased herself to the edge of the stool and rubbed a place next to her as if warming it for his comfort.

"I saved this visit for last." He rested one hip on the stool to give her more room. "I often watch over you until you fall asleep."

"Like my dead boy, Brother, your company brings comfort." Tibia fell silent.

"You said he died as a young man." Even though he could not read her expression, he heard both grief and anger well mixed in her speech. "Was it illness or an accident that took him to God so soon?"

"That man?" With a gesture of disdain, she pointed in the direction Will had disappeared. "The blacksmith?"

Thomas nodded.

"He murdered my son."

His mouth opened in shock.

"But those wise men of the crowner's jury claimed I raised the hue and cry unjustly and that my son died by accident. They fined me for the trouble I caused."

"And Will?" he asked.

"Suffered nothing. Oh, a mild rebuke."

Had grief clouded her reason in this, Thomas wondered. The men could have made a mistake, being imperfect mortals, but were not most fathers themselves? Few of them would fail to sympathize with a parent's agony over a dead child, yet he did think the fine assessed against her most harsh. Had she been a nuisance to them perhaps in other matters? Had they wanted to teach her a lesson? And what reason could there have been to rule against her unless the evidence did unequivocally prove an accident?

In any case, he thought, the lad was dead and it no longer mattered which conclusion was the true one. Kindness, not debate, was required now. "Then I commend you for your charity to him," he said softly, "for you spoke most civilly a few minutes ago."

"Charity? Nay. I must be humble in the face of my wickedness. Priests tell me I'm kin to the Whore of Babylon. When I found my boy's naked body, swinging from a tree with a rope around his neck, his eyes bulging and his face purple, villagers said I should've taken this pain as retribution for my sins." Tibia's next words came out in a gasp of labored breath. "Some even whispered that God had used Will as His instrument to punish me. I couldn't question God."

I most certainly would have and, in truth, did at times, Thomas thought with a shiver, and then took her hand between his two, hoping to soothe her. "Why did the blacksmith hang your son? Was it out of malice?"

"They were all boys. My son fell in love with a girl in the village. When they caught him lying with her in the forest, they mocked him, swearing he must pay for his lust, especially being the offspring of a harlot. A rope was put around his neck and he was hauled up. According to those who stood in judgement later, the intent was honest enough and meant only to scare him. A joke, they claimed, but the rope stuck in that tree. When my son began to choke, they said help was sought, but my boy died before he could be cut down."

Thomas bent his head in silence. Had any son of his been killed in this fashion, he would have found more solace in crying out *murder* and railing against a deliberate killer. There was no intent in an accident, and thus a man might reproach God for lack of caring and the cruel injustice of it. Was it not better for her soul that Tibia believe the death to be murder and choose to curse a man who killed rather than God?

As if she had been reading his thoughts, the old woman added, "It takes time to strangle, Brother. My boy was beyond all help when I found him, but I saw who'd done it running into the woods." Her breathing grew harsh with the torment of memory.

How little most mortals think of consequences when we are that young, Thomas thought. To look up and see the boy slowly strangling and the rope snagged beyond reach must have been terrifying. Although he felt no pity for bullies, he did understand the delay in action as the tragedy dawned. The crowner's men should have demanded some punishment for such a vicious and unnecessary death, but he was not sure he would have called this willful murder either.

Tibia shook her hand free of his. "Go, Brother," she whispered. "Tonight I'd best stay alone." Her lips twisted into a thin grimace. "But I promise I'll think on how well God rewards us when we turn the other cheek."

Watching her hobble into the dark hut, Thomas knew that he had failed her.

Chapter Twenty-Three

The curtain flapped in the sweet-scented breeze. The anchoress caught a glimpse of the pale moon's position in the sky and longed for morning light.

"Why do you condemn me? I listened for God's direction. I heard it. I acted. All this did you advise."

Sister Juliana shut her eyes and prayed, but no answer came to her in the dark silence of her soul.

"Why do you now say I should beg for mercy? Did I not render His justice upon a wicked man?"

"Your sin is grave." Juliana's lips trembled.

"How can you denounce me so? Hasn't God's will been done? He spoke…"

"You must seek a priest," the anchoress cried out. "You must ask for absolution. That I have no right to grant!"

"God speaks through your mouth. I have heard Him."

"I am Eve's daughter: feeble of mind, irresolute in spirit, sinful in body."

The only response was the sharp intake of mortal breath.

The anchoress bent forward until her forehead hit the stone wall. "I may pray that He fill me with His spirit, unworthy vessel that I am," she groaned, "but I am still a wretched creature. Believe me when I say I have no right, no authority, to cleanse your soul. Only a priest has such power."

"My soul is at ease. My act was a righteous one. When you told me to wait for God's voice, you said I would feel at peace when I heard it. I believed your words and I now rejoice. What need have I of any priest?"

"This is murder!" Juliana wailed.

Only the soft whish of tall grass broke the stillness as the figure moved from the window and walked away.

That night God did not grace Juliana with sweet visions or a honeyed voice. Instead she experienced only that bitter despair suffered by lost souls. In anguish, she sought the small whip, bared her back, and beat herself until blood dripped, making tiny circles in the dust on the anchorage floor.

Chapter Twenty-Four

Signy trembled.

Such a reaction might be caused by either outrage or fear, Eleanor decided as she sat back in her chair.

"He lies!"

"One of you does, perhaps both. Were I possessed of a more credulous mind, I might conclude that memory had simply betrayed one or the other of you. I am not, however, nor do I sympathize with trivial fears. Whether or not he was a good man, Martin's soul has been torn from his body by unlawful violence."

The length of the silence, as the prioress studied her, must have given Signy some foretaste of how unpleasant eternity could be. Discomfited, she dropped her eyes.

"By repute, you are a sensible woman. If you are innocent, there is no reason to lie other than shame. Compared to the sufferings of a soul sent to Hell without the chance for repentance, I think humiliation is a very minor thing indeed."

"I did not kill him."

"Then you should be eager to do everything to prove that," the prioress replied. "Surely you agree as well that this killer must be found and punished? In the search for truth, I may ask many questions. Answers to some may not be relevant, and if so, I shall cast them from my mind, leaving those transgressions to your conscience and your confessor. That said, all details must be exposed and investigated further if needed. Justice shall be hastened."

Sweat glistened on Signy's brow.

"Would you like some ale?" Eleanor asked. Although her voice was gentle, she was angry. Lies stank like night soil at midday, and she was concluding that the reek in the room was growing too potent.

"I would be grateful, my lady." Signy's shoulders drooped with resignation.

Against her better judgement, Eleanor's heart began to soften. "Do not imagine that I ignore the beam in my own eye when I see the mote of dust in yours. Not one of us is free from sin; thus I promise to hear all you have to tell me with compassion." The prioress poured a pottery mazer full and passed it to the innkeeper's niece. "Unless, of course, it proves murder."

Signy quickly swallowed the ale. "Will is a hateful man," she said.

"Why would he tell such a story?" Eleanor refilled the woman's cup. "Before you reply, be aware that I heard the tale of what Ivetta shouted out during your argument near the inn. She was quite specific in her details. Many have repeated her words."

Signy flushed deeply. Her hand shook, and she quickly set her cup down, spilling ale in the process.

"The tale will be forgotten soon enough. Since we all struggle with our failings, most of us will readily forgive if another rejects deceitfulness and humbly admits the truth," Eleanor reminded her gently. "God, of course, is always willing to forgive the contrite heart."

"So said your new anchoress, my lady."

Eleanor raised a questioning eyebrow. "You have sought her counsel?"

"Most of the village women have and found comfort from her."

"At night?"

"The Evil One troubles sinners most when there is no light in the world, my lady. Sister Juliana understands that and gives welcome solace to those tortured by Satan's imps in the dark hours."

"Most certainly proof that God is compassionate with the penitent," Eleanor replied with heavy emphasis on the last word. Although refusing to be distracted from murder, she did tuck the woman's testimony away for the next time Sister Ruth brought forth her complaints about the anchoress. "Was the matter troubling you related either to Martin's murder or the allegations that you might be sharing the cooper's bed?"

Signy took in a deep breath. "In part, my lady, but the tale is a long one."

The prioress nodded, offering both ale and cheese. "To give you strength in the telling," she said with a smile.

"I have reason enough to hate Martin," Signy began with evident lack of enthusiasm. "After my parents died and I had gone to my uncle's care, the cooper sought me out and often soothed my battered heart with soft compliments. I was ignorant then of how desire can erupt from a few caresses so let him touch me for it brought a curiously sweet solace. One night he drew me down beside him in a hidden spot near the inn and taught me howling lust. I was frightened at the power of it and tried to break away, but he first covered my mouth and then shattered my maidenhead. I was younger than Gytha."

"You told your uncle of this?"

"I dared not! Without question, he is a most charitable man but he has always treated me as if I were an apprentice, kindly but with no great affection. And so I feared to anger him, lest he cast me out. Martin swore he would claim I had encouraged him if I spoke of what he had done. Had he accused me of lewdness, my uncle might well have turned his back on me and I have no other family." She rubbed her eyes. "I did not give the cooper opportunity to swyve me again."

"Indeed?"

Signy bit her lip.

"Do not think me a fool," Eleanor said, resting her chin in her hand. "I doubt Martin was silent about his conquest even if you were, but the scandal has lost its bite after all this time. Too many other broken maidenheads have since brought greater glee to the withered hearts of tale-tellers. Why should this especially trouble you now?"

"I did not kill the cooper!" Signy protested once again, her eyes round with terror.

"Then confide in me. Let me help you free your conscience as well as prove your innocence. I know you did not consult Sister Juliana because the inn ale had gone sour, nor, I suspect, did you suddenly long to find forgiveness for virginity lost long ago."

"Might I not realize the horror of my sin, even at this late date, and seek advice on how best to repent?"

Eleanor leaned forward, her eyes narrowing with anger. "I believe you and Martin have bedded more recently, something you wish would remain secret. That is why you screamed at Ivetta when she publicly denounced you, not out of shame for a young girl's weakness years ago. In this fresh sin lies a reason for you to have killed the cooper."

"A lie!"

"A word you have used with ease today." The prioress sat back, her expression devoid of pity. "If I can conclude such a thing, others will as well. Even if the blacksmith has told no one else except the crowner what Martin most surely told him, he shall do so now if he thinks he is a suspect in his friend's death. Once the tale is bruited about, our crowner must arrest you, whether he wants to do so or not. You would be wise, therefore, if you told me now why you should not be found guilty of murder and let me keep you from some fetid hole while you wait for a trial."

"Ralf must not hear of this," Signy sobbed.

"That, I cannot promise. If he does not hear it from me, he will hear it from others. Ivetta has detailed moles and marks on your private parts to all in the village square. The blacksmith will shout out anything else he has learned to cast suspicion of murder away from him. I cannot prevent further humiliation and shame, but the truth may protect you from the hangman."

Signy put her hand to her mouth. As she spoke, she looked away from the prioress. "I did let Martin back into my bed some months ago."

"Why?"

"Do not ask. I beg of you!" Her eyes began to flash with anger, although her cheeks now glistened with tears. "You would not understand what I…"

"Understand? No, I do not, nor would others who have not so vowed themselves to chastity. If, as you claim, you hated the man for a rape committed against you as a young girl, why would you now eagerly spread your legs for him again? Many would find cause to ask that, not just I."

Shocked at the prioress' harshness, Signy opened her mouth to reply but all speech had fled.

"You may think me cruel, but my words are far gentler than those you shall hear flung at you during your public trial."

The innkeeper's niece slipped to her knees. "My lady," she said, "I beg forgiveness for what I have both said and thought."

The prioress rose and took Signy by the hands. "Your penance shall be the truthful telling of what happened. If there is violence in your tale, I promise I shall seek some reason to beg for mercy on your behalf."

The woman rose, wiped her cheeks dry with her sleeve, then took the mazer of ale and sipped. "Many months ago," she began, clearing her throat, "I took a man into my bed, someone my heart adored. I believed he cared for me as I did him. Instead, he used me as casually as he would any whore." She squeezed her eyes shut.

Eleanor gently touched Signy's hand.

"Filled with shame and anger, I let Satan possess me. For some time I was blind to either virtue or reason, and I sought out Martin for his charming lies, although I swear I lusted after his false flattery more than I ever did his body."

Eleanor said nothing, her silence proclaiming her skepticism eloquently enough.

Signy flushed. "You are right enough to cast that look at me, my lady. Although I did love the balm of his words, Martin is not only clever in speech but has learned well how to pleasure a woman."

The prioress nodded but quickly closed her eyes to veil her own thoughts.

"But the secret I wished kept was not so much the wickedness of lust. I found myself with child," she whispered. "I sought the advice of old Tibia. The babe…"

"…died?"

As if the word had been a blow, Signy's head jerked to one side.

"Martin knew this?"

"Somehow he learned it, although I did not tell him."

"Who did?"

"Not the herb woman. Not only did she have cause to avoid him after the death of her son, no one would go to her if she were one to tell their secrets."

"Could another have overheard you speak of it? Think back on what you might have said, when, and to whom."

"I confided in no one else," Signy protested but fell silent then, frowning with thought. "Yet I do suspect someone. I would not like to say the name, lest I accuse unjustly."

"Do not fear explaining this to me. I will decide the merit of your thoughts."

"As I left Tibia with her remedy in hand, I saw Ivetta coming around the side of the hut. At the time, I assumed she had come for the same reason I had, but she was surely skilled enough in such matters and had no cause to seek the herb woman's help. Perhaps she listened at the wall? There are enough holes in it that the winter wind finds little resistance." She stopped to think further. "If she heard my plight, she would have told Martin. Perhaps she learned many other secrets at Tibia's walls and passed them on to him. Of course! How else would he have learned so much? And he did find merriment in making others squirm when he revealed vices they thought were buried deep."

Eleanor waited as a renewed stream of hot tears extinguished the fury glowing in the blue eyes of the innkeeper's niece. "And did he find a way to torment you for this?"

"Aye, my lady." Once again, she rubbed her cheeks dry of tears. "Two nights before his death, Martin accosted me in the stable near the inn. He was tiring of Ivetta, he said, and of being a bawd for an aging harlot. He wanted the inn to bring him honest wealth, a respectable business and a profitable one. I must marry him, he said, and pass the business on to his control at my uncle's death. If I refused, he would make sure the entire village learned that I was a whore and a murderer of babies. No decent man would come forth to marry me then, and, even if my uncle honored his promise to grant me the inn, all would assume I would turn it into a brothel."

"Thus losing the custom of pilgrims and other virtuous travelers."

"Aye."

"You could deny his tale as a malicious lie. Others have suffered from Martin's vile tongue and you would have gained sympathy."

"Only the twist he would have put on the story was a lie, my lady. What Ivetta screamed to the entire village may have been humiliating enough, but think how much more credible Martin would be since he had swyved me. My uncle has long protected me from lewd fondling. With this one exception, I have kept my lapses from chastity both rare and discreet. Hence, I own the reputation as a woman no man should approach with sinful intent. That would have ended with the cooper's tale."

"Your uncle is still innkeeper and able to protect you from…"

"He has never married, my lady, and believes women are either whores or virgins. Although he has been kind to me and I am grateful, his opinion in this matter is so inflexible that I wonder how he honored his mother who must have bedded with his father in order to give birth to him."

"Does he not know about your lovers?"

"If he did, I do believe he would have thrown me out to earn my bread on my back."

Eleanor paused while she thought about what Signy had just told her. "You do have a motive for killing Martin."

The woman nodded. "Nor will I pretend I did not long for his death. I have not hidden my transgressions from you, my lady. On that truthfulness I do swear I am innocent of murder. To wish for the crime may be as great an offense as the act in God's eyes, but surely He will forgive the thought sooner than the deed."

Although the prioress longed to believe this woman's tale, she could not quite set aside the conclusion that Signy had good cause to kill Martin. By committing the deed, she would have saved her reputation, avoided an unthinkable marriage, and kept her uncle's protection along with the promised inheritance of a profitable inn.

Yet Eleanor knew that murder was most extreme and surely Signy would have found other solutions to the problems. She was a clever enough woman and could have twisted the tale, just as Martin might have done, to give the facts a more favorable cast. As for her uncle, surely he was not as ignorant of her lapses in virtue as she believed. Finally, as a practical matter, who else would inherit the inn? If there had been any male relative of any talent, a niece would never have been named heir in the first place.

As she pondered further, Eleanor asked herself if Ivetta didn't have reason as well to kill the cooper. She claimed to have loved Martin and still wished to bear his child despite the hardships inherent in keeping the babe. It was true that she was no longer as attractive as she had once been. Perhaps Martin told the truth when he said he found it less and less profitable to be her bawd. If the cooper had married Signy and dropped Ivetta, how would the woman live?

Yet killing Martin solved nothing for Ivetta either. Now the woman was as bereft of support from her bawd as she would have been if he had cut her free of his control through some marriage. Was the murder done out of such strong passion that all reason fled? Was there something Eleanor had yet to learn that might make sense of why the death occurred when it did?

Why not kill Signy instead? Or was that too difficult to accomplish? Was Ivetta even competent enough to make the poison, let alone plan the murder? Surely she would have known that she would be the primary suspect? Why not arrange with Martin for a marriage to someone else as the better solution? Perhaps to Will, a man not known for his quick wits?

As the conversation with Signy now slipped into the ease of pleasant courtesies, the prioress sat back in her chair, more bewildered than ever. There were too many questions, and Ivetta might have at least some answers. The woman must be called back to the priory and soon, despite the loud protests sure to come from Sister Ruth who claimed Satan's stench had almost killed her the last time Ivetta walked through the garth.

If God were kind, a second visit might even inspire the prostitute to seek redemption at Tyndal. If that miracle happened, Eleanor thought with wicked pleasure, she would make sure the sub-prioress was charged with any instruction.

Chapter Twenty-Five

The man fumbled with his braes.

Would he never get dressed? Ivetta thought. Even her skin crawled with impatience to push him out the door, but he must be made to pay first. With Martin dead, she had to worry about earning enough to feed herself—and the babe as well.

"There's a chicken I laid just there." He gestured drunkenly. "That'll do it."

"The price was two, as you well knew."

"For riding an aged slut?"

"For performing a miracle. Did I not transform a drooping stalk into an iron rod?"

"I can get this free, you know."

"From your pigs, for cert, and methinks you've tried. You stink enough of them."

The man cursed and grabbed for the door but hesitated before opening it. "I'll bring the other tomorrow," he said, his voice suddenly gentle. "Sorry about the cooper." Then he was gone.

Ivetta sat on her straw mat and began to twist a strand of greasy hair. Looking down at her naked belly, she smiled at the rounding. "I should give you to the priory if you're a boy. They could use strong arms like your father had," she said. "If you're a girl, I must do so." She nodded. "Other priories would sneer at a whore's daughter, but Prioress Eleanor might take you on as a servant. She wouldn't want you to follow my trade any more than I do, and someone has to scrub the hospital linen. You'd have food enough in exchange for reddened hands, lass, and that is more than I can provide."

Her shoulders sagged as she gazed around the small space. This stinking place with drafty walls made of dung and straw was all she had now, a shelter her younger brother had made for them both before he died in the road, stabbed by another drunk in a fight over something long forgotten.

"Martin promised me more," she sighed. But Martin was dead and she had nothing. Everything she ever earned on her back, or more often on her knees, went to him. In truth, he had fed and clothed her as well as he did himself and made sure she had a soft bed. When the bouncing got rough, she did not bruise as quickly. Standing, she rubbed her buttocks. With only this straw to buffer a man's weight, there would be marks soon enough from that swineherd's pleasures.

Pulling a loose gown over her head, Ivetta went to open the door. As she stared up at the twinkling stars, she felt her spirit plunge into melancholy. What was she going to do? Angry though she may have been over the swineherd's insults, she knew her value as a harlot was lessening. Without Martin to bring clients who were willing to pay for special acts, she was reduced to serving the poor, maimed, the drunk, diseased or aged. Virile lads, who might even bring her a little joy, always seemed to find enough girls with taut maidenheads eager for bursting. She would never feel their muscular arms around her on that rough mat.

She turned, went back into the stifling room, and yanked the badly fitted door shut.

If only I could store this heat for the dark season when the babe is due, she thought. The damp cold will be so bitter then we shall both surely turn to ice.

She took a mouthful of the ale still left in the jug. "Fa!" she spat. The brew had turned foul.

She had nowhere to go. Her parents were dead, not that they would welcome such a wicked daughter back. When she had returned from the field, bleeding after Martin's breaching, they had cast her out with one loaf of bread as a mercy and the gown she wore. The only living kin she had left was an elder brother, but his wife would refuse to let her in their house. That fine woman spent most of her waking hours and, if truth be told, most of the sleeping ones on her knees in prayer. Charity to sinners, especially those guilty of carnal wickedness, was not one of her reputed virtues.

Ivetta was very much alone.

"I'm sure the priory would take me in to do hard labor," she muttered. "They hinted enough that I should repent, but I cannot confess guilt over Martin. I loved him." Her mouth puckered as if she had bitten into sour fruit. "If I'm going to Hell, at least he's there as well. We might as well burn together."

Covering her face with her hands, she began to weep. "I am going to die, and the babe with me," she moaned. "Curses on Signy! The blood of the three of us will be on her hands and she'll just grow fat…"

There was a knock at the door.

Ivetta roughly ran fingers under her eyes to dry the tears. Who was this? she wondered, resentful that she could not be left in peace right now. Yet she did need the trade. If she were fortunate, it would be the swineherd with the other chicken. If not, it might be some lusty leper who knew she could not afford to turn anyone away if she were to survive.

As she opened the door, however, she drew back in shock when she recognized the dark figure outside.

"I have come to make peace," the shadow said.

Chapter Twenty-Six

Returning along the path to the priory, Thomas gazed up at the sparkling stars. Above him was the constellation of the cross and to the right was the lute in the shape of a heart. A faint white light shot between the two, then disappeared. Was that a soul traveling to God?

Perhaps it belonged to the man with the deep sore in his throat who had died tonight. In that suffering creature's last moments of mortal consciousness, Thomas had knelt beside him and taken his confession, granting absolution quickly lest Satan find cause for rejoicing over the capture of another soul.

While Death pulled the throbbing soul away, the widow screamed in protest, throwing herself on her beloved husband's still breast. Tears flooded down his own cheeks as Thomas watched the woman lying there and trembling with both irrational outrage and better understood grief.

Although he had reassured her that her husband should find sweet peace in heaven and would wait for her with open arms when her time came, he suspected none of this would be of comfort until her wild anguish had run its course. As she alternated between howled curses that her husband had deserted her and sweet pleadings for him to return to her arms, Thomas knew that her heart only begged God to keep the misery of her remaining life on earth very short, an existence that most certainly would be both difficult and forlorn.

"Cursed be the Devil's darkness!" he growled, a profound loneliness weighing his spirit down like some dark and sodden cloak. Why had God not utterly destroyed men after Eden if human life was so wretched that only death held joy? And if death was man's only pleasure, why deny him the right to claim that delight by calling self-murder a sin?

"Get thee behind me," Thomas cried out, shaking his fist at the shadows, but Satan, with especial cruelty, now cast the image of Giles into his weakened soul. Until he had gone to Amesbury, Thomas had achieved some peace from this torment, but the events last year at the old priory had shattered that little calm and driven his spirit back into the stinking hole of despair he had suffered in prison.

Had Giles found peace with his older and quite wealthy wife, he wondered, and had he banished all thought of Thomas from his heart? Was it worse if Giles remembered him but only with hatred and disgust?

"I need sleep," he groaned. "I need…" He fell silent, terrified of pursuing that ill-defined longing any further. If God ever answered his prayers for understanding, he might take courage and face the dreaded thing. Until then, his soul remained as firmly chained as his body had once been in prison with rusted and chafing irons.

"Sleep must come," he muttered, shoving away all the prickling aches of body and spirit. "Then I can seek answers for my sins."

As he thought more on that, he wondered if this lack of rest was meant to goad him to the chapel night after night—or even to seek out Sister Juliana. After all, what force had thrown him to his knees by her tiny window that night? Was it God's hand?

"Perhaps," he murmured. "Aye, I think so." After he had spoken with her, he had followed her counsel and filled his soul with silence the next night when wakefulness drove him out of his narrow bed. That night, an unfamiliar peace had caressed his soul, briefly but sweetly. Was it a sign that God was at last willing to grant him mercy?

When he arose afterward, his heart fluttering with hope, he had tried to seek for the meaning and cause of this perplexing experience. Instantly, the calm vanished as if God had once again deserted him. Or was He telling him, as the anchoress had suggested, that he must listen only with the stillness of his heart and reject mortal logic?

Surely the heart was the frailest of man's organs, a woman's refuge and most subject to sin. Yet hadn't God spoken to Elijah in such a small voice that the prophet might only have heard Him in silence? A man's mind stirred to debate and roaring speech; the feminine heart stayed still like a rabbit with a fox about. Might Sister Juliana be right in suggesting that God spoke more clearly from the organ condemned to silence by Adam's imperfect sons?

Thomas stopped and glanced up at the moon. No longer full, it gave off a lesser light, and the man in the moon, Cain with his bundle of thorns, had a bleak aspect. The monk looked down the road and realized he had gone beyond the village and was near the gate by the priory mill. Perhaps he should visit the anchoress tonight, if no one was waiting to speak to her. Might she be able to explain the meaning of what he had experienced in the chapel and guide him further in his search for God's wisdom? He quickened his pace, choosing the path that followed the fork of the stream flowing into priory grounds.

As he entered the forest, he suddenly hesitated. Something caught his attention, a thing that did not seem quite right.

Just to the right of the path was a crudely built hut almost hidden between two trees. Hadn't it been long abandoned? he asked himself. Yet the door was open, and one guttering candle inside now cast a misshapen, twitching circle of light on the ground without. In the wavering shadows, Thomas saw a darker mound as if a dog had fallen asleep there, or else some person.

Thomas grew uneasy, sensing malevolence, but he felt compelled to draw nearer, albeit with caution. If this were a dog, even one of the hounds of Hell, surely the creature would have lunged at him by now.

Slowly, ever so slowly, he approached the strange object.

Falling to his knees, Thomas reached out and touched it. The familiar warmth convinced him this was no imp or hound but rather a human body. When he rolled it over to look more closely, he saw the face in the flickering candlelight.

"God have mercy!" he cried out.

Ivetta, the whore, was dead.

Chapter Twenty-Seven

"Yew," Sister Anne said, then bent over the corpse again.

Those attending her remained silent as the sub-infirmarian continued her examination.

"Unless we find a witness, I should only make a tentative conclusion about the poison. Other evidence might point to another method."

"I saw vomit inside the hut," Thomas said, his voice low as if he feared humiliating the dead woman with what he had discovered. "Outside the door, her bowels had loosened. In the dark, I could not examine thoroughly, but the odor was strong. What I did not find was any potion. There was some ale in a jug, but it had turned and was probably undrinkable. I smelled it. Perhaps we can find more after the sun rises."

Anne nodded. "I am grateful for your observations, Brother. Note, too, that her lips are blue, and, if you come closer, you will see that her pupils are enlarged. This poison takes effect quickly…" She hesitated, glancing at Eleanor, Ralf, and Thomas in turn. "She aborted. Either that was her intent, and she took more of the herb than was wise, or else she was murdered. The purpose is not evident in the results."

In the flickering light of the hospital chapel, Ralf's eyes narrowed, perhaps from the candle smoke or even from anger.

"I am troubled that two people, so well-known to each other, have died by the same method and with little time in between," Thomas said, his words still softly spoken.

Eleanor watched her monk as if carefully considering his words, then turned away. Although the lateness of the hour should have cast the pallor of fatigue on the prioress' cheeks, her color was high. "If she intended to abort, why was she found outside on the hard ground?" she asked, her voice trembling. "What woman would lie near a public road when she had the comparative ease of her pallet close by? Is it not strange as well that no evidence of the drink was found, if she deliberately took the poison?"

"I doubt she would have chosen to lie in the path as any form of penance," Thomas said. "She had shown no inclination to atone for her sins. Thus I find her place of death most troubling."

"Would we even question any of this if Martin had not been killed?" Ralf folded his arms in disgust.

"Why do you say that? Because she was a harlot?" Anne rested one hand gently on the corpse. "All mortals have souls, even if they are filthy with the Devil's touch."

The crowner did not reply.

"I incline to a presumption of murder," Thomas said. "Were we to assume she intended to abort, I doubt Ivetta would have been ignorant of the dosage needed. According to old Tibia, whores are familiar with the methods, having the need and, as a consequence, the experience. Perhaps yew is one way to get rid of a quickening, but is it not a dangerous one? Surely there are safer means to accomplish that intent, and surely she would have known them. I do not think she would have taken too much of any remedy, and I doubt she would have used yew. Thus I suspect a foul motive."

"There are safer methods, Brother, and she might well have been experienced with them. Nonetheless, I cannot agree that she would have known the correct dosage. When my husband and I were apothecaries, we treated enough women who thought they knew these matters well and almost died as a result." Anne turned around to examine something on the body.

"I suspect she either killed herself deliberately, maybe from despair," Ralf suggested, "or else wished to rid herself of the child and died accidentally. Maybe she took the poison in the ale, not caring how it tasted. Does a sweet drink matter when someone commits self-murder or wishes to abort quickly?"

Eleanor stared at the face of the corpse which was frozen in gape-mouthed horror. "I agree with Brother Thomas, Crowner, and fear we have not one, but two, murders to solve. I do not think this woman died by accident because of an abortion attempt, nor do I believe she committed self-murder. Ivetta loved the quickening life inside her, as she loved the man she named *father* to this new soul. In this, I think she told the truth, although I have doubts about other things she said and had planned to call her back for questioning." She glanced up at Anne "Was there any sign of struggle? Might she have been forced somehow to take this poison?"

"There is minor bruising on the buttocks and arms, but none of that recent, my lady," Anne replied. "In her profession, such marks would not be unusual." Her tone was subdued.

"When I looked around her dwelling, I found nothing to suggest violence, other than what I mentioned." Thomas hesitated. "There was a freshly killed chicken by the door, yet she kept no fowl. I point that out because it seemed odd."

"Perchance that was her fee for relieving a man of his pent-up seed," Ralf said. "Had she suffered blows, I would look for a fellow who quarreled with the value he got for that price. Considering the method of death was poison, that possibility seems unlikely."

The group fell silent. All eyes, except for those of the prioress, turned away from the corpse.

"We have failed you," Eleanor said to the dead woman. "This should not have happened."

"Do not blame yourself, my lady," Ralf said. "Sister Anne has stated there is no reason to believe this was murder."

"I said I could not be certain without more evidence."

The prioress tapped her heart. "Illogical woman that I am, Crowner, this tells me it was."

Ralf bowed. "Your heart holds more reason than most men's minds."

"Might not the killer be the man who had just lain with her?" Anne sounded almost hopeful as she reached for a rough cloth and covered the corpse.

"Were we to assume murder, and she had been killed by another method, that would be the obvious explanation," Ralf replied with some reluctance. "I still argue that we do not use poison as a common weapon in this place. That was true with Martin's death, and I see no reason to change my mind for this one either."

"Both Martin and Ivetta, it now seems, have been killed by yew poisoning," Eleanor said.

Thomas' forehead furrowed with doubt as he turned to the crowner. "So you think she died accidentally from taking too much yew, perhaps in an attempt to rid herself of the child if not to commit self-murder?"

The crowner nodded.

"I still cannot believe Ivetta would choose to abort her child," Eleanor said.

"I concur." Anne moved slightly closer to her prioress.

The crowner did not reply but instead walked over to the body and lifted the cover to expose the face.

Thomas whispered what sounded like a prayer.

"May I be blunt?" Ralf asked, still studying the body.

"Were you otherwise, I might fear you were sickening." The prioress' lips turned up with a brief smile.

"Few men pay to swyve a woman big with child. How, then, would the whore live if she had no means to feed herself? To my knowledge, she was not one to hide coin in some hole under her straw pallet for the day she must earn her meat other than on her back." He dropped the cloth back over the dead woman's face. "That said, I shall assume I am wrong and she was more prudent. Even then, I must ask how she could care for the child with neither family nor maid to help while she plied her trade. There are few women in a village as small as Tyndal who would be willing to serve a harlot." His expression flickered with pity. "Maybe she did love the child but realized both of them would die if she birthed it—and chose to save herself."

"Once a woman holds life within her, she does not let go of it effortlessly." Anne's words were sharply spoken. "Never so casually dismiss the depth of love a mother holds for her child."

"A woman of Ivetta's profession does not commonly debate moral questions," Ralf retorted.

Anne's face turned scarlet. "You were not her confessor, nor were you the one drenched with the tears of those women John and I saved from death when they tried aborting." She took a deep breath. "If you condemn Ivetta because she was but a wretched common woman of the village, go back to court, Crowner, where whores come in finer dress and eat enough in one day to keep any poor but honest mortal content for a week!"

"I have never thought a woman more virtuous just because she dresses in brighter colors and softer cloth, Annie. That you should know." Ralf's eyes softened. "I have no argument against anything you have said, but surely you must agree that some women do not rejoice when they quicken with child. I meant only that Ivetta was such a one."

With obvious reluctance, Anne nodded. "Yet even among those who willfully rid themselves of the quickening, because they believed there was good reason for their act, most bewailed the loss far more than the sin. Motherhood holds a woman's heart with a fierce hand, Ralf. I have known women to smile at the sight of their new babe while they lay dying of the birth."

"Forgive me, Annie," Ralf whispered. "I should have thought on my wife before I spoke so cruelly."

"I think we might consider a different way of looking at this situation," Eleanor interrupted.

"We are getting nowhere as it is." Ralf nodded, his expression betraying hope that the conversation would move in another direction.

The prioress gestured at the crowner. "For the sake of argument, let us conclude for a moment that this death is murder. With that assumption, I have some questions for consideration."

"Please continue, my lady," Ralf said.

"After I talked with both the innkeeper's niece and the prostitute, I discovered there was ill-feeling between them, and I did not sense that the reason was simply Ivetta's trade. Can you tell me what other reason Signy would have to dislike Ivetta, or why the latter would attempt to cast suspicion on Signy in Martin's death?"

"The matter of the whoring at the inn," Ralf suggested. "Signy did not approve. Martin, if not Ivetta as well, profited from it."

"Is that cause for killing?" Anne asked.

"Even if it were, how are both deaths connected? Now that Martin is dead, there would be no more whoring at the inn and certainly not with Ivetta," Thomas added.

"That is the trouble," Ralf said. "I do not think the deaths are related. Even if each is murder, the killers must be different."

The sub-infirmarian pointed to the corpse. "Poison was used in both cases, and it is probable that the poison is the same one. The reasons might be different for each death, but I suspect the murderer is the same person."

Thomas turned to Ralf. "And as you said, the method is unique. Therefore, Sister Anne must be right. There is only one murderer. Would you agree?"

"I admit there is merit in the argument."

Eleanor began to pace. "Despite all, I cannot see what motive there could be in slaying both Martin and Ivetta."

"The blacksmith said Martin planned to replace Ivetta with Signy. If Martin was more to Ivetta than a source of steady business, would she have seen the innkeeper's niece as a rival?" Anne asked.

"Then she might have killed Signy, Annie, not the reverse."

The prioress stopped and considered her words before continuing. "If the two women were rivals for the cooper's affections, Signy might have sought retribution for something said or done before Martin was killed. What if she knew that Ivetta was pregnant and decided to destroy the prostitute's child in revenge? What if she gave the woman some herb in a drink and left, not knowing the result would be more calamitous than she intended?"

Ralf shifted uncomfortably. "Signy would never do such a thing, my lady. A woman may have poisoned Martin, but I think it far more likely that the harlot killed herself, willingly or no."

"Do you think Ivetta killed the cooper and then herself?" Thomas asked.

Ralf shrugged. "I would not be surprised."

"Although my meandering thoughts may be flawed, Crowner, I am equally convinced that Ivetta would not kill either her child or the father of that babe. She mourned the death of Martin and found comfort in bearing his child."

"She was the Devil's creature, my lady."

"As are all of us, Ralf. Never forget that. Robert of Arbrissel, our Order's founder, followed the example of God's Son and spent time winning over the souls of many prostitutes. Their eagerness to listen to him suggests that their hearts might be more likely to understand God's message than many deemed less sinful. For this reason, and charity, I cannot condemn Ivetta more than others."

The crowner opened his mouth, seemingly to protest, but then fell silent. Instead, he nodded.

Eleanor went on. "You may dislike the idea of a man using poison as a murder weapon, but that might also be a clever device to avert discovery. For instance, Will might have wished to kill Martin after the latter publicly mocked his manhood. Could the blacksmith have felt his humiliation so keenly that he killed the cooper and then Ivetta, a woman who witnessed his impotence and possibly ridiculed him as well?"

"Although Will may be obsessed with his sexual failures, I never thought him quick enough in wit to be that devious, my lady." Ralf suddenly turned to Thomas. "I forgot to ask you. Did you ever query the old woman about what she might have seen at the inn that night?"

"Her pain has been too great when I came with her potion. I did not wish to trouble her with murder."

"I was hoping she had seen some odd thing that might lead us to a killer we have yet to consider." The crowner shrugged. "But if she suffers that much, I doubt she would remember anything of value. Pain that severe must sharpen the soul's fear of God's judgement while it dulls interest in more trivial worldly matters."

"What of Hob?" Eleanor asked. "Might he have had reason to kill?

"Of the two brothers, he is possessed of greater wit. He is also loyal to his brother, even if he does not always follow his lead any longer. Maybe he did something to protect..." The crowner angrily rubbed his eyes as if they annoyed him. "The suspects grow in number. Will cannot be entirely discounted. Nor, it seems, can Hob."

"Nor Signy," Eleanor added with sadness.

Ralf bowed his head in weary resignation.

Silence fell with the bleak chill of sea fog on everyone in the room.

Chapter Twenty-Eight

The day had dawned with pleasing warmth, tempered by a cool breeze from the coast.

Eleanor, however, was not soothed. "What am I failing to understand?" she asked, seating herself on the stone bench in the middle of the cloister gardens.

The previous night had been a restless one for the prioress, her dreams filled with writhing shapes and troubling images. This time, the creature shattering her sleep was not an incubus in the shape of Brother Thomas but the tormented soul of Ivetta. Even now the woman's screams echoed sharply in her ears.

The sight of the blackened burns from Hell's fire on the woman's naked body was terrible enough, but her piteous cries had so distressed Eleanor that she abruptly awoke with hot sweat streaming down her trembling body. Mercifully, sleep failed to return. The prioress could bear no further meetings with the dead woman's spirit.

Eleanor now shut her eyes, but the most terrible image from the night remained as if burned into her eyelids lest she try to forget it. In the dream, Ivetta had held the image of a perfectly formed but tiny child in her hand, stretching it out for Eleanor to take. "I promised her to the priory when she was born," the spirit had howled. "I may deserve this eternity of fire, but she never had the chance for salvation. For pity's sake, take her to your heart!"

The voice, as piercing now in bright daylight as it had been in darkness, chased Eleanor from her seat. She ran a few steps, then dropped to her knees and wept.

After a few minutes, she calmed, breathing in a fragrance of almost holy sweetness as if the breeze from the North Sea carried the scent of Heaven. "I shall find your murderer," she whispered. "To deny a soul the chance for absolution is grave, but to deny a babe baptism before death is an unspeakable and most cruel sin."

Prioress Eleanor rose and walked back to her chambers with a determined step, swearing that she would do more than she had in this matter. Martin's murder may have been a secular concern, but God had made it quite clear that Ivetta's death was her responsibility.

As she walked into her private room, her attention was drawn to the tapestry hanging on the wall at the end of her bed. The depiction of Mary Magdalene at the foot of Jesus never ceased to fascinate her, the expression of love and compassion between the two figures bringing comfort on dark nights when the wind howled outside her window. Now they seemed to rebuke her for not casting aside all other concerns when justice should have been the foremost one.

"Had I dealt with Ivetta differently, she might have repented and sought our cloister, thus saving her life and that of her child. I must find the killer," she murmured, closing her eyes to banish all possible distractions.

"My lady, do you have need of anything?"

The prioress spun around and faced Gytha.

Her maid did not need to express her concern. Her eyes conveyed it eloquently enough.

"Stay, if you will. I have need of your advice," Eleanor said, smiling as an idea struck her. "Indeed, I may even ask for gossip."

"Of that I have some knowledge, my lady." Gytha grinned with both humor and evident relief.

"It is about a priory matter. What does the village say about Sister Juliana?"

"Most believe she is a holy woman who speaks as if blessed with the tongue of Heaven's Queen. A few are troubled that she sits by her window only at night. These voices are the same who question whether it is seemly for any woman to go to her after the sun sets. Yet others counter with the argument that our anchoress' virtue might be more truly doubted if most of the visitors were men."

The prioress reached down and petted the cat now rubbing against her robe. "Men do not seek her out?"

"I know of only two from Tyndal village, although a few strangers may have visited. Each of our local men came away uneasy, wondering why she did not seem to welcome them. My brother spoke with her and left as terrified as if God Himself had spoken. When he told me about it afterward, he said her words may have been wise but he could not convey the tone with which she spoke them. The very thought of returning filled him with dread. He mentioned only one other man from here who had sought her out. It was he who told my brother that he understood at last what it must have been like to talk to God in the burning bush."

"Tostig is not a man who frightens easily," the prioress remarked. "Who among the women have told any tales?"

"Signy. When she visited, she found both welcome and comfort in our anchoress' words, unlike my brother and his friend."

Eleanor clutched her hands tightly, hoping to hide her delight in the way this discussion was going. "She felt no terror?"

"Sister Juliana did beg her to kneel farther from the window, but Signy was not disquieted, believing that our anchoress would rightly fear corruption from a mortal woman if she came too close to her."

"Did the innkeeper's niece say why she had sought counsel?"

"I did not ask, my lady, nor did she offer to tell me."

"Has anyone mentioned if Ivetta visited Sister Juliana?"

"Aye! Signy herself told me that she had seen the woman once or twice and wondered why a harlot, who did nothing to change her ways, would seek out an anchoress. As you must know, the innkeeper's niece and Ivetta were not friends. There was no reason for either to confide her reasons for visiting or even acknowledge that one might have seen the other. If it would help you find who committed this crime, I could ask about. Someone might know why Ivetta wanted to speak with our anchoress."

Either I have failed in subtlety or else Gytha is too clever by half, Eleanor thought with affection as she noted her maid's eagerness to be involved in hunting down a killer. "I will not involve you in murder, and the asking of questions might bring you harm."

The cat gave up trying to gain his mistress' full attention, went to sniff at Gytha's shoes, then left the chambers in pursuit of those things deemed important by his ilk.

"I am troubled by accusations against our anchoress, Gytha. As you are also aware, I am also concerned with two deaths, one of which we know to be murder and the other I believe must be."

"We have a market day, my lady. No one would question my presence there as your servant, and I could carefully listen for any tales that might be abroad about the deaths. That would be safe enough if I do not show undue interest."

"I will think about consenting to that but only if you promise to take care."

Gytha eagerly agreed.

"In the meantime, I may be glad that Sister Juliana has been of service to the village, a mercy that most seem to agree upon, but Sister Ruth complains she cannot find any proper woman who is willing to wait upon her. I hear that our anchoress can be most frightening when she is possessed of this spirit that may be most holy."

"If I may be honest, my lady…"

"…as I have always permitted."

"Sister Ruth chooses servants much like herself. If our anchoress wishes to pray quietly all day and serve as a conduit of God's wisdom by night, she does not need a woman in attendance who loves the sound of her own voice. Nor should she be cursed with a woman more desirous of a heightened reputation because she waits on a holy woman than any longing for true service."

Eleanor laughed. "Methinks you have touched upon the truth of it. Nonetheless, I have no solution to the problem. Our sister cannot wait on herself and still spend every hour serving God. In addition, she has expressed horror at the very idea of any servant."

"If I might suggest someone, my lady?"

The prioress looked delighted. "You know of a woman?"

"A cousin, my lady. She is younger than those Sister Ruth has recommended."

"Not a young girl, surely? Will she not be terrified when our anchoress falls into her fits? And what of marriage? She could not continue serving an anchoress when a husband would need her by his side."

"My cousin has no expectation of marriage and is possessed of a quiet, calm temperament. She will be content to sit until called upon and will not tremble when God's spirit enters Sister Juliana."

Eleanor frowned. "Why has Sister Ruth not suggested her to me?"

Before Gytha had any chance to reply, the door to the public chambers flew open and crashed against the stone wall. The aforementioned sub-prioress stormed into the room like Satan's imp cloaked with the form of a wild-eyed horse with a stitch in its side.

"My lady, you must come immediately!" Sister Ruth's face was gray.

"What has happened?" Eleanor exclaimed. The genuine fear in the woman's urgent tone chased all annoyance from her heart.

"Sister Juliana has murdered a lay sister!"

Chapter Twenty-Nine

"Troubled?" Ralf stood at the door to the smithy.

The fire in the pit burned low while Will leaned against the wall, his eyes staring at nothing. One hand played absently with the tongs. At the sound of the crowner's voice, his expression refocused with sharp anger. "What're you doing here?" he snarled.

"Ivetta is dead."

"And you're now accusing me of her murder too?" Although the smith's tone hinted at outrage, his brow furrowed as if he were more befuddled than wrathful.

"Did I say anything about murder?"

"Why else would you come with this news? Not out of some recently discovered courtesy. I know that much."

"We were lads together, Will, and I knew Ivetta as well. Should I not share your grief?"

"Perhaps you *knew* her as we all did," the man snorted, "but that was the sum of your acquaintance of her. As for any affection you claim to bear me from some boyhood shared, I'm not that slow of wit to believe your tale."

"When did you see her last?"

The man pointed at him in triumph. "Ha! Caught you out. I was right, wasn't I?"

"When you refused my sympathy, you reminded me that I am the crowner with murders to solve. When did you last see Ivetta?"

"The night Martin died."

"Not since? Not even to console her after his death?" He winked.

Will struck out at Ralf. The crowner caught his hand, spun the man around, and twisted the smith's arm behind him.

Will yelped but his struggles only made the pain worse. "Loosen your grip, Crowner!"

"Gladly, should you decide to tell the truth."

"She was a *whore*! Why would I care about her?"

"I think you envied the extra coin Martin gained from her and went to visit her last night, hoping to take his place in her bed and as her bawd."

The blacksmith spat.

"You've always had a hot temper. When she said she would not tolerate your useless fumblings and other rough ways, especially since she was with child, did you lash out?"

"With these visions of yours, you belong in the priory. I had little to do with the whore and most certainly not last night."

Ralf tightened his hold on the man's wrist. "She bedded you when the cooper was feeling generous. No woman would have you, including her, if she hadn't been well paid for the effort. And effort it must have required, if what I hear of you is true."

Will roared in fury.

"So you liked her. Maybe too much? Is that why you killed her? Were you jealous of the babe? Or could you not bear her rejection when she mocked your feeble manhood?"

"How often did you try to mount her, Crowner, or at least until Signy opened her legs to you? Maybe you killed her." The blacksmith jerked and pulled but could not break the crowner's hold.

Ralf twisted the hand.

The man screamed.

"Maybe you took Hob with you, thinking he's the better looking and she might agree to be his whore. And being a loyal and generous brother, he would surely share Ivetta with you often enough like Martin did. Maybe Hob killed her when she spat in your faces? Or did he just hold her down while you…"

"For the love of God, Crowner!"

Ralf wrenched the man's hand, then dropped it.

"You've broken my wrist!"

"Learn to work one-handed."

"I'm innocent!" Tear were streaming down the man's cheeks.

"Prove it. Tell me where you were last night."

Cradling his limp hand, Will fell to his knees. "I went to see old Tibia last night," he whimpered.

"Will she vouch for you?"

"She wouldn't open her door. I waited. Then left."

"Any witnesses? Her hut is close to the inn."

"I hid. Who wants to be seen with Satan's bitch?"

"I don't blame her for barring her door. Even old crones aren't desperate enough to let you try to swyve them."

His face purpled with rage, the smith leapt to his feet, grabbed the tongs with his good hand, and swung at the crowner.

Ralf ducked, then quickly straightened and rammed his knee into Will's groin.

Writhing, the man dropped to the ground and wailed like a beaten dog.

The crowner's victory was short-lived. The moment he stepped away, something struck his head. As he fell into darkness, the last thing he remembered thinking was how foolish he had been not to guard his back.

Chapter Thirty

The buzzing of some bees, finding brief respite from their labors and the day's heat, was the only sound that broke the silence in the close confines of the anchorage.

The woman knelt and clutched her body as if fearful it might otherwise break apart like a carelessly scattered handful of dust.

Gently, the prioress took Sister Juliana's chin in hand and raised her face until their eyes met.

"I did nothing to harm the lay sister, my lady."

"Truly, I did not think you had," the prioress sighed. "Only once have I seen you behave with cruelty to another and that was at Wynethorpe Castle."

"An act for which I perform daily penance." Tears began to flow down her cheeks. "How does the lay sister?"

"The wound is grave enough, but Sister Anne believes God may be gracious and it should mend."

Juliana lowered her eyes and whispered a prayer.

"Although I know you did not strike her, there was something that caused the lay sister to trip and hit her head on the stone floor. What so filled her with blinding terror that she fled this anchorage? "

Juliana turned around on her knees, slipped her robe down with careful modesty, and exposed her back.

Eleanor gasped.

"Do I not have the right to discipline myself alone?" Juliana said, her jaw tightening despite her humble tone. "Formerly, I blocked the door to my tomb while I used the whip, but, in obedience to your command, I have ceased to do so. In return, I expected kind courtesy from her, but she never asked permission to enter, my lady. Had I known she was opening the door, I might have prevented her from seeing what she cannot understand."

"Then I, too, must perform penance since my orders contributed to this cruel accident," Eleanor said after a moment's pause. "My judgement has been proven to be a feeble thing, and I shall seek counsel from those more knowledgeable. Your actions have surpassed my own poor abilities to comprehend. Although I do not quarrel with the need to discipline an unruly body, I confess honest doubts about the value of such extreme mortification, Sister."

"I take full blame for this near-tragedy and will seek absolution from priest and victim," the anchoress replied, easing her robe back over her shoulders.

"We both must beg forgiveness."

"Punish me as you see fit, but I beg you to believe me! I had no idea she was watching until I heard her scream. When I turned around, I saw the door to my tomb wide open and she was lying on the ground, motionless. Since my vows prohibit me from leaving this space, I prayed loudly and God showed mercy by sending Sister Ruth. When she saw the lay sister on the ground, blood pouring from her head, she cursed me. After that, I remember nothing."

Eleanor lifted Juliana from her knees. "Until now, I have shown much tolerance and defended your singular ways, although Sister Ruth has complained of your conduct since you arrived at the priory. With this incident, she has proved to be the wiser. In addition, I confess to finding your choice of self-mortification a strange act to perform in a place dedicated to the worship of a forgiving God. I can understand why the lay sister fled from the sight of your gory back. That said, I would listen to your reasons for…"

"Then I plead with you, once again, to let me stay in solitude! Send no one to serve me. I cannot bear it nor, it seems, can they." Juliana's boldness suddenly failed her. "Do not, I beg of you, cast me from this sanctuary!" she whispered. "In this place lies my only hope for salvation."

"I will not send you from your anchorage. That I may promise, but you must have a woman to watch over you, even if she does not serve you in other ways. You fall into convulsions. You whip yourself most cruelly. Once, you beat your head against the walls until all sense left your body. Were you to die of your wounds without a priest to hear confession, you would not only die unshriven but also be guilty of self-murder."

Juliana's eyes grew large, her body now trembling. "Murder?" she murmured. "My lady…"

"Aye, murder. Nor is that the only concern that must be addressed. Although many of your calling commonly receive visitors at different hours, you do not sleep and keep court by your window only at night."

"None of this is by my will!"

"Then whose will demands this of you?"

"God's, my lady. I have begged Him to choose another, someone far worthier than I, but He has not answered those prayers. Indeed, that is the reason for the mortification. I have committed such grave sins He has not come to me at all since…"

"You quickly point to God, claiming He supports many of your questionable desires, Sister." Gazing into the anchoress' pleading eyes, Eleanor instantly regretted her harsh words. How darkly circled with fatigue those eyes are, she thought, and I should know well enough what secret torments God chooses not to spare us even when begged to do so. "He will comfort you again with His presence," she promised in a softer voice.

"All I wish to do is spend my days entombed here with no voice to disturb my prayers on their way to Heaven. If God did not demand me to speak His words, I would seal that window with bricks or stone and have cause enough…"

Eleanor waved that aside. "Before any decision is made to keep pilgrims from your window, I shall seek counsel from a priest and ask him to question you. Satan has been known to speak with honeyed tongue to mortals, Sister, and is oft mistaken for God. If the priest finds no sin in your words or thought, then you must be His instrument. You have no choice."

"I will welcome that examination with prayer and joy, my lady. In the meantime, leave me here in solitude so I will not endanger another innocent like the good lay sister. I beg it!"

"Why are you so stiff-necked in this matter of servants?"

"If God did not protect me, I would bear worse wounds than these paltry welts on my back. I do not need a warden."

With both hands, Eleanor cradled one of Juliana's. The bones and flesh were so delicate that the prioress wondered how tenuous a connection the anchoress had to anything of this world. "Then consider this," she continued. "As humble service, most anchoresses are obliged to give modest guidance to pilgrims seeking comfort, but no one else, to my knowledge, welcomes troubled souls only at night. No matter what I might say, others will contend that women, who come at night when the Devil is dancing with his imps, must brush closely with evil. When men kneel at your window, some doubt your virtue. An attendant would confirm that you commit no sin during this time of dangerous shadows."

"And at such dark hours, many souls are unsettled, my lady. Not all are women, although I confess that most are. Those men who come are few, and I believe God protects my virtue by setting cherubim with blazing swords at my window, much like those standing at the gates of Eden. As for the women who come to me, they have returned home safely enough. Is that not proof that God gives them protection when they come to hear His words through my mouth?"

"Did Ivetta ever come to you, Sister?"

"Not being from this land, I would not know her voice." Juliana looked puzzled by the question.

"She was the harlot of Tyndal village."

"I do not take confessions, my lady. Many at my window bemoan lust, cursing the terror and pain of childbirth. Lust is one of Satan's most powerful afflictions. When women fall victim to carnal longings, I may hear bitter weeping but I cannot say if any earned her bread thereby."

"Signy, the innkeeper's niece? Did she seek counsel?"

"Nor do I ask names." Juliana hesitated, then whispered: "Unless it was she who came to seek confirmation that God would agree…"

"It is no matter." Eleanor dropped the anchoress' hand and turned away. "I will ask Brother John to come here and pose questions. Afterward, he will report his conclusions to me."

Juliana lowered her eyes, her face ashen in the pale light. "Might you not send Brother Thomas instead?" she murmured.

Eleanor tensed. "Why the one rather than the other?"

"At Wynethorpe Castle, it was the sight of him that confirmed my belief I would find sanctuary in this priory. He is a gift from God, my lady, and has always understood what lurks in my heart with clarity and compassion."

Color rose to the prioress' cheeks. "How can you speak of his perceptions with such familiarity? You have not met him since that winter when you begged an anchorage at Tyndal."

"He has come to my window, my lady."

"To seek advice?" Eleanor hissed.

"I think not," the anchoress said softly. "Rather to raise issues for honorable debate."

"Brother John will visit you, Sister. That is my decision," the prioress snapped, each word as sharp as a dagger's point. Without any courteous word of farewell, she spun on her heel and stormed out of the anchorage.

Shocked, Juliana raised both hands in futile supplication.

The door slammed, the very wood shuddering from the force of Eleanor's fury.

Chapter Thirty-One

"You breathe, Crowner. Corpses cannot say the same. For that, you owe God much gratitude." Brother Beorn skillfully applied a poultice to the back of Ralf's head. "Stop squirming. Ponder instead why God has been merciful to a shameless sinner like you when others are more worthy of His kindness."

Since boyhood and for reasons lost to memory, the two men acted like threatened hedgehogs raising their quills in defense whenever they met. Neither could point to any fresh argument over the subsequent years, but their querulous banter had become a matter of habit. So much so, in fact, that some suspected each had discovered an odd but companionable pleasure in tweaking the other.

Ralf grunted.

"I'm done with you."

"Perhaps Sister Anne should check your work."

A tall nun stepped into the crowner's sight. "I have never found that necessary. Our brother is a skilled healer."

Ralf flushed. "I beg pardon, Annie. I meant no ill."

"*Sister* Anne," the lay brother growled.

The sub-infirmarian smiled at Brother Beorn and nodded. He walked away without further word.

"You might have granted him a word of appreciation, Ralf. He took you out of turn when Cuthbert pointed to the black blood on your neck." Sister Anne bent over and looked at the skin around the poultice. "I would have thought that becoming a father might have gentled you a little and taught you some courtesy."

"Murder roughens me, but the sight of my daughter soothes the rawness like one of your salves."

Anne sat down beside him. "I have heard you named her after your wife?"

"A woman who bequeathed much joy to me with the gift of this wondrous small creature, although she died from her beneficence."

"You loved your wife for herself, not just her lands?" Anne asked softly.

Ralf stared at his clenched fists, then opened them as if in humble appeal. "I honored her with fidelity and courtesy, Annie, but felt no tenderness. Yet she was a good woman who deserved a far better husband than she got in me. I am not so rude a man that I did not understand that."

They fell silent, and the nun started to reach out, as if give the crowner a consoling touch, but quickly drew her hand back. "I doubt not you were kind to her, Ralf, but do not be so fearful in loving. Let your daughter teach you that."

He sighed. "Loving my child demands no effort from me. As for grown women, you well know the most grievous and festering wound my heart has suffered and why I have little hope of any affection from your sex."

"Each of us is given what God deems best for us, Ralf. You alone know why we two could not have married, and why I have found sanctuary at Tyndal where my husband led me. And if you still believe you do not deserve a good woman as wife, remember you have a daughter now, one who deserves a loving mother. Do not wallow like some pig in rank selfishness!" Her voice was light and teasing. This time she did not hesitate to put her arm around his broad shoulders for just a moment, an act that would have brought her censure if observed but one that was no more sinful than compassion ever could be.

Despite the pain in his head, Ralf laughed. "As always, you have the right of it, Annie, but since you must continue to refuse me, show some mercy and reveal the name of this good woman to whom I must give my heart."

"She will reveal herself to you—and prove her suitably meek nature by giving you no choice whatsoever about marrying her." The sub-infirmarian stood and walked a short distance away, one deemed more appropriate to her calling. Turning around, she smiled and gestured at his head. "While we wait for that miracle to occur, tell me why this happened to you."

"I had questions of Will and twisted his hand to force answers from him. When he cried out that I had broken it, Hob must have heard him and struck me. Cuthbert saw him running from the smithy, dragging his brother with him. I swear Will did not deserve such a defense, but I do not blame the brother for his loyalty. As the king's man, I might seek vengeance, but I will not trouble Hob if he is otherwise innocent of murder." He grinned weakly. "An old soldier who forgets his battle wisdom deserves what he gets."

"Do you truly suspect the blacksmith of murder?" Anne asked, frowning.

Ralf shrugged.

"If not, why treat him so harshly? That is not like you."

"He is a coward!" the crowner barked, then winced. "In truth, I do not think he killed either Martin or Ivetta. Will is too hot-tempered and more likely to swing his fists than poison anyone. Making a potion of yew requires planning and, as I have already said, more wit than the man owns." The crowner cautiously shook his head. "My quarrel with him lies in his malicious attempt to divert suspicion from himself and bring it down on the head of Signy, the innkeeper's niece. I also believe he knows who did kill the two but fears he will be blamed himself."

"Or else the blacksmith was afraid he would be accused just because he and the cooper happened to quarrel that night." She hesitated before asking, "Why do you set aside the possibility that Signy might have killed both Ivetta and Martin?"

"It is not in her nature."

Anne smiled at his quick defense. "Even the most virtuous may be vulnerable to Satan's corruption given the right cause and temptation."

"Guilty we each might be of lust, greed, gluttony, or all these things, but murder is the cruelest act. I cannot see Signy killing anyone."

"Might you not suffer some blindness about her, Ralf?"

He hid his face in his hands.

"Speak truly." She touched her heart. "Haven't we known each other long and well enough to set aside petty things and all fear of shame?"

"Aye, we have," he said, looking at her with affection. "Forgive me, Annie, and pray for my soul. I bedded the woman in lust, albeit with affection, then humiliated her, but without malice. As penance, my heart demands that I must find her innocent in these crimes."

"Even if she is guilty?" Anne shook her head at the crowner's mournful expression. "A poor jest, Ralf. I, myself, find it hard to imagine that she killed the two, although I agree she might have reason as well as opportunity most certainly—and is a woman, that creature you think most likely to use poison."

Ralf snorted. "It is the weapon of the devious, the weak, or the fearful."

"Woman may be weak by nature, thus fearful and often devious, but a man can be all that and especially the last by design. Nothing you mention disqualifies any man from poisoning another. Might Will have used poison to cast suspicion elsewhere or even because he was fearful of confronting Martin in a fair fight?"

"Our blacksmith is possessed of no subtlety. As for fear, he strikes first when enraged and thinks, if ever, later. Only then does he turn pale at the mention of a hangman."

Anne pondered that. "I agree that he is not as clever as his younger brother, but Will speaks well enough when he so chooses or when he is sober enough. That aside, what do you think of Hob as a killer?"

"When we were all lads, especially after the murder of old Tibia's son, I might have agreed, but Hob has become more of a man with the years. That experience changed him, and now I would doubt his guilt in this matter. Even Tostig claims he has grown almost somber."

"I have heard that the crowner's jury found the death accidental."

"I did not mean that I questioned his involvement in the boy's death, only that Hob seems to have repented of that sin."

"Yet he struck you from behind at the smithy. Might that act suggest a man who does not wish to face another? He may have changed, as you claim, but he could still be the bully he was as a lad only in different guise."

Ralf considered her words in silence and then shook his head.

"Teach me your reasoning, Ralf. What causes you to conclude that Will is more capable of killing than his brother?"

"Will once threw a young cur into the smithy fire because the creature barked, causing him to damage an object he was working on. Hob burned his own hands saving the animal. That is but one tale out of many I could mention."

Anne grew pale at the story. "Is that the dog that follows Hob everywhere?"

"Aye, the one with scarred bald spots where the fur could not grow back."

"I understand," she said, her eyes narrowing with rare anger.

"Yet Hob has always been a loyal brother, loving Will more than the elder merits. Whatever evil Hob committed as a youth, he now works hard, complains little, and sins only in fighting for his brother's honor and sometimes drinking more than he should."

"And so he nearly killed you out of loyalty this day?"

"He might well have done so if he had wished it. Instead, he led Will off to safety so his temper could cool and left me to wake up when Cuthbert threw a bucket of water over my head. Some might say my suffering head was penance for the sin of almost breaking the smith's hand, or else the near drowning I got with my sergeant's tender concern." He gingerly touched his neck where the poultice lay. "For this I should have cracked the blacksmith's wrist in two!"

"You said you suspected Will of knowing something more than he is saying. Will you question him further?" Anne looked at the crowner with that stern expression common to mothers with troublesome sons. "Without breaking any part of him?"

The crowner's grin was wicked enough to warm any imp's heart. "Additional inquiry I may promise you, but I cannot say the blacksmith might not suffer a minor scratch or bruise!" Ralf's expression shifted from jest to determination. "You have given me reason to ask Hob more questions as well, Annie. Perhaps he does have something to hide. Or, if he is such a loyal brother, he might know secrets belonging to his brother, matters he wishes to conceal as much as Will does. If he understands that telling me everything would keep Will from the hangman, he might speak up."

"Then go," Anne replied. "But you might do worse than remember Brother Beorn's words about mercy."

Perplexed, Ralf raised a questioning eyebrow.

"Should you forget your past principles and use untoward force as a method of inquiry again, God might not protect you the next time you forget to watch your back."

Chapter Thirty-Two

Had the sea turned the color of Prioress Eleanor's eyes, sailors would be howling prayers for deliverance. Brother Thomas found himself wishing for some safe haven as well.

"I care not that Sister Juliana is an anchoress with a line of pilgrims at her window, no monk should spend time there. It is unseemly," the prioress said. "After witnessing that matter in Amesbury last year, you, of all people, should know how quickly any priory may garner accusations of lewdness."

"I beg forgiveness, my lady. Never would I deliberately bring shame to you or this priory. If I have done so out of foolishness, no penance you demand of me could be more severe or painful than my own remorse."

"What was your purpose in visiting her?"

Faced with his prioress' wrath, Thomas began to wonder if it was truly God that had drawn him there. In any case, he was sure of one thing, even if it was his only certainty: "My intent was innocent," he replied weakly.

"Indeed."

The monk opened his mouth but no words came forth. He cleared his throat. "Without question, I have erred, but I swear to you that I was drawn to the window for the same reasons others have had. I wanted..." He hesitated. "I sought understanding." How else could he explain it?

Eleanor folded her arms. Her look did not soften. "When I questioned our anchoress, she succeeded in providing more detail, declaring you came to debate questions of faith. That is an admirable activity in principle, Brother, but your wish for disputations of that nature are best satisfied with another monk or with your prior. Sister Juliana may pose what queries she has with her confessor."

Lacking any response, he bowed.

"She might even properly seek my counsel."

Thomas winced at her sharp rebuke and kept his eyes lowered. He could not quarrel with a thing his prioress was saying, yet something urged him to resist in this matter. Was it Satan? What of his vow to obey this woman without question?

The meeting between him and the anchoress had been chaste. Even if his wicked nature had wanted it otherwise, his manhood would have shriveled in Sister Juliana's terrifying presence. And hadn't her advice already brought him more peace than he had previously known? Where was the sin if she taught him how to pray? Were there not holy women who were blessed with God's speech? Hadn't abbots and bishops begged advice from many?

"That said, I have not forgotten that you have served both Tyndal and my family well in the past."

Thomas blinked at the abrupt change of subject. Her comment might have pleased another, but uneasiness pricked him with an icy sting. Was she listing factors that would modify the severity of his penance, or was she about to pursue some new direction for reproach? His heart longed for the former. His mind feared the last. Opting to remain silent, he raised his eyes and hoped his demeanor revealed only a suitable meekness.

"For this reason, I should have no reason to doubt either your commitment to your vows or your fealty to me as head of this priory. Am I correct?"

"I may have been a most sinful man in years past, but I swear to you that I have not broken my vows since I took them."

"Vows of both chastity and obedience? While you have been here?"

Had Death's finger just caressed his heart or had that organ simply frozen with indefinable dread? Her questions were often deceptively simple, and he suspected this was one such occasion. Most monks wrestled with lust, but he had remained as chaste as most—and more than some, if truth be told. Other than in dreams, when he swyved imps dressed in mortal flesh, he had not broken any vow, even at Amesbury. "Aye, my lady," he said with caution and hoped his simple reply had been adequate.

The prioress studied him in silence, her head tilted to one side and her eyes showing determined patience.

She is waiting for something more, he thought and knew he had not satisfied her. Who had accused him of lewdness? Or, he suddenly thought, who had questioned his obedience and why? Thomas met her eyes, allowing his bewilderment to show.

Eleanor turned away from him and walked toward the window. For a long time, she stared out at the priory grounds as if they might give her answers she was not getting from her monk. "What reason did you really have for visiting our anchoress, Brother?"

Although her voice had softened a bit, Thomas wondered why she would not be plainer in her concern. Had she mentioned obedience only because he had not sought permission to visit the anchoress? He considered his response.

"I do not wish some fine speech, but rather blunt honesty." She turned around to face him. "Some time ago you confided a secret to me, a troubling admission I honored with silence. Did that not teach you that I respect frankness and do not abuse a confidence?"

"I hesitate only because I am not sure myself why or by what power I was drawn to Sister Juliana's window, although my purpose was not lewd. In that, I am most certain. Have I been so accused?"

Eleanor's sigh was heavy with weariness. "Nay, Brother, but as you well know, some might condemn if they witnessed you there. I must ask if our anchoress said or did anything that might be construed as sinful, whether or not you think it justified." She raised a finger. "Be as forthright as your vows require. I will decide the meaning of what you tell me, praying that I do so with the fairness God demands."

"A few may blame her for welcoming the sleepless at her window. I have seen an increasing number of those troubled ones during the weeks I have been assigned to the sick of our village, as well as on nights I have sought the chapel."

Eleanor nodded more thoughtfully and with less anger evident in her expression.

"Rarely have I seen men waiting in the shadows, and, if my experience is common, she is most likely to strike fear into their hearts. That is a most powerful antidote to lust, my lady."

Her eyes widened in surprise, and then the prioress smiled.

She is amused, Thomas thought with relief. "Although there are those who will most certainly condemn her for allowing any man to approach her window at night, I doubt Sister Juliana has longed for anything but the anchorage. Did she not fight against a marriage to one who would have been a most devoted husband? Were I required to swear an oath on this, I would say our anchoress seeks only God's arms about her."

"Although you and I might argue over whether she found the proposed husband distasteful for reasons other known only to herself, I do agree that your conclusion holds no other significant fault, Brother." Once again, the prioress turned away from him. "Do you swear without reservation that you felt no lust for her?"

"I swear that without hesitation." If she is so concerned about my chastity, he asked himself, why allow me to travel to the village at night to deliver medicines? Were I inclined to those sins of the flesh, would I not find opportunity there to find some woman to swyve? If not, why should I be tempted by Sister Juliana? "Was our anchoress offended by anything I said or did?"

"Nay, Brother, but I must answer all complaints with persuasive truth, especially those based on misconceptions."

Although he thought the prioress was going to continue in that vein, she fell into a distracted silence. As her brow furrowed, he began to tremble. He could not read her thoughts, but he was suddenly filled with a cold but ill-defined dismay.

Instinctively, he fell to his knees.

Eleanor caught her breath.

"My lady, I have vowed to protect and obey you as the earthly representation of Our Lord's mother and to do so with the devotion sworn by the beloved disciple at the foot of the cross. That oath is more sacred to me than any other; therefore, if I have committed any sinful act, seeming or real, involuntarily or simply ill-considered, give me what penance you will and I shall embrace it, no matter how onerous."

Eleanor shakily reached backward, seeking the security of her chair, then fell into it as if she had lost all strength.

Thomas gasped with apprehension.

She shook off his concern and gestured for him to rise, then continued. "I have taken your oath as a loving and dutiful son to my heart, Brother, and shall not forget your words." She took a deep breath, and her color returned. "In the meantime, I would hear more of what you have seen at night when you have passed by our anchoress' window. There may be much of use to me as I counter criticism. As you would surely agree, her behavior invites that even if evil has no part in it."

"From what I have heard in the village, she is known for giving solace to those who seek that."

"What comfort did she offer you?"

Hearing the bite in these words, Thomas again felt perplexed. Hadn't he just sworn he felt no lust for the woman, an oath his prioress seemed to accept? What was disquieting her? "The night I felt drawn to her window," he continued, "I admitted that I was troubled in spirit. She advised prayer."

"Has she taken on a priest's role?"

Thomas hesitated. "She said nothing inimical to her sex, my lady. She quickly asked if I had spoken with my confessor, then called herself a foul creature." Was her advice against spoken prayer wrong, an admonition that was contrary to Church practice? Although the prioress had ordered him to tell her everything, he balked. Was he not a priest, able to decide these matters himself? Or was Sister Juliana speaking with Satan's tongue, when she told him he had the right to hear God's truth directly, and had he been seduced into sin?

"You said you felt drawn to her window, as if you were driven there and not of your own volition. Could the Prince of Darkness have pushed you there? I ask, not to accuse, but to gather information."

"To my imperfect knowledge, the Devil brings joy only to our lesser nature. My soul found ease. That was all." At least he was able to speak the truth there.

"Did she claim to speak with God's tongue?"

"She does, but, as we all know, He has spoken through many holy women. Perhaps He has chosen her? Yet she did not proclaim this with pride. I found her humble, quite terrified that she might be His chosen vessel, and filled with longing that He pick someone else."

"I had best leave that decision to Brother John, whom I have sent to question her. Although you say the village proclaims her holiness, I know other voices hiss of sin. Our sub-prioress is amongst those." She fell silent as if troubled, then continued. "Tell me what seekers come at night when Evil prevails, frail creatures of either sex who should be asleep in chaste beds and not walking about freely at such a time."

Thomas closed his eyes, trying to remember those he had recognized. "Some, I did not know, but they may have been pilgrims…"

"I am not concerned with those." Eleanor smiled gently. "Nor will I ask you to list all you could identify, or else I fear I shall hear the names of the entire village. Tell me if Martin, Will, or Hob ever visited our anchoress. Did Signy or Ivetta?"

Ah, it was murder that troubled his prioress, not his secrets or his sins! Thomas brightened with relief. "In the darkness, it is hard to see with clarity, but I do not think either the cooper or the two brothers ever came. Although I did see the shadows of a few other men, I can name only Tostig with certainty. Most of the men seemed to be strangers, pilgrims on the way to or from Norwich, or so the rumor from the village declares."

"Do you know why any of the men came to her?"

"I do not listen where I should not, my lady." Hearing his own aggrieved tone, Thomas forced himself to moderate his speech with a smile. "Unless, of course, you order me to do so in the name of justice."

Eleanor acknowledged his attempt with a short laugh. "What about Signy?" she then asked.

"Aye. I have seen her there more than once."

"Ivetta?"

"As often as the baker's wife."

"A woman who found our anchoress most well-informed about bread, if the tales passed on are true," Eleanor replied dryly. "From what you have already said, I will not ask if you overheard what troubled either Ivetta or Signy, but were you aware of any rumors from the village?"

"Nay."

The prioress shook her head in frustration, her expression suggesting she was about to end the discussion.

"I might question old Tibia," Thomas said. "Although Crowner Ralf asked me to question her about anything she might have seen at the inn the night of Martin's murder, I have not done so yet. Her pain has remained severe, yet she did tell me that she has also visited the anchoress and swears by her counsel. Perhaps she knows what brought Ivetta or Signy to our anchoress' window."

Eleanor nodded approval. "I thank you for what you have told me. As for your visit to Sister Juliana, I must order you not to repeat it. Surely you understand why."

Thomas bowed his concurrence.

With that she dismissed him.

Thomas left. Outside the chambers, he stopped briefly to wipe sweat from his eyes, then went down the stairs and back to the hospital.

The moment the door had closed, Prioress Eleanor began to weep.

Chapter Thirty-Three

Ralf's mood was as pained as his aching head, and the market smells did not improve either. Normally, the butcher stalls did not trouble him, but the metallic stench of blood and offal only reminded him of his failure to bring a murderer to justice. The crowner turned around and walked back toward the sellers of vegetables.

"Isn't it a fair day for market?" A young widow, with three children trailing behind, shifted her basket filled with green leeks and yellow mustard. Tilting her head to look up at the crowner, her smile revealed an almost full complement of teeth.

Ralf nodded with an abrupt but courteous enough gesture and walked on. Feeling uneasy, however, he glanced back.

The widow was still watching him. She waved, then reached out for one straying child and pulled him closer with a mild rebuke.

"I think she likes you, Crowner."

Ralf felt his cheeks flush as he spun around.

Gytha stood just to his left.

"Have you been too busy rendering the king's justice to notice?" She grew more solemn as she saw the injury to his head. "Surely that wound has only recently addled your wits."

His face grew hotter. "A minor thing," he muttered, fingering the tenderness. Ever since she was a wee lass, he had liked Tostig's sister. She made him laugh with her frank wit. Now that she was a young woman, however, he sometimes found her ways oddly disturbing.

"Brother Beorn's work," she concluded, but her brow remained furrowed.

Unable to come up with anything else to say, he went back to the subject of the widow. "Her husband and I fished together as boys. When I heard he had drowned in a storm last winter, I was saddened."

Gytha raised an eyebrow with her unspoken question.

"I am not interested in marrying her," Ralf growled.

Two plump wives, and longtime friends, passed by with bright smiles and friendly nods. After a few steps, they drew closer together and began to giggle in whispered conversation.

It was Gytha whose cheeks now turned pink.

But not unattractively, Ralf thought, then grinned with gentle delight. "Your basket is full, I see," he quickly remarked, wanting to soothe whatever had caused the girl's embarrassment. "What can Prioress Eleanor possibly lack with her fine priory gardens?" Curious, he reached into the basket and began to sort through the contents.

She swatted his hand. "Hush, Crowner! I'm here to listen. 'Tis for deception that I am buying a few things."

"And the reason for this?"

"Gossip. I wanted to learn what the village is saying about these murders."

"What!" he roared.

Gytha grabbed his arm and pulled him away from the crowd.

"Do you think…?" One of the plumb wives asked the other as they stared after the departing couple. With a beaming smile, her friend nodded.

"I'm sorry," Ralf muttered as he and Gytha found a quiet hillock where they sat down in the warm grass.

"You were as loud as your stomach often is," she replied, but her tone did not suggest she meant these words as her usual jest.

"You should not be getting involved in this matter. It is not your concern, and I do not want you to get hurt," he hissed.

"Because I am Tostig's young sister," she snapped.

"That, too," he replied and then suddenly realized he may have suggested more than he intended. "I..."

"Oh, be silent, Crowner! Your tongue always has balked at your teeth unless you are tormenting suspects. Let me tell you what I learned, and you will see that no harm could come of this." She dug through her basket and pulled out a small fruit tart. "Eat this while I talk. It will keep you quiet while I chatter. Anyone passing will assume you were hungry and I am simply amusing my brother's best friend with childish babble."

He took the tart and bit into it. "Where'd you get this?" he asked. "It's good."

Gytha scowled. "Methinks you need a nurse to take care of you more than your daughter does!"

"I, rather, *she* most certainly needs a good woman..."

"...and I'll find her one. That, I promise. Do you want to hear what I have to say or not?"

Ralf nodded sheepishly.

"The news abroad is that Ivetta and Martin were poisoned by drinking a potion of crushed yew berries. When I was examining these onions, a group of women nearby were complaining that their husbands now refuse to drink anything without having some creature lap at it first. One said she must be grateful her husband didn't want her to test it rather than the dog!"

"Is there growing concern over these deaths?" Ralf licked his fingers and looked hopefully at the basket resting between them.

Gytha found another tart and tossed it to him. "Despite the priory's efforts, some do still think the Devil is involved. The baker's wife told me that Will, the blacksmith, was seen in conversation with old Tibia just before he disappeared."

"Disappeared?"

"He has not been seen at the smithy for many hours."

Ralf swallowed his bite. "Did she say what passed between the two?"

"No, but she thinks the herb woman is a witch, and Will sold his soul to the Devil through her. That would explain why he has vanished, she says. As for the other deaths, the baker's wife believes Satan killed them because he had grown impatient waiting for those wicked souls to come to him."

"She doesn't think they were poisoned?" He gestured expectantly at the basket.

This time, she ignored his hungry look. "No one doubts that yew was involved, but, according to the baker's wife, that proves Satan's hand in the deaths. Everyone knows how poisonous the tree is. Would you allow Sibely to even play in the shadow of a yew? Only the Devil can handle it without harm."

"Are there no suspects mentioned?"

"Only the Prince of Darkness."

"Thus panic grows," Ralf muttered, covering his face with his hands. "And I am no closer to finding the guilty one."

Gytha rose and picked up her basket. "You will, Crowner. You always do."

He looked up and smiled with gratitude at her gentle words.

"Oh, you are quite welcome to the help I have given you." She tossed her head, and then left him before he could find words to reply.

Ralf watched her walk away, his mouth still open. When she did find a husband to suit her, he wondered if he should pity the man or envy him for winning the heart of such an amazing woman.

Chapter Thirty-Four

"Silence that cur."

The growl grew deeper.

"He doesn't like anyone who threatens me, Crowner." Hob's grin was not pleasant.

"Answer my question then, and you both will be treated with the benevolence due all honest creatures." Ralf glanced under the inn table.

The dog covered his eyes with a large paw.

"How can I tell you where Will is when I don't know myself? Must I lie to convince you I am honest?"

Ralf was tempted to grind his foot into the blacksmith's arch but remembered the dog. "Perhaps you can explain to me why he ran if he is innocent of murder?" Anger made his face grow even hotter in the already warm air.

"Knowing you is cause enough."

"Must I ask this a second time? Have you ever seen me act unfairly in the pursuit of justice?"

"You hate my brother, even if you have been honest enough in other matters."

"Your brother is not known for his generosity to those less gifted with mortal goods than he. He does not possess a sweet nature. All that is true enough. Nor, I confess, am I fond of those who torment the innocent." The crowner shrugged. "None of those qualities is likely to foster love in my heart for any man."

Hob leaned across the table, his face so close to the crowner's that Ralf could smell the ale on his breath. "None of that means he's a murderer either, but Will told me you'd arrest him nonetheless."

"Your brother did kill, as you well remember. Why shouldn't I think he would do so again?"

The man turned his head and spat. "That one time with the boy was an accident. Besides, Will only threw the rope over the tree limb and held him. It was Martin who dropped the noose around his neck and hauled him up."

The crowner sat back and folded his arms.

Hob did the same.

"Very well. I do not accuse your brother of murder. But he does know more than he admits, maybe to you as well as to me. All I want from him are frank answers. Then he can return to the smithy in peace and beat hot metal into submission all he likes. Tell him that. His rank stench is enough to keep me far away, unless the king's justice demands it."

Hob nodded, his expression softening. "If I tell you what I know of this, will you leave my brother alone?"

"You shall confess your knowledge whether I decide it proves your brother's innocence or not." Ralf's tone indicated some hope of concession.

The man thought for a moment, then shook his head. "I've already told you that Will could not have murdered Martin. He wasn't at the inn…"

"The cooper was poisoned, not beaten to death as rumor should have told you by now. Your brother could have slipped the stuff into the drink before he left."

"Poison?" Hob threw his head back and roared with laughter. "My brother not only has no skill with herbs, Crowner, he wouldn't know a beet top from that of a carrot. Nor does he seek the skill of those who understand the healing herbs even when he falls ill which, thanks be to God, has been rare. Like most of us, he fears mortality and rejects any reminder of it. As for the night of Martin's death, Will was more interested in proving his manhood by rubbing up Signy. Whatever else you might think of him, my brother is a simple man with simple desires."

"And the night Ivetta was killed?"

"He went to see old Tibia…"

"What business did he have with her? Surely she is too old to find a use for his limp rod, and you have just said he had no love of herbs. Was it to make cruel fun…?"

"My brother left her alone after her son's death! He was hot-tempered but not cruel."

Ralf pointed under the table. "Tell that to your cur."

Hob swallowed hard and turned away.

"When did he go to the herb woman? When did he return? Why did he want to speak to her?"

"I told him to forget the night with Ivetta—although he had more than one such failure to overlook. As much as he hated potions and powders, the one thing Will could not bear was the loss of his manhood. He admitted to me that he would seek out Tibia's cure. Others had praised her for it, but, when he went to her hut, she would not answer his knock. He stayed for some time at her door."

"Perhaps she knew who it was and did not wish to help him."

"She had promised earlier that she would."

So far Hob was confirming what the elder brother had already told him. "Are there witnesses? And, again, what time was this and when did he come back to the smithy?"

"Enough questions! He left the smithy not long after the sun disappeared, for that was the hour she told him to come. When she did not let him in, he went to the inn, thinking she might be there since the innkeeper and his niece often fed her for the good of their souls. When he didn't see her, Will drank until the thatcher carried him home and dropped him outside the smithy. I know this because I awoke from the noise and pulled him to his pallet. The next morning he cursed the herb woman for going back on her promise."

"Someone saw your brother talking to her just before he disappeared."

"Maybe that was when they agreed to meet at her hut?"

Ralf silently cursed himself for not asking Gytha exactly when the baker's wife had seen the two together. Perhaps Hob was right. "Did he ask anyone where she was when he did not find her there?"

"You think Will would let a man besides his brother know he had need of her special skills?"

Ralf turned thoughtful. "And you, Hob? What were you doing that night?"

The blacksmith winced as if pricked with a nail. Bending toward the crowner, he beckoned for him to bring his ear closer. "Swear you will keep this secret?" he whispered uneasily.

"If it has naught to do with murder."

"I had a woman in my bed. Her father does not know we meet...."

"Will she confirm this to me?"

"I would prefer you not ask her, but she will answer readily enough if need be. Aye, Crowner, I read your thoughts in that frown." Hob sheepishly lowered his eyes and studied his open hands. "She is a praiseworthy woman, sensible, and far too good for me. When I can prove to her father that I am steady enough, we shall make public the vows we have spoken to each other in secret. In God's eyes, at least, we are married."

Casually fingering the hilt of his sword, Ralf leaned back. As he continued to glare at the man in front of him, he knew that those with greater reason to fear him would soon break down into tears and confession. Would the blacksmith?

Hob did not blink.

"Tell your brother to come home," Ralf said at last, conceding defeat. "He has nothing to fear from me."

Those anticipated tears now threatened to overflow from the younger blacksmith's eyes. "I would if I knew where he hides. In that, as in all the rest I've said, I did tell the truth."

Chapter Thirty-Five

Brother John was a wiry man, well over a foot taller than the woman who accompanied him, but he was having difficulty keeping pace with the tiny prioress of Tyndal.

She glanced behind and said with a hint of impatience, "Did you not say that Sister Juliana begged you to bring me quickly?"

"Aye," he panted as he raced after her.

"What brought about this plea? Did you question her as I asked? Was it that?"

"I do not know the cause, my lady. I did question her."

"Do we have God's creature or Satan's in our anchorage?"

Although sweat was now beading on his gaunt face, a sweet look conquered his usual somber expression. "God's, I think."

"Yet you would agree that her behavior is most strange."

"Many holy women have behaved in ways men have found questionable. Beatrice of Nazareth cinched her waist with a girdle of thorns and even feigned madness to show the depth of her ecstasy, but Jesus favored her by speaking in Latin only. Saint Mary of Egypt lived over five decades on herbs alone. Saint Euphrosyne dressed herself as a man and lived chastely with other monks in a monastery for almost four." He gulped in a breath. "I find no fault in our own sister here."

"How do we know she does not commune with Satan in secret?"

"After I spoke with her, I hid and watched her from the squint that opens into the church. She prays, either on her knees or lying with her face pressing into the ground. I did see her shake once as if convulsing, but her expression glowed with a most holy joy afterward."

"Does she eat or sleep?" Eleanor's pace did not slow.

"A rat ate the meal placed on the floor just inside the door. As for rest, God may grant it to her in some marvelous way, but I never saw her lie on her bed. Not that I was there for long…"

"She has asked to be given nothing to eat that was once living flesh, including both fish and fowl. Although we all should reject venison and other such meat to keep our bodies free from lust, I have heard that such extreme renunciation may suggest unorthodoxy. Those of the Cathar heresy often denied themselves in a similar way, did they not?"

"She strives to follow the desert fathers who fasted in a similar manner, not to deny or punish the body, but to cleanse it of those sins that drove Adam and Eve from Eden. I myself see no problem with her wish to live as if Lent must extend the length of her days on earth."

"What of her sleepless nights at the window, waiting to attend all those souls in pain?"

"Satan and his imps may have claimed the night as theirs, but is not God mightier than evil?" He stopped for a moment but his prioress did not and he hurried to catch up. "Not one frail woman has suffered ill effects. I would suggest that God smiles on her and protects those who come to hear His words, spoken through her mouth. She may be unusual in greeting seekers to come to her window only after the sun sets, but other anchoresses have ministered to the suffering who prostrate themselves at the curtained window during the night. Her ways are not without precedence."

"And her resistance to having any woman serve her? What is the point of that?"

The monk brushed the burning sweat from his eyes. "Sister Juliana told me that the women sent by our sub-prioress do not understand that she does not want to hear their voices while she is listening for God's. A few have tried to tell her when to eat or sleep, while others frown or wince and in other ways express silent criticism of behavior they find troublesome or incomprehensible. Some have even tried to gossip and chatter with her, finding the solitude of an anchorage uncomfortable."

"She wants a monk to serve her. Did she tell you that?"

"My lady, have mercy on me!" The monk bent forward, hands on knees. "God has given you a fleet foot whereas I have ever been a sluggish man and find it difficult to answer your concerns properly when I lack the breath to do them justice."

Eleanor skidded to a stop. "Forgive me, Brother, for my thoughtlessness."

The monk did his best to smile while gasping for air.

"Let us sit over there in the garden and rest before we see Sister Juliana." She gestured toward a bench, hesitating briefly. Rarely did she come here without remembering the day, soon after she had first come to Tyndal, that a dead monk was found nearby. She prayed Brother John had forgotten.

The monk settled on a corner of the bench, apparently more grateful for the chance to rest than unsettled by any distressing memory. When his breathing returned to normal, he continued. "Had I not heard of Saint Euphrosyne or Christina of Markyake who lived chastely with the hermit Roger, albeit hidden in a miserable hole from which only he could release her, I might have questioned this desire more. Yet I find nothing lewd in her request. She seems to think men more peaceful creatures." He pondered that for a silent moment. "I wonder what our new king would have to say about that."

"Then it seems we must ask God to send her a woman with a man's nature," she replied.

A rustling sound came from the shrubbery a foot or two away, startling the prioress, but it was only the hospital cat. Trailing behind the creature were two kittens, one of which bore the distinctive markings of the prioress' own orange tabby.

Brother John smiled. "You ask for a difficult resolution, my lady."

A small bird landed a short distance away.

"We must continue to believe in miracles," the prioress replied.

The cat hunched into the hunting pose. The kittens mimicked their mother.

The monk bent his head in modest agreement. "I shall add my prayers to yours."

The bird flew off, accompanied by the high chirps of feline annoyance.

Eleanor rose. "Perhaps we should continue to the anchorage," she said. "How did Sister Juliana learn that you were watching her?"

This time, Brother John kept pace. "I do not know how she could have discovered me, my lady, for I crouched close to the wall and held my breath when I thought she was near. Nevertheless, when she threw herself on her knees near the squint, begging that I send for you and crying that her soul was cursed, I did not ask questions but came for you at once."

"We shall soon find out the source of her pain, Brother." Then the prioress looked back at the kittens. They had forgotten all birds and were now engaged in an intense new hunt for bugs.

Suddenly Eleanor knew she had a solution to at least one of her problems.

Chapter Thirty-Six

Tibia clutched her staff with such force that her knuckles shone bone-white.

"You must go to the priory hospital," Signy urged as she eased the tortured woman onto an inside bench near the inn door. "I will take you there."

Her jaw tight and eyes squeezed shut, Tibia shook her head with the impatience of the suffering.

"You need not fear walking. We will find a cart or men to carry you."

Tibia's groan was like the cry of an animal, uncomprehending yet instinctively fearing the cause of its torment. She opened her eyes and turned her pale gaze on the innkeeper's niece. "You're a good woman. My son should have married you. He'd have lived then," she gasped through lips thinned by pain.

Signy said nothing. What merit was there in reminding this woman, whose mind seemingly wandered with grief and agony, that she had been too young to wed when Tibia's son had died?

"Methinks it's easing," the old woman whispered. Indeed some color was returning to her face.

The innkeeper's niece gently pushed a steaming bowl of pottage toward her.

"I can't eat."

"You must." Gently, Signy rested her hand on a bony arm.

"The Devil's coming soon enough for my soul. I don't mind if it be sooner than later. Give this to another in need, one whom

God might love more." The old woman sucked in her lips. With
so few teeth, her sharp nose almost touched her chin. "Is it true
the crowner thinks you killed Martin and his whore?"

"I do not know what he thinks. We rarely speak." Signy's words
sounded brave enough, but her trembling lips betrayed her fear.

"He must know better!"

The innkeeper's niece shrugged. "He thought Ivetta killed
Martin, but she has proven her innocence by dying herself. Perhaps
I'll be next. If so, I needn't fret about the hangman's mercy or
whether my uncle will show kindness and pull my legs to break
my neck as I dangle and choke." She laughed in bitter jest.

"What reason would anyone have to kill you?" Tibia's eyes
narrowed.

"Why murder Martin, or why Ivetta?"

"Does anyone mourn them? Martin was a skilled cooper,
but he was a cruel man and another will come to take over his
trade. Ivetta was evil. Simple as that."

"My heart held no love for either," Signy said, reaching out to
stroke the old woman's arm, "and confessed as much to Prioress
Eleanor. Perhaps I should not have done so. My honesty may
suit our crowner well if he cannot catch the murderer but must
find someone to hang."

"You're innocent! Unlike the man before him, this crowner's
an honest man."

"The crowner before was honest enough, but he did make
mistakes. Is Ralf so different?"

"Honest?" The old woman snorted. "Perhaps he was for those
who could reward him for it. Since I couldn't, he ignored my
son's death. I don't think the current king's man is as blinded
by the glow of a coin."

"So you believe our current crowner is less fond of gold or
inclined to error? In the past, we did think him different from
his two brothers, but hasn't he come back from court a richer
man? Methinks he is now beholden to the powerful and become
much like you think his predecessor was." Her voice cracked on
that last and she bent her head, perhaps to hide tears.

Tibia drooped wearily. "You think he'd find an innocent guilty of murder then?"

"Have you not heard the tale?" Signy asked, rubbing her eyes.

"I hear little from my hut."

"The thatcher said the butcher told him that Ralf had gone to seize both Hob and Will for the murder of Martin." Signy turned thoughtful. "Although the fishwife did claim she heard the men arguing, she said there was no mention of any arrest. In short, the crowner did not take either into custody because Hob struck him on the head and hurried Will away. Now Will has disappeared, and even his brother does not know his whereabouts. Or so my uncle has said."

"Do most think either is guilty?"

"No one does, except our crowner. Why should they have killed Martin? The blacksmiths and the cooper have been like brothers since they were all lads."

"And Ivetta, their sister," Tibia muttered, her eyes glowing with anger. "Incestuous whore!"

"Well, she is dead in any case, and Will is gone. If he has any sense, he is on the road to the west. Of those our Ralf thinks guilty of murder, only Hob and I remain. I think he prefers me to Hob in this."

"Why?"

"Because the weapon was poison, a woman's instrument according to the crowner."

"Most of the women in the village could poison a man if they wished. It's a poor wife that doesn't keep a good herb garden well tended for her family's ills. There's no reason for our crowner to set his mind on you in particular." Tibia shook her head as color began to fade from her cheeks again. "Methinks no one will be arrested for murdering either Martin or Ivetta."

Signy raised a questioning eyebrow.

"Satan owned their souls. If the crowner wants an arrest, he better try to set his chains on the Evil One for 'twas the Fiend that called them to Hell."

"Surely a mortal hand helped?"

Tibia lurched forward, groaning with a spasm of pain.

Signy cried out as she reached out to comfort the woman. "Please! Someone find Brother Thomas and tell him that old Tibia desperately needs his potion!" she shouted to a nearby table of men.

The herb woman began to cry out with agonized moans.

A young man rushed to help. Another ran from the inn in the direction of the priory.

"Carry her back to her hut," Signy begged.

The man nodded, then carefully lifted the trembling old woman into his arms and took her home.

Chapter Thirty-Seven

"I have failed," Eleanor muttered. As the prioress walked back to her chambers, she was oblivious to the lush perfume of summer that drifted gently around her. Instead, her soul was heavy with thoughts of murder and disgust at her own imperfections.

Juliana's cries of pain were still fresh in her ears. When Eleanor heard the source of her anguish, she had comforted her old friend but quickly left so Brother John could offer God's consolation. The moment the door to the anchorage closed, Eleanor had fled out of fear that she might contaminate this wounded soul with her own foulness. Was she herself not guilty enough in this matter?

The good brother she had left behind was her confessor as well, to whom she would admit her worldly errors in due course, but now she needed time alone to let God know how much she understood her failings.

In fact, the anchoress had done little wrong. Eleanor herself often begged audience with God and listened with blank mind and in silence until she felt, more than heard, His voice. In this, Juliana's advice to those who sought her out held no error. Where the woman may have failed was in not recognizing a killer seeking justification for revenge.

Could anyone else have seen the evil? Would she have done so any more than Juliana, a woman who feared the world and longed only to escape from it? On the other side of the argument, a reasonable person might say that a holy woman should have read the sinner's heart even if a lesser mortal was incapable of it. Eleanor frowned, then dismissed the latter thought.

Others might cast blame on Juliana, but the prioress of Tyndal could not. Neither she nor the village was worthy to determine the blessedness of any other mortal. Meanwhile, all she could feel for the anchoress was compassion. Even though Juliana might continue to bring trouble to the priory, her questionable ways likely to invite criticism from those with Sister Ruth's cast of mind, Eleanor knew her old friend well.

No matter how changed, Juliana was still the girl she had met as a child, a person with a kind heart who bore the world no malice even if she wanted nothing to do with it. Yet to atone for her one act of cruelty, God must have decided that Juliana should provide solace to many pilgrims filled with much grief and many sins. That would most certainly be a hard penance for the anchoress to bear.

Nay, the prioress thought, she had no cause to condemn the anchoress. Had she herself not been so concerned with the worldly reputation of Tyndal, she might have heard the begging in Juliana's voice when she confronted her just yesterday. If she had not been driven mad with jealousy over Brother Thomas' visit to her old friend, she might have listened instead of interrupting when the anchoress tried to tell her about the murderer's visit to the anchorage window. Although Eleanor had never used the whip on her back, this was one time she felt she merited that extreme penance.

But who was the murderer? Juliana knew only that the voice belonged to a woman. That would eliminate both Will and Hob from the list of suspects. Since Ivetta was dead, surely she was innocent as well.

Or was she? Had the prostitute killed Martin, only to be poisoned by someone else as revenge? If Signy's story was true about Martin's methods of seduction, more than a few women in the village might have killed him—and killed Ivetta out of anger, jealousy, or even spite. After all, if a prioress dedicated to the pursuit of God's perfection could grow enraged when her monk chastely sought the company of an anchoress, any other mortal should be more easily blinded by evil.

Eleanor shook her head with frustration. "There must be some clue that would solve this crime," she said. "Why am I failing to see it? Why does my logic keep circling with such futility?"

Not wanting to go back just yet to her chambers, she turned into the cloister garth and began to pace amongst the flowers of the gardens. What had Gytha told her about the women rumored to have visited the anchoress for advice? Who amongst them might be the killer?

"I must look at each with dispassion. Surely logic may discount several as possible suspects, either because they or their kin have no obvious or serious quarrel with Martin. Try as I might," she continued with a wry smile, "I cannot see that the baker's wife would poison the man because her husband's bread had not risen for three days after the cooper tried to put his hand up her dress. Would the fishwife do so after Martin jested about her husband's infidelity? Perhaps, if she were not grateful he did bed others so she did not have to pay any marriage debt."

Martin had enough enemies, but she did think Ralf was right in his conclusions. Most men would have settled any quarrel with the man by a blow. Some already had. Many women would have found brothers or husbands willing enough to retaliate on their behalf for any insult or wicked jest. The number of suspects was now considerably reduced to a woman who had no such man to strike a good blow for her and must seek revenge in another way.

Ralf had initially preferred Ivetta as logical choice for the killer. After her death, he assumed she had committed self-murder out of guilt. Eleanor never did agree with either conclusion. Was she wrong?

"Ivetta discovered she was with child," the prioress said as she settled down on the stone bench she had earlier shared with Brother John. "True or not, she believed the father was Martin. Yet surely she had quickened before now with his seed, as well as

others, and most likely had sought remedy to hasten the ending
to any pregnancy. Why would she choose not to do so now?"

Ralf suggested she might have thought the cooper would
marry her, Eleanor thought. Whether or not Martin had said
anything in fact about this, the important point was that Ivetta
might have thought he did or ought to have done so.

Had he mocked her for thinking he would marry a woman
he had sold to others? Did she then poison him in hurt anger
and soon after attempt a fatal abortion? Brother Thomas was
right, as Sister Anne confirmed, that many women were aware
that yew was a most effective poison. Mothers even warned their
children not to climb the tree out of a fear of it.

Or was Ivetta killed by the person who killed Martin? According
to Sister Anne, the poison was probably the same, although she
had expressed cautious doubt and would not firmly decide that
such was the case. "I am inclined to conclude that Ivetta was
murdered as well," Eleanor said, reaching down to draw a single
line in the gravel. "I met with the woman. She was proud of her
pregnancy! Even if I wanted to suppose she killed her bawd, a
man she inexplicably followed like Hob's dog does his master, I
cannot believe that she would kill that babe. Surely she would not
have taken a draught of yew willingly, knowing full well what the
properties were," she decided, "and therefore I think it unlikely
that she killed Martin and tried to abort later."

If she eliminated Ivetta as the culprit, was it Signy? Once
again, Eleanor bent down and drew another line next to the first.
Thoughts swirled in her head like squalling mews looking for
a safe landing after a fright. Attempting to bring back rational
order to her mind, Eleanor took in a deep breath and let the
pleasant scent of budding fruit from nearby trees fill her.

"Aye," she mused thoughtfully, "this is God's blessing to us,
His bountiful season, full of life's vigor." In just a short while,
however, the frosts would come to give apples that sharpness
needed for Sister Matilda's tarts, simple treats to delight monas-
tics. Then the snows would fall, breaking branches with cruel
weight and killing young trees with bitter cold.

Wasn't the innkeeper's niece much like that, Eleanor asked herself, a woman cruelly hurt who had rebounded like a hardy tree blossoming after a hard winter. Could such a person be a killer, a woman whose strength made a mockery of cowards like the cooper? And if he had pushed her beyond her ability to endure, might not Signy be more likely to take a broom to him, or even a knife? She was a strong woman, after all, and might well have surprised him enough to injure if not kill him.

"Signy has faults enough," Eleanor continued softly. "Lust has a strong hold on her, but she has never sworn herself to a chaste bed, only to break the vows as I have. Yet she has virtue enough, as I have heard. Many men have been cheered innocently enough at the inn with her merry ways, and no wives betrayed. And she has shown charity as well. Old Tibia is one whom she feeds without charge as God demands."

Yet the innkeeper's niece had reason enough to hate Martin. He had taken her against her will as a girl, and then recently filled her womb with a child in her moment of blind weakness. When he threatened to make all this public, if she did not bring him the inn with marriage, she had reason to fear her uncle might cast her out. Whether or not the innkeeper would have done so, Eleanor understood Signy's terror at being faced with following Ivetta's trade to stay alive.

Viewed rationally, many must know that Signy was no virgin. Surely her brief affair with Ralf had been suspected, even if not mentioned above a whisper. Now there were rumors about Tostig. Although Gytha did not think he had bedded the woman, others must have concluded otherwise. As for the abortion, old Tibia would never speak of that, and, sin though it might be, many women shared her guilt. Surely Signy had confessed the deed and done penance.

Overall, Eleanor could understand why the villagers saw little cause to condemn Signy and why they chose to keep their gossip to a murmur. The innkeeper's niece brought no grief to any, only laughter to those whose lives were hard. Although people often damned others whom they did not like, they rarely had a quarrel with those that brought them cheer at the end of a tiring day. Besides, how many would care to encourage Martin's lewd tales when they had suffered themselves from his stories?

Was she making a similar mistake, ignoring sins and assuming innocence just because she found the woman pleasant? Gytha and Tostig also found her worthy enough. Until recently, that might have settled the issue since both were people whose judgements she respected. Now she had cause to distrust the good opinion of honest folk. After all, didn't the two speak of Brother Thomas with high regard? Yet wasn't he no better than a venomous snake, treacherously enjoying warmth in her breast?

She rubbed her forehead just over her left eye. One of her severe headaches was coming on, and she knew she must quickly seek Sister Anne and take that feverfew remedy before the pain got worse. "This is not the time to be distracted by the blinding pain daylight causes." She rose hurriedly to seek ease in the more subdued light of her chambers.

Closing her door carefully behind her, Eleanor lowered her head to keep the brightness of the day from searing her eyes. Circles of color drifted in front of her, and, had she not known what these auras of beauty presaged, she might have taken them for revelations from God. Instead, she knew well enough that she was too sinful a creature for visions. She cupped a hand over her eyes to lessen the throbbing pain.

"Very well," Eleanor muttered, as the headache forced her to deal more efficiently with this problem of murder. "Perhaps I should retain confidence in the wisdom of those whom I respect. Despite my aunt's disclosure about Brother Thomas' falseness, she has carefully reminded me that I may still have reason to trust him and win his complete and true loyalty. This knowledge of his treachery has unbalanced my better judgement and let Satan whisper ill counsel. I must trust as I have before and not dismiss either Gytha's or Tostig's opinion about Signy's character, for they both have known her for many years. But if she did not kill Ivetta and Martin, who else had cause?"

The prioress slipped gingerly into her chair and held her head as the pain began to pound with more insistence. "Who knew poisons well enough? Ivetta did, and may have been skilled enough about yew to know dosages. I do not believe she was the killer," she whispered. "Signy went to old Tibia when she quickened. That suggests she is ignorant of such matters. Who, then, knew herbs and potions and understood them well enough that she could kill with efficiency and stealth? Who had no one to seek revenge for some hurt on her behalf…?"

Suddenly a possible answer came to her, and she begged God to forgive her for caring more about her petty jealousies and pride than putting facts together to catch a killer.

Headache now forgotten, the prioress called to Gytha and, when the maid arrived, told her to summon both Crowner Ralf and Brother Thomas to her chambers as quickly as possible. The sharing of everything each had learned and what the sum of those facts might mean was long overdue.

Chapter Thirty-Eight

"She was in her hut, I swear it!" The young thatcher trembled under Ralf's fierce look.

Hands on hips, Signy's eyes glittered with equal fury. "Why should you not believe him?" she retorted, tossing her head at the youth. "Tibia was in great pain, and I asked him to carry her home until Brother Thomas could come. He did so as a mercy. Has kindness now become a crime, Crowner?"

Ralf opened his mouth to reply, then opted for the wiser choice and shut it.

"There is no cause to disbelieve him," Thomas suggested gently.

"I did not say he had lied," the crowner growled, attempting to retain a semblance of control in this discussion.

Gaining courage from so much support, the young man bravely turned indignant. "When I laid old Tibia on her pallet, she sent me away, telling me her son would come to care for her."

"Her son is dead," Ralf countered.

"When her mind wanders with pain or age, she often thinks I am he," Thomas explained.

"In any case, she is gone." Ralf gestured at the miserable hovel. "Where did she go? Did someone come for her? Where are witnesses?"

Signy's expression shifted to one of concern. "What could have happened to her? I have rarely seen anyone in such pain. How could she have walked anywhere?"

"Her agony ebbed and flowed. When it did ease, she moved well enough for an aged woman with such a bent back," the monk said.

"That has been true enough, but the severity and frequency did increase of late." Signy shook her head. "And with so much evil about, I cannot be the only one to fear the worst!"

Thomas glanced at the king's man. "How I wish you and I had thought to speak together sooner. Now we don't know where she has gone or why…"

"Perhaps you should find her, Crowner," Signy snapped. "Or are you the only person in the village to have forgotten we have a murderer amongst us? We tremble while you do nothing."

Ralf winced. "My men and I are not ignoring the danger," he replied, and then turned to Thomas. "Your prioress did not say what we should do if we did not find the herb woman. If her theory is correct, we had best seek Hob or…"

"What new crime now rattles the wits of our valiant crowner?" Hob sauntered toward the group clustered around the old woman's hut, his dog trotting close behind.

"At least that is one less person we have to worry about," Thomas whispered to his companion.

"Depends on whether we find another corpse and whose it is," Ralf replied softly, then moved apart from the group and gestured for the blacksmith to follow him. "I would speak to you at some distance away, Hob."

"So you can shackle me and take me off for hanging?" Hob stepped back. "I think not!"

"I give you my word that he wishes only to ask you a question," Thomas said.

Hob did not move. His dog began to bark.

"'S Blood! A man of God has sworn an oath to my intentions, and you dare to doubt it?" Ralf stepped forward. "I am no boy that spends the day playing games. Come with me as ordered or I shall…"

Hob clenched his fist.

"I share your misgivings about the king's man," Signy called out, casting a dark look in the crowner's direction, "but Brother Thomas has earned the trust of the village. I'd take his word on this."

The monk put a restraining hand on his friend's arm. "If it will save time, let me ask the question. We have little enough to spare if another life may be lost."

Ralf retreated a short distance.

Thomas walked slowly toward the blacksmith, avoiding the now growling cur's eyes. "Tell your dog that I mean you no harm," he said softly.

Hob turned to pet the creature. "He'll not bite, Brother. Let him sniff and he'll stay, unless I tell him otherwise."

The dog calmed, Thomas put a hand on the man's shoulder and directed him some few steps away. "We must find old Tibia," he said after a moment.

"Since you ask, I assume she's not in that hut. Why should I know where she's wandered off? I've been working hard at the forge like any honest man to earn my bread, Brother. Now that my brother is gone, I labor for two."

"Where is Will?"

Hob tensed. "Why do you ask?"

"He may be in danger."

The blacksmith shook off the monk's hand. "From the crowner, aye!"

"I swear not on my hope of heaven. Whatever your reason to dislike the king's man, in this matter he is on your side."

The man hesitated, then bent his head. "Brother, may God strike me if I lie to you. I do not know where Will has gone. I told the Crowner this. When my brother left, he said he'd return when the killer was found. Nothing more."

"Would he have gone far from here?"

"I doubt it. He believed dragons lived outside Tyndal village and only the priory kept them away."

"If you do not know his hiding place, tell me who might? Surely someone must. How else could he learn when it was safe to come home?"

Now sweating with panic, Hob gestured helplessly.

"Do you have any suspicion, no matter how vague? If not you, might he tell the innkeeper, the thatcher, some woman, a..." Thomas was counting off guesses on his fingers.

"I do not know and didn't think to ask! It just wasn't me."

"Where did you hide as boys?" Thomas asked, desperation evident in his voice. "I am not from here. I would not know these things."

"We had many places, Brother. I don't know which are still here or if he would have chosen any of them."

"When the stream near the village swells with rain, it carves out hollows and caves in the banks. Might he be in one of those?"

"And the stream just as often destroys those things the next year. I swear to you that I don't know where he might have hidden!"

"Help us find all the places, then," Thomas said, gesturing for Ralf to join them. "Cuthbert will search as well. With four of us, we can each look in a different spot."

"If Will's life is in danger, why not call the whole village out to find him? Someone may even know where he hides." Suspicion warred with panic in Hob's eyes. "Or do you want to keep secret what blows you will rain down on my brother if you catch him?"

Ralf shook his head. "The person who knows your brother's hiding spot will not be here, Hob. As for calling out more men, that would take time to organize efficiently. I think the four of us will find your brother faster if we start now." The crowner pointed to the path leading to the stream. "You go in that direction, and I will send Cuthbert over there."

"Why not send out others?" Thomas asked in a low voice. "It would not take that long..."

"I want justice, monk," Ralf replied. "As Signy has suggested, the village is frightened. Frightened men hang first, then ask if they did the right thing. As for Will's safety, we may have naught to worry about."

Chapter Thirty-Nine

Cuthbert's mind was not on murder. The air was hot, and he slashed away at the lush underbrush with minimal enthusiasm. A soft spray of dampness misted his face from the cut greens. With unconscious pleasure at the unexpected coolness on such a warm day, he stopped and listened for a moment to the rushing of the nearby stream and hum of lazy insects. Nay, he no longer fancied rousting out thieves and murderers, although he knew he would continue to do whatever the crowner wanted.

Ralf was a good fellow. Unlike his one arrogant brother, Sir Sheriff, and the other, lordling of the Church, the crowner cursed those who protected their own while condemning the evil of others with sanctimonious ardor. He also told good tales of the soldiering life, while drinking at the inn like any other man, and never arrested someone just because he was the popular choice for hanging. Querulous the crowner might be, but Cuthbert would take an honest, bad-tempered fellow any day over a sweet-smiling hypocrite.

And hadn't Ralf just told Cuthbert that he needed a bailiff, then asked if he would take the job even though the sergeant could barely read and could not write? "I need someone who knows how to run a farm, and your father tells me you're as good as your elder brothers at that," Ralf had said to him and slapped him on the back. As a landless man, Cuthbert would have been a fool to refuse—and foolish he most certainly was not!

Due to bad stewardship in the past, the land, now owned by the crowner, had brought little enough good to the village. If he ran it well, the farm would be more fruitful, and Ralf would be pleased to hire more poor men at harvest time. Given time and hard work, Cuthbert would also gain much status in the village for his success.

His mind more on his new position than where he was walking, the sergeant stumbled and his foot dropped through the forest floor into an invisible hole. Cursing from the pain, he fell awkwardly to the ground, then lay still, praying that the sharp stabbing in his ankle meant the injury was only a sprain.

"Aie!" he groaned, and then let his thoughts go back to happier things. Might he not even seek a wife, he wondered, swatting at gnats as they swarmed in a beam of light. He would have position enough now, and there was one lass he had always fancied, even as a boy, taking her nosegays of forest flowers until her father had chased him away.

Smiling at the thought of her, Cuthbert stared through the leaves above him to the pale blue sky of an East Anglian summer afternoon. She was a pretty one too, that girl, and not married yet, although rumors had circulated that her father wanted to marry her to the tanner's son.

The pain eased and the sergeant pulled himself upright with care. Testing his ankle, he decided it was not broken. "But no reason to chance a break," he muttered. "I'll quit the forest and find the clearing where I won't injure myself again."

Tanner's son? A good match if one discounted the stench, Cuthbert thought as he found a clear path without things to trip him up. But wouldn't marriage to a bailiff be a finer one? The crowner might even sell him a bit of land in time. With some work, that would suit a wife and a few babes. If she was even half the woman he knew her to be, she would work alongside him with as much eagerness as he to build a home and some standing in Tyndal village. And he had always thought she liked him well enough even when he was just a peasant's younger son with no land and few prospects.

The pain in his ankle eased with the balm of sweet imaginings, and Cuthbert now thrashed more eagerly through the lesser brush, keen to finish searching his assigned area so he could return to the village and seek out that father who had once scorned his blushing attentions to the daughter.

At least his heart was filled with joy until he burst into that clearing and found a corpse swelling in the summer heat.

Chapter Forty

Hob wept.

With practiced gentleness, Thomas pulled the eyelids down over dead eyes. "His soul fled not all that long ago," he said, touching the back of the dead man's neck where the sun had not kept the skin warm. Although he spoke with calmness, anger honed an edge to his words.

"What killed him, Brother? Can you tell?" Ralf stood slightly apart as if understanding that his presence might not be appreciated by the blacksmith as he grieved over his dead brother.

"I would guess it was the same poison that killed both Martin and Ivetta." The monk stretched out and picked up a small jar on the ground close by, then sniffed at it. He poured a few remaining drops into his hand. "See the seeds from the berries? Yew, or at least it looks enough like what Sister Anne showed us." Carefully, he wiped his hand on the grass. "There he vomited." He pointed. "From the stains on his clothes and the rank stench, I'd say his bowels loosened with great violence."

Ralf scowled. "Who all knew he was here? Was it more than one?"

"Our prioress had the right of it, I think. It was but one person, and that over there should prove it, Crowner." Thomas stood up and walked to pick up a forked root topped with dried, apple-like fruit from the ground nearby. "Mandrake. A remedy for impotence," he said. "See where it's cut? Methinks he was given a small bit and told to wash it down with the poisoned drink. If we looked, we might find more of it growing around, but that matters not. His killer could have brought it or even left the mandrake for Will to find. Arranging a meeting point within easy walking distance of the village would have been important. He must have been told to come here."

Hob wailed in anguish. "While you baited him and harassed me, the murderer remained free!" He jumped up and shook his fist at Ralf. "Now my brother is dead, and you have still done nothing."

"Nothing?" Ralf roared. "Take blame enough on yourselves for acting like dishonest men!"

Hob lunged at the crowner.

Thomas grabbed the blacksmith around the waist and tried to hold the struggling man from attacking. "You cannot bring Will's soul back by striking a king's man!"

"Will and I were honest enough with you," Hob shouted. "Tell me where we lied."

"Your brother fled. Men who do that are usually guilty. You claimed you did not know where he went, and, when I asked who might know, you named no one. Yet Tibia must have learned." Ralf glowered.

Hob calmed, a shocked expression replacing his fury.

Thomas stepped back.

"Why did you not tell me they had spoken again just before he disappeared? I should have been told earlier by you that he promised he would find whatever she needed to cure his impotency. Mandrake is the plant. She must have told him where to find it and that she would meet him here. She knew. I did not."

"In truth, I did not think his conversations with the old witch meant anything." His anger now dampened by sorrow more profound than any insult, Hob turned around and fell back on his knees beside his brother's body. "Now you must know that Will was innocent of any crime. For all his faults, he was my brother, and I loved him."

"He was obsessed with shame at his failure with the whore as you well knew…"

Thomas raised a cautioning hand to the crowner.

Ralf nodded and fell silent, then glanced down at the scarred dog snuffling and whining at Hob's feet. "Very well. He was innocent enough of killing Martin and Ivetta, at least," he finally said.

"What man did this then? You said my brother was in danger. Now he's dead. Who?"

Thomas looked up at Ralf, warning him with a small shake of the head to remain silent.

"She cannot have gone far, monk," the crowner said.

"Be silent, Ralf!" Thomas hissed.

"*She*?" Hob's eyes grew wide with horror as the truth finally broke through the walls of his grief. "That's why you were looking for the herb woman, wasn't it? Tibia is the killer!"

Ralf chose not to reply. Thomas could not.

To Hob, the cause of their silence was irrelevant. The fact of it was answer enough. With a cry of brute anguish, he jumped to his feet and tore off into the forest, his dog racing behind him.

Thomas turned to Ralf. "We must follow," he urged. "You should not have spoken so plainly."

"Let him go," the crowner replied, not moving except to rest one hand on his sword. "I do not want him, and his grief has driven him wild for the moment. He will calm…"

"I did not mean to catch Hob, Crowner. I fear for Tibia," Thomas cried out. "What if he comes across the old woman before we find her? She should be close to hand and we must get to her first!"

Ralf bent his head in the direction the blacksmith had disappeared. "There is no path through the forest where he went. Why would an old woman with a twisted back choose to walk home through vines and dense brush? Methinks she is hobbling down the path to the village."

"We came that way and did not see her…" The monk stopped in mid-sentence. Perplexed, he studied his friend for a moment. "If Hob catches old Tibia, he may kill her. Surely you know that."

Ralf shook his head.

"Come with me!" Thomas urged, his voice edged with frustration

"Not through the forest. We should go back along the road."

"Then do that! I shall take my chances with the blacksmith alone," Thomas angrily countered. He took a few steps toward the forest, and then turned around. "When you catch the herb woman, will you hang her?"

"Perhaps not," Ralf looked around with an expression of uncharacteristic indecision.

Suddenly they heard a high-pitched scream.

The crowner sprang off in the direction of the sound.

Thomas was right behind him.

Chapter Forty-One

Thomas grew breathless. His feet pounded the earth. Branches slashed at his flesh as he pushed through the thick brush. Thorns from a wild berry cane cut into his ankle. Soon his lungs were screaming with pain.

Running in front of him, Ralf cried out and fell.

The monk leapt over the crowner, avoiding the vine that had tripped his friend.

Were they too late?

Rushing around a thick clump of bushes, he burst into a small clearing.

A tall tree stood near a steep embankment. Hob stood at the brink, looking down. His dog leaned against his leg.

"Where is she?"

The blacksmith pointed to a spot just below him.

The monk crouched on his heels, then carefully eased himself over the edge and down the several feet to the stony stream bed, grabbing at rocks to slow his pace, gravel and dirt filling his shoes as he slid.

Tibia lay at the bottom, her body broken on the rocks. Her wide eyes turned to stare at him, eyes that screamed more of terror than pain.

"My son," she gasped.

From the angle of her body Thomas knew that the fragile bones of her spine must have shattered beyond hope. "Mother," he whispered as he knelt by her side. Then he took her hand.

A strange look of peace came over old Tibia. "I killed them," she said. "For you."

What point was there in reminding her who her was, he thought. "You killed them because they hanged me?" he asked, raising his tone into a soft and youthful tenor. "Martin, Ivetta, and Will?"

Tibia's lips twitched into a brief smile. "God was kind to send you, Brother," she whispered.

"He wants you to confess so He can hold your soul in His hand," Thomas replied, reverting to his own voice as quickly as he had the dead boy's.

"I have given no joy to any and sinned for no reason, even pleasure. All that I confess and regret." She lost breath for a moment, then continued, "Aye, I killed the three who murdered my sweet lad. No remorse."

"You must repent or all hope of salvation is lost."

"My son went to Hell on that tree above us. Ivetta lured him to her bed. He'd been as virginal as a saint 'til then. The others waited until he was covered in spent seed from wicked lust. Then they killed him."

"It was an accident."

"God knew otherwise, though I didn't understand that. Spent years weeping for justice from Him. Then our anchoress said I must fall silent. To hear His voice." She groaned. "He told me the time had come for vengeance."

Thomas felt tears stinging his eyes. Surely God would never order or consent to these murders. Satan must have found a way to twist the anchoress' innocent advice.

She cried out, her eyes round with pain, and dug her nails into Thomas' hand. When it eased, she continued. "The crowner's jury blinded themselves to their own sins when they found the murderers innocent. Some lay with me as a girl, others had Ivetta." Her eyes squeezed shut. "Muttered that a whore's son caught swyving a harlot was a sinner twice over and deserved to die. Puffed out their chests with righteousness. Thought to hide their own guilt and..." She screamed. "Punished me!"

"Say you repent!" Thomas pleaded.

Panting with weakening breath, the old woman whispered, "Of those deaths, I can't. God said I needn't wait longer. I was dying. He let me have justice."

The killings were wrong. Of course he knew that, but his heart ached with both sorrow and understanding. She had been spat upon by the very men who had once used her as a girl no older than their daughters. Then she lost the one thing that gave her joy and was mocked when those who had killed him walked free. If she had heard God's voice in Satan's seductive words, how many others might not have done the same? But the deed was still against God's commandments and Tibia must repent. He begged God to show him how to persuade her, for he would not let Satan have this soul.

Then it came to him, a cruel thing to tell her but something that might force Tibia to see the error of flawed mortals rendering vengeance. She had adored her son and that love had brought some redemption, despite the harshness of her life. This news might grieve her deeply enough to provoke remorse.

"Did you know that Ivetta was with child when you killed her?" he said, bending to whisper into her ear.

"Didn't know!" Tibia convulsed with fresh agony. "I deserve Hell."

"Nay! Your son begs you to cleanse your soul. God does. I do."

Another spasm hit her. "Give me comfort and pity. I die!" She rolled her eyes in the direction of the embankment. "Of the four, I poisoned three. I saved Hob. He begged forgiveness. Left wood at my door in winter. He could live. God said."

Thomas glanced up at the man standing in silence above, his arms casually folded as he gazed down at them. The dog looked intently at Ralf who stood but a foot away. Did the crowner think the younger blacksmith had killed Tibia? Had the man done so?

"Did Hob push…?"

"Dog. Scared me. Fell." Her lips drew back, exposing her gums, and her eyes began to roll back. "An accident," she mumbled.

With her soul struggling to depart a body it had long hated, Thomas knew he had no more time for questioning or argument. He must cleanse her of sins. "I bring the comfort of forgiveness. Just say *repent*," he beseeched.

For a long moment, the only sounds were the rattling whisper of Tibia's fading life and the bubbling of the nearby stream. Then she murmured something so softly that Thomas had to press his ear near her lips to hear.

"God'll grant mercy if due. Punishment, too. I'm ready."

"Then you do repent," the monk decided and quickly repeated the ritual of absolution.

With a harsh scream, she reached out to him, her eyes turned white and blind with death. "God's terrible face! Take my hand! Oh, sweetest son, hold me! I can't bear this..."

Thomas raised her hand to his lips and tenderly kissed the gnarled fingers.

The herb woman convulsed once and slipped into silence.

Tibia was dead.

Chapter Forty-Two

The monk released her hand, pressed his eyes shut, and begged God to take pity on her. Would He take her final words as sufficient repentance and deflect her soul from Hell? Thomas believed she understood the nature of her sin but he had grown fond of her and his heart might be untrustworthy as a result. Certainly her spirit had cause enough to rejoice when it tore away from that body. Hadn't she suffered too much pain and a life with too little happiness? Wouldn't God feel compassion…?

The rattle of small rocks tumbling against his feet brought him sharply back to earthly matters.

Ralf skidded to a stop and knelt beside him.

Thomas nodded at the body. "With two corpses to carry into the village, we will now need more men." His voice echoed in his head with an odd hollowness, as if his thoughts and tongue were separated by much distance.

"She died quickly then?" Ralf looked hopefully at his friend.

"She confessed first."

"To the killing of all three?"

"Aye. Signy is innocent," Thomas snapped, answering what he assumed to be the crowner's primary concern, but his face grew hot with swift regret. He had not meant to speak so harshly. After attending the dying, he often found himself impatient with the living, their concerns flat and pallid in the face of death. As a former soldier, however, Ralf might well understand and forgive his abruptness. To temper his words, he added, "Tibia did kill them for their part in murdering her boy, as our prioress suspected."

"Did she die quickly, monk?" Ralf shifted his weight in the gravel.

"Soon enough. Within minutes, Crowner." Thomas expression turned quizzical.

"You asked if I hoped to hang her. The law would have demanded that I put her neck in a noose, but she'd have died long before any trial, in misery, with foul water, hard bread, and rats for company. This was a better death for an old woman. Murderer though she was, I find no fault with that. Her soul will pay the price."

"She was dying already and may have stayed alive only for her revenge."

The crowner looked at the tree looming above, its dark branches stretched out like the arms of a condemned man praying on his scaffold. "Yet I find it strange that she did not return home along an easy path? Why fight her way through that brush to this place after poisoning Will? This was where her son died." He twisted around and stared up at Hob still standing on the edge of the embankment. "I wonder if she was to meet someone here?"

The blacksmith did not move. His dog whimpered softly.

"Perhaps it was the Devil. Some claim she was a witch. She might have traded her soul to the Prince of Darkness for that of her son and come here to make the exchange," Thomas murmured as he went back to studying the body, his forehead furrowed with dark thought. "Yet Satan does little in the brightness of God's day..."

Suddenly, the monk reached out and pulled over a small but damply stained bag from where it lay under the dead woman's hip. "If this holds what I suspect, she may have done with life. Perhaps she wanted her soul to depart the world under that tree where her son had been hanged?"

From inside the bag, Thomas drew forth two small pottery bottles: one intact; one cracked and leaking. "I fear I am right. For once, I grieve to be so," he murmured.

"What is this?" The crowner took the undamaged bottle and uncorked it, sniffing at the opening with caution.

"Don't drink that unless you are in need of profound sleep," Thomas' smile was thin with bitterness.

"Poison?" Ralf's eyes narrowed with suspicion.

"Not in moderation." The monk shook his head. "A very effective draught for easing pain and bringing sleep that was brought to our priory, when it was still a Benedictine house, by an old crusader. On his way to join the monks at Shrewsbury, he fell ill, and in gratitude for his care here, he gave the infirmarian some poppy seeds for the garden. Their usefulness was forgotten until Sister Anne recognized the plant and remembered how her father had prepared and used this draught."

"Two bottles?" Ralf gave the monk a questioning look as he gestured at the broken one.

"Sufficient to fall into death's sleep," Thomas replied. "There I take full blame. She asked me about the dangers of the draught, and I must have explained enough for her to conclude the dosage needed to die. When I found her without pain, or so she claimed, she begged me to leave the bottle each time, saying she feared the agony would return after I had gone. These two, it seems, she set aside for this sinister purpose."

"Can you be sure we do not have another poisoner?"

"Sister Anne makes the potion only when there is a need and allows no one else to do so. These are priory jars. If you seek another killer, then you have found him in me."

The crowner jumped to his feet and tossed the intact bottle into the stream. It shattered, staining the rocks before the water washed the potion away.

Thomas watched, his face devoid of expression.

"What of him?" Ralf asked, gesturing at the figure still standing on the edge of the bank.

"She said he had naught to do with her death."

"An accident?"

"When the dog ran out of the forest, he startled her. She must have been standing there at the brink and fallen backward."

Ralf hesitated, his expression suggesting some internal quarrel with himself. At last, he nodded and then pushed himself upright. "Hob!"

The blacksmith let his arms drop to his sides but did not speak.

"Find Cuthbert, will you? We need more men to carry these bodies back to the village."

The man turned and walked off. Behind him, his dog followed, tail wagging.

"Will you stay with her body, Brother, until the men come?"

Thomas nodded.

As he watched Ralf pull himself back up the embankment with deliberate slowness, he realized that the crowner was allowing Hob to get far enough away to understand that no one was following to arrest him for murder.

◇◇◇

Did the forest ever quite grow silent, Thomas asked himself, as he sat back on his heels and waited. From the safety of trees, birds warned each other that an ominous creature was still in their midst. Insects were less cautious. He swatted at a few brazen enough to land on his face and hands. Even the leaves made noise brushing one against another in the sea breeze. Nay, the woods were not quiet at all—unlike the forsaken shell of Man.

Thomas looked at the motionless corpse and bent over to close the gaping mouth. Tibia's expression was calm, her face smoother now that the pain of age and anger was gone. Sinner she most certainly was, but whose fault was it that she had felt justified in poisoning those who had murdered her son?

Was it Sister Juliana's advice? Surely the guidance to seek silence in order to plainly hear God's voice had been much the same as the anchoress had given him and others. These words may have been innocent enough, but might Tibia have heard another voice and interpreted that to mean that God would both actively encourage her take matters into her own hands and forgive her for doing so? Surely her spirit had mistaken the seductive lilt of Satan's voice for God's and heard only what she longed to hear. Her heart had been bitter enough to be easily wooed by the Devil.

Thomas stared up into the bright sky. He blinked with confusion and felt a slight shiver of fear. There were other conclusions. Dare he imagine that God would use her as an instrument of justice against the three when mortal sinners had failed to render it? Was it not heresy to think that God might have demanded their deaths without any opportunity for confession? What if God knew that none, except Hob, had ever felt the slightest anguish over what they had done? If they did not, could they have been truly penitent even though they spoke the right words? Surely God could not be so easily fooled.

Terror filled him. Was it a sin to wonder about such things! He was a priest. Had he not granted Tibia absolution when many reasonable men would have doubted the sincerity of her regret? Had he been present at their deaths, would he not have given the same consolation to Martin, Ivetta, and Will? His heart began to answer but he silenced that untrustworthy voice. Wasn't he already cursed enough?

What of his own part in this cruel tale? Why had he not realized the danger of leaving her these potions? She was not the first to commit self-murder when pain of body or soul grew too great. Had God blinded him or had he blinded himself to what she might do with the extra bottle? At least she did not use the draughts—but she might have done so and that would have made him a companion in murder.

Closing his eyes, he suddenly felt as if Tibia's soul were still hovering like a mother longing to give comfort to her orphaned child. "I shall pray for you," he whispered. "God may have used you as a hand of vengeance for a brutal killing. I should not question that. Sinner you most certainly were, as am I, but perhaps He did speak to you. If He has now forgiven and taken your soul into His comforting arms, would you intercede on my behalf? Please ask if He will finally pardon me and answer my pleas for understanding."

Tears began to run down his cheeks, and he rubbed his face dry with his sleeve. A light breeze brushed against him as he stood. Suddenly he began to shake with horror at the next thought that came to him.

"An *accident*?" he murmured. "You said your death was… That was the verdict in your son's death. Did Hob kill you after all?" he asked. Looking around as if expecting to see the herb woman alive and standing close by, he continued, "If so, why did you protect him? Did you think God used him to punish you for following His direction? Or did Satan direct Hob's hand while God did nothing but stand by and watch?"

"Answer me!" he shouted, all tolerance for uncertainty at an end. But the only sound he heard was the twittering, rustling, and humming from the woods.

Raising his fists, his body tensed with outrage. He shut his eyes and willed himself into the silence Sister Juliana had promised would open his soul to God's voice.

No words came. God most certainly did not speak.

Instead, Thomas found himself pondering two new questions.

Should he, like Sister Juliana, abandon the world completely and seek a hermitage? By hiding in the forest away from all men, he would never have to face his human demons again, as he did in Amesbury, and might find the strength to fight those imps who came to him in dreams. Even his spymaster might leave him alone then, for no priest would ever dare to pull a hermit from his holy cave.

Or should he stay in Tyndal Priory, working with Sister Anne in the hospital until his prioress demanded otherwise? Since his arrival here, he had begun to think that Prioress Eleanor might well be one of those avenging angels sent by God to wage war on evil men. And had he not fallen to his knees just the other day, breaking his previous oath to his spymaster, and sworn to obey her in all things henceforth? At the time, he had done so without thinking. Had God inspired him?

Opening his eyes, Thomas groaned. "I am still confused." Indeed, he meant no complaint in that statement, only resignation. God may not have spoken to him from the stream or the rocks, but an odd kind of peace had been bestowed. Instead of answers, he had been granted questions. Only two, in fact, and for that he feared he should be grateful. Would his torments be eased once he had answered them, or were these only the beginning in a series of troubling queries?

Now hearing men's voices in the distance, he knew his time by old Tibia's side was almost over. If her soul still hovered nearby, perhaps with a lingering regret for the loss of earthly things or even some fondness for a man she sometimes called *son*, he had best dismiss it.

"Go in peace," he whispered. "If you were acting on God's behalf, you need no mortal blessing. If He did not make you into His avenging angel, I have given you absolution. Wherever your soul may go now, I beg you to pray for me as you did your murdered boy. I shall miss you."

Then he bent down and kissed old Tibia's cool cheek, took hold of her hand for the last time, and wept like a son who had just seen his mother die.

Chapter Forty-Three

A few days later, in the tiny cell of the anchoress, Juliana, two women knelt together in front of the small, plain altar and prayed silently. When they had done, each opened her eyes and turned to the other. Neither spoke, nor did either doubt the other had finished her talk with God. Their smiles suggested a mutual understanding that words were sometimes mortal things, best left unspoken owing to their imperfection.

Prioress Eleanor opened her arms and embraced the anchoress. "Am I forgiven?"

"Am I?" came the reply.

"It is up to God to decide the severity of each of our sins. Yet He is merciful."

"Mine led to murder."

"As did mine."

Eleanor rose, then helped the anchoress to her feet, and the two went to the small opening in the wall that provided entry for light from the world. Eleanor pushed aside the curtain and peeked out. "The earth still sings with joy, and the sun brings warmth to all creatures," she said. "Despite men's sins, God's handiwork finds ways to rejoice overall."

"My heart believes that is God's message of hope, my lady."

While the birds turned their babble of voices into a unique but strangely appealing polyphony, the two women fell silent and enjoyed those gifts of creation.

Eleanor turned at last to Juliana. "When I told my aunt in Amesbury that I wanted to take my final vows in our Order of Fontevraud, she asked whether I longed only for the sequestered life of prayer. Being yet a child, I must have answered with predictable eagerness, although I have no memory of my exact words. She put her hands on my shoulders, pushed me to my knees, and said, 'You must pray daily that God gives you the strength to do whatever He requires.' I have had cause of late to remember her advice and regret that I have failed, until now, to follow it."

"I do not understand."

"The nuns and monks of Tyndal, with some few exceptions, spend their days praying for souls in need. Had I stayed in Amesbury Priory with my aunt, I might have remained like them, but God had other trials for me and inspired King Henry to appoint me leader of Tyndal."

"Your friends and family rejoiced at the honor given," Juliana replied with a rare smile.

"As prioress, I must deal with worldly matters and even more worldly men. If our house does not prosper, our religious will lose the roof that shelters them, the altar before which they pray, and the food that gives them strength. In guaranteeing wealth and prominence enough to provide all this, I know I serve God's purpose well."

The anchoress nodded agreement.

"Nonetheless, my duties bring temptations, and I was led away from righteousness by concern with worldly reputation. Fearful of men's censure, because I allowed you to welcome tortured souls at night, I stopped my ears to the words of warning you wished to speak. Had I listened, I might have prevented the blacksmith's death." She knelt and bowed her head. "I have begged God to pardon all my sins in this matter. He demands that I humbly seek your forgiveness as well."

Juliana said nothing for a long while, her eyes sad as if she had seen or heard something in the prioress' gesture of humility that troubled her. Finally, she spoke: "My lady, whatever forgiveness you have been commanded to seek from me is most heartily given, whether or not you ask it."

A high color may have risen from Eleanor's neck and spread over her face, but she did not reply.

"God has read our hearts, yours and mine, but He promises solace for our sorrows and forgiveness for our weaknesses. When we show our strengths, He praises us." The anchoress knelt as well and took her prioress' hands. "Like any mortal, we have longings held secret from other men. Seek His guidance."

Eleanor nodded.

"Will you forgive the grief I have brought this priory, my lady? Believing that God may have chosen me as His vessel blinded me with pride. I failed to see the evil I let loose. If you blame yourself for one murder, I bear the burden of three."

"This priory has not suffered from your presence, nor did your advice cause the Evil One to dance. When the herb woman sought solace for the tribulations she had suffered, she surely closed her ears when God spoke and instead beckoned Satan to come nigh. He urged revenge. Thus her soul bears the weight of the crimes she committed in his name." Then the prioress kissed the anchoress' hands. Her smile twitched with a hint of mischievousness. "There is only one sin of which you are guilty and must seek forgiveness from me. Will you hear what it is and the penance you must bear?"

"Tell me and I shall perform it."

"It is the intolerance with which you greet all women who serve you."

"We have spoken of that…"

"And I promised to find you a maid who would do honor to your calling."

"You have discovered such a person?" Juliana's words may have been spoken with submissive enough acceptance, but they most certainly did not sing of happiness at this prospect.

"Not yet, but I shall. In the meantime, I have discovered something that may teach you forbearance." Eleanor rose and walked over to a covered basket she had placed near the door when she arrived. It was a small thing, of a loose and open weave.

The anchoress watched with a puzzled but curious frown.

The prioress lifted the cover off the basket, reached inside, and pulled out two small objects.

Juliana stared in amazement.

Eleanor gestured for the anchoress to stretch forth her hands. Then she carefully placed two sleeping female kittens in them. "These shall help teach you the sweet nature of good women," she said, "and how to accept service from our sex."

With that, the prioress kissed the anchoress on her cheek and quietly left the cell, pulling the heavy door shut behind her.

Sister Juliana looked down at the soft, purring creatures resting easily in her palms, and then held them gently against her face. Although she now began to weep, these tears were most certainly born of joy.

Author's Notes

This story takes place in the summer of 1273, a reasonably peaceful time in England—at least in retrospect. King Henry III had died on November 16, 1272, and his son, now King Edward I, was on his way back from the Holy Land. When he received word of his father's death, he was in Sicily but took his time getting home and did not arrive in England until August of 1274. One of the reasons for this delay may have been his slow recovery from the wounds suffered from an assassination attempt before he left Acre, although he did participate in a tournament in Chalons during which, once again, he found himself in danger of either losing his life or receiving a serious wound.

In the meantime, the English government was run by a council under the direction of his clerk, Robert Burnell. While the new king visited in Rome and Paris, his mother's family in Savoy, and handled a crisis in Gascony, that council dealt with the ongoing aftermath of the Simon de Montfort rebellion. Not only were there rumblings from the former rebels, assessed huge fines for the recovery of their lands, but there were also droves of pilgrims from all social classes coming to Evesham to venerate the dead Simon. Fear of the renewal of this civil war was certainly a legitimate one, added to which was the lack of any money to fight another.

It seems that Edward had full confidence in his council, and his journey home was hardly a pleasure tour. A far more astute politician than his father, Edward was carefully renewing and building alliances while settling disputes on his continental lands. To the grief of the Welsh, he also met in Savoy the master mason and architect, Master James of St. George, a man he later invited to join him in England to design and build such famous castles as Beaumaris and Harlech.

Anchoresses are both fascinating and often misunderstood. Although some were bricked up in their cells, most were not. In the early 13th century, *Ancrene Wisse* (Guide for Anchoresses) was written in England for a group of anchoresses living in individual cells, with servants, and sharing common space for meals. Many decades earlier, Aelred of Rievaulx wrote his guide, a work the author of *Ancrene Wisse* knew well, for his sister who seems to have been a solitary anchoress in the mid-12th century.

An anchoress (or anchorite, if a man) was a person who did not necessarily belong to any Order or take vows other than chastity, obedience, and fixity of place—although, like Juliana, a few might choose to do so. Many of these women, but not all, lived in a building attached to a church. If the anchoress was alone, her space was small (one such cell measured twelve feet square) with three windows: one, called a *squint*, opened into the church interior so services and Mass could be observed; another was used to pass food and waste; and a third, curtained, let in light from the outside and allowed villagers to visit for comfort and advice.

Within this cell, the anchoress had a bed (often made of stone), an altar, and a crucifix. Some cells did have space for a maid or two. Many also held a coffin, or else a grave already hollowed out from which the anchoress dug up earth daily with her bare hands to remind herself of death and her hopes for life thereafter. Although these women might be buried in their cell, the anchorage was often passed on to another.

The anchoress might have wished for more solitude, but she was not alone in fact. Practicality demanded some human contact. According to legend, the desert fathers were fed by birds and beasts, but, by the 12th and 13th centuries, the animals seemed to have wearied of the task and turned the duties over to humans. Even solitary anchoresses usually had one indoor servant (who cooked, mended, and attended to other physical needs) and an outdoor attendant (who carried wood, did laundry or other heavy work). Both maids were expected to be modest in behavior, above reproach morally, and plain of dress. Their wages consisted of the glory they received for service given to these holy women, plus food and shelter. Many of these servants moved into the cell after their mistress' death and became anchoresses themselves.

Although the practice was discouraged, some anchoresses received visitors in their cells. A few taught young children, although Aelred made plain his dislike for this activity. Needless to say, contact with men was pretty much forbidden. An elderly, sober priest of unquestioned reputation could visit for confession and counseling. If a prior or abbot wished, he might do so as well but only rarely and in the presence of a third person. In the company of any man, the anchoress heavily veiled herself.

Setting apart her particular jealousy, Prioress Eleanor had good reason to be outraged when Brother Thomas visited Juliana because tongues did wag about improprieties. Both the author of *Ancrene Wisse* and Aelred of Rievaulx talk about the dangers of touch between the sexes (even if hands met only in the act of alms-giving), sexual imaginings after innocent meetings, and how some anchoresses enlarged the outside window so a lover could slip into the cell. If the building was made of stone, the latter must have required quite the dedicated effort.

A man or woman who chose this life was expected to emulate the suffering of Jesus. For this reason, the wearing of rough clothing, flagellation, and significant fasting were common. That noted, moderation was recommended and urged. The author of *Ancrene Wisse* particularly advises against the wearing of hairshirts and says that diet should be meager but most certainly adequate for maintaining strength. He also recommends bathing (filth did not please God) and says that a cat was the only suitable animal to keep—unless otherwise advised.

Some suggest that the Celtic Church, known for its solitary religious, had an influence, but Britain seems to have had a larger number of anchoresses than the continent, especially in the 13th century. Two of them are especially famous: Christina of Markyate (c. 1097 to sometime after 1155) and Julian of Norwich (1342-c.1416).

Christina probably wanted to be a nun, not an anchoress, but Roger, the hermit, helped to hide her from her family who wanted the young woman to marry and produce children. For four years, she suffered incredible agony and deprivation from remaining motionless in a tiny space during the daytime, the effects of which probably shortened her life. Roger willed his anchorage to her in Markyate when he died.

For a woman who wanted to live a chaste life, she suffered much from lust and the lust of others. One unnamed cleric, friend to Archbishop Thurstan of York, was so driven by his passion that he visited her naked. Nor was she immune to his pleas. Mary Magdalene finally had enough and ordered him in a dream to quit the nonsense. To cool her own ardor, Christina ate only raw herbs, scourged herself, and prayed instead of sleeping. Finally, she seems to have entered into a chaste but loving relationship with Geoffrey, Abbot of St. Albans, a man who was amazed when she, like most saints and not a few ordinary women, read his thoughts.

Julian of Norwich probably took her name from the St. Julian of the church to which her anchorhold was attached. A woman of middle age when she entered this new life, she was not a nun but did dedicate herself to seeking God's voice in the silence of her small enclosure. Her particular findings were written down and published as *The Revelations of Divine Love*, a most interesting work in which she discusses the compassionate and feminine nature of the Divine. During the Reformation, her cell was destroyed, and, although the church survived, it was almost obliterated by a bomb during World War II. When the church was reconstructed, the foundations of what was believed to have been Julian's cell were discovered. Although many such cells were built on the north side of churches, to deprive anchoresses of any joy from the sun's light, Julian's was placed on the south. I'd like to think that the man who built her cell believed that she, as an author, was worthy of a bit more comfort.

On the other side of the chastity issue lived the prostitutes. Prostitution is an ancient profession, albeit not always called an honorable one. How it is viewed has changed from era and culture and locale. Many have considered it part of the religious experience or a rite of passage; others condemn it as immoral and/or degrading to women. Whatever the point of view, the profession has always been supported by society in fact, either openly and legally or covertly but just as enthusiastically.

Both the Church and secular authorities in the medieval period were as uncomfortable and conflicted about the business as we are today—with a slight shift in emphasis. The commercial aspect of prostitution did not define who was or who was not a "whore" in Prioress Eleanor's time. That concept seems to be our inheritance from industrialization and the rise of the mercantile class. Rampant female sexuality (and the obligation to control it) balanced against the need for unmarried men to find an outlet (literally for the good of their health) were the prime concerns in the 13th century.

Unlike good Victorian women, who supposedly closed their eyes and thought only of England, all medieval women were believed to suffer from such lust that they were often driven to seduce otherwise decent men into bed. Virginal nuns, who vowed chastity, were deemed more virtuous than monks because of their greater struggle to honor that oath, and repentant prostitutes were especially venerated, in part because they knew what they were giving up. As one man's property, wives and women in monogamous/ longtime relationships were of less danger to social order than an unattached single woman. The husband or "significant other" was expected to keep them sexually satisfied and thus unlikely to tempt innocent men with their wiles.

As a single woman, Signy had good reason to fear for her reputation. Since men and women of the lower social classes in

England often married later for financial reasons, premarital sex was common and even reasonably accepted. As long as she was discreet and limited her affairs, the single woman could hope that the community (defined as men of authority in a village) would opt to ignore what she was doing. In this way, she might escape legal action as well as the inability to follow any remunerative occupation besides prostitution should she be publicly accused of "whoredom".

Of course the Church found prostitution reprehensible, but they and the secular authorities both decided it was socially necessary. Despite believing all men should be chaste, they also assumed that public order (protection of another man's wife, daughter, or female servant from lewd activity) and a man's health (release of "seed" was needed to keep a man in trim) required the availability of "common women". With prostitutes, unmarried men such as priests, students, and apprentices could find necessary relief, although no one liked to admit that this went on. Like modern officials who think the problem of the homeless is eliminated by shooing them off somewhere less visible to tourists, the medieval authorities justified their uncomfortable acceptance of prostitution by limiting the women to sections or streets in a town where "honest folk" didn't have to see them.

Most of us know that the term "common woman" does not have the same origin as "common man". It may be a more ancient one, however. In the medieval period, the concept meant any woman who was sexually and publicly available to many men (not a series of husbands), including priests. Pay was often involved but volume business was more significant in defining who was and was not an official "whore". As is true now, that particular term could and was used casually as an insult against any woman for any reason and often had little to do with any sexual activity.

A short note on single women owning or inheriting property in the Middle Ages: they did, although it was not the preferred method of passing land on. Sons always trumped daughters in inheritance. With mortality being what is was, some tradesmen or landowners had no living children. When Signy's uncle chooses her to inherit the inn, he does because he has no possible male heir or even a married niece. No matter how competent the innkeeper may have thought Signy was, however, he also assumed she would marry and that her husband would take over the running of the business.

The story about Tibia being fined for falsely raising a hue and cry was inspired by an actual incident. In 1302, Matilda Coleman of Brigstock raised the hue and cry against Adam Swargere whom she accused of doing some injury to her daughter. Her act was found to be unjustified, and she was fined, as it were, for bothering everyone. That said, the tithingmen also decided that Adam had mistreated the girl, for which they assessed him a financial penalty. A very strange, split decision, but it meant that Adam was assessed only one fine, not two. Had the raising of the hue and cry been found appropriate, he would have paid for that as well as for committing the offense. To us, the logic of why a proper complaint was punished may seem strained at best, but Dr. Judith Bennett provides illuminating background on the rationale in her fascinating book, *Women in the Medieval English Countryside: Gender and Household in Brigstock Before the Plague.*

There are a few period terms used in the book which I hope are made clear enough so no reader will be jolted out of the story. Nonetheless, the following ones may merit additional detail.

A hobby-lantern (*hobby* is short for *hobbedy* or the devil) is also known as a corpse candle or a will-of-the-wisp. There are many other expressions used for this form of eerie light seen at night in marshlands, but the tales behind it range from Satan punishing a man who promised his soul if the Evil One would pay his bar tab (and then reneged) to a kinder, gentler Devil who tossed a lost soul a burning coal to keep warm as it wandered the earth.

A bawd in the medieval period (14th century) meant either a man or a woman. This individual arranged for those sexual encounters where marriage was not at issue. He or she could be a pimp, a brothel owner, a prostitute, or someone who arranged meeting places for lovers, either or both of whom were married to others.

A tithing was originally a group of ten men, over the age of twelve, who took responsibility for other group members coming to answer for any accused crime.

When Hob says that he and his unnamed companion are husband and wife in God's eyes, he is referring to a common medieval marriage practice. Many marriages were performed in secret, with or without witnesses. These were quite valid under both ecclesiastical and secular law. Even if there were no witnesses, a man and a woman could exchange vows "in the present tense" and become as bound in marriage as those are today who get a license and go before a justice of the peace or religious authority. Vows spoken "in the future tense", on the other hand, were the equivalent of an intent to wed and were closer to our current concept of an engagement. Needless to say, such marriages were often hard to prove or disprove. Barring strong evidence to the contrary, the ecclesiastical courts often found that a wedding had occurred. The practice eventually lost favor with both Church and State.

And, finally, a bit of information new to me but one of those delightful discoveries that brings pleasure, even if belated, and is common enough knowledge to others. According to Janet Backhouse in her beautiful book, *Medieval Birds in the Sherborne Missal,* the term *mew* was used in England for *seagull* until the 17th century. My cats have told me that they will never look at those birds quite the same again…

Bibliography

The following are a few books I found helpful, educational, and just plain fascinating while writing this story. Hopefully, I have not misinterpreted the concepts or information. If such proves to be the case, I apologize deeply. The authors are hardly to blame for my ineptitude. That said, I cannot thank them enough for the pleasant hours spent reading them all.

Treatises and Pastoral Prayer (Rule of Life for a Recluse) by Aelred of Rievaulx, Cistercian Publications, 1971.

A Medieval Life: Cecilia Penifader of Brigstock, c.1295-1344 by Judith M. Bennett, McGraw-Hill College, 1999.

Life in a Medieval Village by Frances and Joseph Gies, Harper Perennial, 1990.

Common Women: Prostitution and Sexuality in Medieval England by Ruth Mazo Karras, Oxford University Press, 1996.

Lives of the Desert Fathers, translated by Norman Russell, Cistercian Publications, 1980.

The Life of Christina of Markyate: A Twelfth Century Recluse, edited and translated by C.H. Talbot, University of Toronto Press, 1997.

To receive a free catalog of Poisoned Pen Press titles, please contact us in one of the following ways:

Phone: 1-800-421-3976
Facsimile: 1-480-949-1707
Email: info@poisonedpenpress.com
Website: www.poisonedpenpress.com

Poisoned Pen Press
6962 E. First Ave. Ste. 103
Scottsdale, AZ 85251